Wataru Watari
Illustration Ponkan⑧

6

Contents

Haruno
Yukinoshita

MY YOUTH R♥MANTIC C☻MEDY iS WRØNG, AS I EXPECTED

Wataru Watari

Illustration Ponkan⑧

VOLUME

6

YEN
ON

NEW YORK

MY YOUTH ROMANTIC COMEDY IS WRONG, AS I EXPECTED Vol. 6
WATARU WATARI
Illustration by Ponkan⑧

Translation by Jennifer Ward
Cover art by Ponkan⑧

YAHARI ORE NO SEISHUN LOVE COME WA MACHIGATTEIRU.
Vol. 6 by Wataru WATARI
© 2011 Wataru WATARI
Illustration by PONKAN⑧
All rights reserved.
Original Japanese edition published by SHOGAKUKAN.
English translation rights arranged with SHOGAKUKAN through Tuttle-Mori Agency, Inc., Tokyo.

English translation © 2018 by Yen Press, LLC

Yen On
1290 Avenue of the Americas
New York, NY 10104

Visit us at yenpress.com
facebook.com/yenpress
twitter.com/yenpress
yenpress.tumblr.com
instagram.com/yenpress

First Yen On Edition: November 2018

Yen On is an imprint of Yen Press, LLC.
The Yen On name and logo are trademarks of Yen Press, LLC.

The publisher is not responsible for websites (or their content) that are not owned by the publisher.

Library of Congress Cataloging-in-Publication Data
Names: Watari, Wataru, author. | Ponkan 8, illustrator.
Title: My youth romantic comedy is wrong, as I expected / Wataru Watari ; illustration by Ponkan 8.
Other titles: Yahari ore no seishun love come wa machigatteiru. English
Description: New York : Yen On, 2016–
Identifiers: LCCN 2016005816 | ISBN 9780316312295 (v. 1 : pbk.) | ISBN 9780316396011 (v. 2 : pbk.) |
   ISBN 9780316318068 (v. 3 : pbk.) | ISBN 9780316318075 (v. 4 : pbk.) | ISBN 9780316318082 (v. 5 : pbk.) |
   ISBN 9780316411868 (v. 6 : pbk.)
Subjects: | CYAC: Optimism—Fiction. | School—Fiction.
Classification: LCC PZ7.1.W396 My 2016 | DDC [Fic]—dc23
LC record available at http://lccn.loc.gov/2016005816

ISBN: 978-0-316-41186-8

10 9 8 7 6 5 4 3 2 1

LSC-C

Printed in the United States of America

MY YOUTH R♥MANTIC C♥MEDY iS WRØNG, AS I EXPECTED

six

Cast of Characters

Hachiman Hikigaya.......... The main character. High school second-year. Twisted personality.

Yukino Yukinoshita........... Captain of the Service Club. Perfectionist.

Yui Yuigahama................. Hachiman's classmate. Tends to worry about what other people think.

Yoshiteru Zaimokuza......... Nerd. Ambition is to become a light novel author.

Saika Totsuka................... In tennis club. Very cute. A boy, though.

Saki Kawasaki.................. Hachiman's classmate. Sort of a delinquent type.

Hayato Hayama................. Hachiman's classmate. Popular. In the soccer club.

Yumiko Miura................... Hachiman's classmate. Reigns over the girls in class as queen bee.

Hina Ebina....................... Hachiman's classmate. Part of Miura's clique, but a slash fangirl.

Minami Sagami................. Hachiman's classmate. Member of the second-highest caste among the girls.

Meguri Shiromeguri.......... President of the student council. Third-year student.

Shizuka Hiratsuka............. Japanese teacher. Guidance counselor.

Haruno Yukinoshita.......... Yukino's older sister. In university.

Komachi Hikigaya............. Hachiman's little sister. In her third year in middle school.

FANGIRL APPROVED

◆ **Outline:**

A full theatrical version of the famous book *The Little Prince*, cast with popular students such as Hayato Hayama!

◆ **Target audience:**

Girls in Soubu High School, girls from other schools, female guardians.

◆ **Characters:**

☆ THE NARRATOR...A rather sulky pilot. Ever since his crash landing in the desert, he's gotten even sulkier.

☆ THE PRINCE...A pure and innocent pretty-boy. His purity makes him highly seductive.

☆ THE KING...Arrogant and desperate to maintain his image. The way he gives orders tells you he's the type with a swelled head. Makes you want to crush his pride.

☆ THE VAIN MAN...Fame has made him conceited, but he's actually a shy and diffident young man. The easiest type to get into bed.

☆ THE DRUNKARD...Drowns himself in alcohol. Is probably also drowning his sad life and the memories of a certain man from his past. The pickup line for nabbing this one is: "Don't drown yourself in booze. Drown yourself in me."

☆ THE BUSINESSMAN...A romantic who cries out about how important he is as he insists he owns the stars. Makes you want to pull on his necktie.

☆ THE LAMPLIGHTER...Bound by rules, covered in soot, he labors on. A diligent, unrefined blue-collar type. His dirty overalls are tempting.

MUSICAL:
The Little Prince

☆ THE GEOGRAPHER...A curious shut-in who wants you to teach him about many, many things. Famous lines of his include "Show me your Matterhorn" and "Look, my Chomolungma..." They're very well-known.

☆ THE FOX...The first friend the Prince makes on Earth. Patiently teaches the Prince about what's important.

☆ THE SNAKE...The Prince falls victim to him.

◆ Summary:

☆ The Narrator, a pilot, has a hard crash landing deep in the desert. He's in serious distress, attempting to repair his plane, when the shota "Prince" appears. The two have many conversations, gradually becoming more and more attracted to each other.

☆ Eventually, in an attempt to provoke the Narrator, the Prince reveals his incredible history with other men. While this makes the Narrator burn with jealousy, they never share their feelings for each other, and the Snake steals the Prince away.

☆ Finally, the Narrator comes to realize...that what is essential is invisible to the eye, and now he understands what real love is...

Hina Ebina's musical is homoerotic, as expected.

…Lovely story.

Definitely not.

Silently, I finished reading the presentation proposal and set it down on the desk. The rather thick stack of paper exuded an indescribable, unique aura, not unlike the one you might expect from the *Necronomicon* if it were real. Written on the cover of the proposal was *The Little Prince: The Musical.* With a title like that, I was expecting more over-the-top tennis matches.

The season was fall, and with fall comes cultural festivals. The whole class bands together during this time, which is tiresome for those with a policy of proud independence. I don't fit in with Class 2-F enough to call it "my class," but today was the day they started buckling down for festival prep.

After much ado about the project for 2-F, the class decided that we would put on a play. When things are decided by majority rule, it's not my place to speak up. I'm always in the minority.

They put out a call for ideas, and one story in particular was submitted as a potential topic: *The Little Prince.*

I figure a lot of people have heard of Antoine de Saint-Exupéry's classic, even if they haven't read it. You might assume that Prince of Curry is a related product, but that's completely different, just so you know.

The story can be summarized thus:

The protagonist/narrator, a pilot, makes an emergency landing in the Sahara desert, where he meets the eponymous prince, and the two of them discuss a variety of topics and discover what's really important in life. It's an appropriate choice for a high school theater production, and it's fair to call the tale a world-famous masterpiece.

But the one thing that was different about this script...was that Ebina wrote it.

Right from line one, the characters, setting, and outline of Ebina's version of the story nearly broke my spirit. But even so, I willed myself to go on. Once I reached lines like "I've been to eight hundred different varieties of stars!" and "A certain pilot and a pervert prince," I gave up.

What does that girl think about her life? I fearfully glanced over at Ebina and discovered she was acting oddly coquettish and shy.

"This is a little embarrassing..."

"A little"? No, no, no, it's mortifying! Without a word, I folded up the printouts and decided to wash my hands of the whole thing.

A heavy cloud descended over our long homeroom period.

"Are we about done?" Hayama called out, scanning the room when most of us had finished reading Ebina's proposal. Typically, this task was in the class rep's purview, but since he was a naive and artless sort of boy, he hadn't built up a resistance to these topics and was now frozen.

"U-um...so what do you all think? If anyone has any questions or sees any problems...," Hayama said.

What *wasn't* a problem here...?

One of the girls in the class raised her hand. "Are there no girls in the play?"

"Huh? Why would there be?" Ebina tilted her head in bafflement. *Hold on there, Miss Naughty.*

There are no human women in *The Little Prince*, but the Rose is drawn to look feminine, so a girl could play the role, in my opinion. And they could consider how they wanted to portray the Fox or the Snake, too. They'd probably end up doing an anthropomorphized version, like that Shiki Theater Company production of *The Lion King*.

Another classmate raised their hand. "Is this even morally acceptable?"

"It's rated for all ages, so it's okay!" Ebina chirped.

Who mentioned ratings?

Most of the others seemed to be struggling with how to take this, too. Oda and Tahara were smirking, along with the other guys who knew a thing or two about fangirls, while most of the girls were perplexed.

Meanwhile, a certain someone was waving his hand around obnoxiously as he tried to get our attention. "I think it's a good idea, though."

Oh-ho, do I spy a desperate bid for Ebina's approval, Tobe? It was weird, whether you called it the guilelessness of a boy in love or an attempt to be cute. But, well, I guess that's universal. I mean, like, back when I was in middle school, I had a crush on this one girl, so I always found a way to make it so we happened to be walking home together, and so people ended up calling me a stalker behind my back until I almost cried... E-everyone does that, right? It's not just me...?

The reception was still decidedly lukewarm, so Tobe pushed even harder. "This stuff can be fun! I think it'd be more popular than a normal play!" An effective argument, apparently; the others all looked at one another as they began considering it.

Well, he had a point. This wasn't a BL novel, and a musical wouldn't hit the audience the same way as text on the page. A bunch of boorish high school boys professing their love to each other in weird costumes onstage would feel more like a sketch comedy.

Cultural-festival plays were judged most heavily on humor and originality. This script had both in spades. Leaving aside the pros and cons of the BL-esque elements as well as Ebina's proclivities as the author, I thought it would probably end up more or less okay.

"Yeah, I think we could take it a little in that direction. Besides, I wouldn't bring out the real deal here at school. Give me some credit!"

So Ebina is self-aware... If anything, the fact that she had arrived at this conclusion only added to my horror.

"Well, for now, we can ignore the character descriptions... So are we okay with emphasizing the comedic elements?" Hayama asked. No one raised any objections.

Well, it was a play for our school festival. It was the right choice to make it comedic rather than taking the whole thing seriously. Not only would a sincere take be awkward, with comedy, you can forgive a flub or two since it's just for laughs anyway. It'd be preferable to include those elements and just have fun with it.

"All right, then it's decided," Hayama said, and there was a smattering of applause right when the bell rang.

It had taken the entire long homeroom period, but the class had finally settled on what to do. There was still a lot left to decide, but now we could get things started.

There was just about one month until the festival. Yet another boring iteration of the yearly event.

Feeling a bit melancholy, I stood from my seat.

In the storm, **Hachiman Hikigaya** continues to slide.

The curtains swayed in the fall wind. Crimson-tinged wisps of cloud peeked out from behind the fluttering cloth. The window was open a crack to let the air in.

My eyes flicked over to it two, three times, and my hand stopped in the middle of turning a page. Those tiny, distracting movements in my periphery were getting on my nerves. I couldn't concentrate at all.

Sitting diagonally opposite me at the long table was a girl.

Yukinoshita had not so much as twitched in some time. Her gaze was pinned to the paperback in her hands, silently tracing the lines on the page. Since her back was to the window, the curtains were out of her field of vision.

Maybe I should've sat on that side, too, I thought, but since we'd both already settled in, going to the trouble of moving now would literally put me in an awkward position. Usually, I seated myself a little farther away from the window in the shade, while Yukinoshita always sat with the gentle touch of the light on her back. But now that we were entering into fall, the setting sun was looking dark. The days were getting shorter.

Summer vacation had ended, and we were a few days into September. Daytime weather was still very summery at this stage, but around this time, when sunset was approaching, cold winds would suddenly blow in.

The second semester had begun, but that didn't mean my lifestyle had changed much. Yukinoshita and I were still coming regularly to club. Even though all we did there was read. As Yukinoshita and I diligently buried our noses in books, Yuigahama fiddled with her sparkly, gem-studded, obnoxious cell phone.

The window frame rattled noisily in an especially strong gust.

The curtains flapped and waved, and my book blew to a different page. *Curtaaaaaain!* The curtains had really been asserting their presence for a while now. *Curtain, curtain!* Are you Bonchuu now?

It was irritating the hell out of me, so I glared at the window and clicked my tongue. The wind was obnoxious, too, but the curtains were far more so for just going along with it. *Do you guys have no sense of individuality?* The only things allowed to sway in the breeze are the balls flying over Marine Field and the skirts of cute girls.

Then, out of the corner of my eye, a skirt did indeed flutter as Yuigahama stood from her seat, about a chair and a half away, and went to shut the window with a snap. Her skirt had been so animated, I'd wondered if there was a Pokémon under there. I almost tried to capture it. *Phew, nearly lost control of my pocket monster, there...*

"The wind's picking up, huh?" she said.

The only reply was the rattling of the window.

Not one to be discouraged by the lack of reaction, Yuigahama spoke again. "I heard there's gonna be a storm." Now that she'd spoken twice, both Yukinoshita and I were forced to lift our heads from our books. Yuigahama looked a little relieved. "The weather was nice all break, and now this happens, huh?"

"Was it? Seemed pretty dark to me." I thought back on it, but I didn't have many memories of bright, sunny days. I only remember those when I go outside...

"You wouldn't know, Hikki, 'cause you never leave the house." Yuigahama gave me a little snort. Yeah, that was true.

"I mean...it's just, blackout curtains do their job, you know?"

"Were they doing maintenance on your grid all summer or something?" Yuigahama asked, her expression puzzled.

"What?" I asked back, equally puzzled.

"Huh?" Confusion on both our faces, we stared at each other until we both figured out we weren't talking about the same thing. *Hey, come on, now. She can't have been asking that question seriously. Oh man, this girl is scary.*

Yukinoshita, who was probably listening to this hopeless exchange, closed her book with a snap and ventured, "Just…in case, I'll explain… Blackout curtains are curtains that block out light. You're thinking of a rolling blackout."

Yuigahama paused briefly before she answered with some surprise. "Huh? Oh…o-of course! Yeah…I—I knew that…" At the end, she was avoiding our eyes completely.

I had pity on her and made a token attempt at helping her save face. "Well, you know, light blocking has an ancient and honorable origin for us Japanese. We even have those light-blocking clay figures. Historically speaking, it's in our blood." Abhorring the light, we are the people who have shouldered the fate of an affinity for darkness—the Japanese. Whoa, that was a pretty M-2 way to put that.

"Oh, really?! Yeah, now that you mention it, maybe you're right. I don't think pit houses and stuff like that had windows." Yuigahama gave me an appreciative *ohhh*.

Yukinoshita, meanwhile, had her hand on her forehead to hold back her headache as she breathed a short sigh. "*Shakouki doguu* are called 'light blocking' because they appeared to be wearing the snow goggles the Inuit wore to prevent snow blindness. It has nothing to do with blocking light in any way." Her voice was quiet and gentle as a whisper, but perfectly clear in the otherwise deathly silent room.

"Oh, really? H-huh…"

Yukinoshita was acting abnormally shy, considering she was in the middle of smugly revealing Yuigahama's ignorance. Nobody was going to talk now that she was like this. Worst of all, I couldn't come up with a snappy retort for her.

"…"

"…"

Maybe Yukinoshita decided to have mercy, since she ended her criticisms there.

After that, she went back to her reading, while I leaned on my cheek and flipped through my paperback with my free hand.

I could hear the wind howling in the distance. *Phew, phew*—I guess even the great outdoors is tired of this.

Someone cleared their throat, and it sounded incredibly loud.

Before I knew it, I could hear the second hand ticking.

I doubt humans differ much when it comes to sensing awkward silences.

As if she'd just remembered something, Yuigahama took a deep breath. "Hikki, you should seriously go outside more. Isn't that how you make vitamin C?"

"I think you mean vitamin D," I replied. "Making vitamin C? Are you Lemon-chan or something? Humans don't generate their own vitamin C."

"They don't?"

"Yep. And by the way, you can make enough vitamin D just by getting some sun for thirty minutes twice a week. Therefore, there's no need for me to go out of my way to leave the house," I told her pompously. I may be a humanities type, but I know plenty of trivia. In fact, that might even be part of being a humanities type.

Apparently shocked by my wealth of knowledge, Yuigahama shuddered. "Why do you know so much about this? Are you a health maniac? Creepy…"

That was pretty harsh. "…My parents said something like that to me, too, once, so I looked it up."

"Are you that desperate to avoid leaving the house…?"

"How very like you, Hikikomori-kun," said Yukinoshita.

"Leave me alone…" I was about to add, *And how do you know my middle school–era nickname?* But I stopped short. Yeah…no need to mention that. I mean, like, that comeback just wasn't funny enough to say out loud. You know what I'm saying? Keeping my mouth shut was the right choice. It happens sometimes: Someone starts a conversation, you get carried away with your witty remarks, and then everyone goes dead silent.

Suddenly remembering a similar situation, I squirmed.

But even though I hadn't said it, everyone was still silent.

"…"

"…"

Yukinoshita didn't so much as twitch an eyebrow. She seemed bored as she looked at the pages of her paperback.

Her lack of response must have bothered Yuigahama, as she laughed to fill the silence. "Ah…ah-ha-ha… Hikki is a total *hikki*, am I right?"

"Hey now, ever since ancient times, this has been the most righteous and sacred lifestyle. Even the chief goddess of Japanese myth, Amaterasu Oomikami, went full shut-in." I will emulate the myths and stay in my house. I will follow in the footsteps of the divine; in other words, I will become the god of the new world.

"The gods of Japanese myth aren't all righteous, though," said Yukinoshita.

"Huh? Really?" Yuigahama asked.

"Yeah. It's pretty common in polytheism." The gods actually do a lot of crazy stuff. If you read a lot of myths, you'll find a whole host of outrageous tales.

Yuigahama *hmm*'d appreciatively in response. "The word *god* gives you the impression they're perfect, though."

If we're talking the capital *G* "God," that might be the rule, but when you say *kami* in Japanese, that's not all they are. These gods are not all-knowing, all-powerful beings of absolute justice.

As I ruminated on these thoughts, the following words suddenly rolled out of my mouth: "Well…you shouldn't try to fit anyone into a specific mold. Not gods or anyone else." I wasn't particularly expecting a reply from anyone. I was just making the most of my talent for monologuing.

After a long pause, the quiet reply was nearly drowned out by the sound of a page turning. "…Indeed." I doubt she was looking for a reply herself. She wasn't looking at anyone or talking to anyone.

You can't fit people into a mold.

Gods are the only ones you're allowed to expect perfection from.

You can't expect anyone to meet your ideals.

It's weakness. An evil to be abhorred. Carelessness to be punished. It's a spoiled and naive thing to do, both to yourself and to others. The only person you're ever allowed to be disappointed in is yourself. The only person you're ever allowed to hurt is yourself. Just hate yourself for failing to meet your ideals.

The only one you can't forgive should be you.

"…"

"…"

The conversation came to a halt, and the air turned thick with tension. The seconds ticked by. Even though the windows were closed, the frozen time was making the room very cold.

"Uh, um…" Yuigahama's head whipped back and forth between me and Yukinoshita, and then her shoulders slumped dramatically.

Lately, all our exchanges had been like this. For days on end, we'd done our best to talk, tried to take a conversation somewhere. After two or three days of this, Yuigahama was, unsurprisingly, tired.

The wind slapped against the window, shattering the silence. The glass rattled, and the air in the clubroom shivered. Yuigahama glanced outside for an opportunity to continue the conversation. "It's gotten real bad out there, huh? If the Keiyo Line stops, you won't be able to go home, huh, Yukinon?"

"Yes."

Right, Yukinoshita took the Keiyo Line to school, if I recalled.

When a really large, powerful typhoon hits the Kanto area, Chiba becomes a lone island off its shore. All the railway lines on the network are paralyzed: the Keiyo Line first, then the Sobu Line, Joban Line, Musashino Line, Keisei Line, Tozai Line, and Toei Shinjuku Line. All of Chiba gets cut off from the rest of Japan, and it's halfway down the road to independence.

Come to think of it, Chiba does have a lot of railroads, doesn't it? Aside from all the above, we have ones like Choshi Dentetsu and Kominato Tetsudou that are all nice and gone to seed. The Uchifusa Line and the Sotofusa Line are also pretty major, but unfortunately, when you're living close to Tokyo, you can't tell the difference. Sometimes you get

them mixed up in an honest mistake, and people get really pissed. The anger of the people of Chiba is like a blazing fire!

Anyway, when a typhoon hits, it causes a number of interruptions in the transportation network around the metropolitan area. Yukinoshita would probably be affected one way or another.

"Right? So, I live pretty close…" Yuigahama trailed off.

The silence struck me as odd, so I looked and saw that Yukinoshita was utterly miserable. "…It's all right. If that happens, I'll walk home."

"O-oh. So it's not so far you can't walk…"

Yukinoshita lived about two stations away from the school. It really wasn't an unwalkable distance.

Yuigahama mustered her cheer again and spoke to me. "You ride your bike, Hikki?"

"Yeah," I answered, then glanced out the window. Fortunately, it wasn't raining yet. I had brought an umbrella, but I'd have preferred to avoid walking home with it up in these strong winds.

"Why don't you take the bus home on days like this?"

"Buses are crowded, so I don't wanna." Besides, most of the riders would be students from our school. If a classmate ended up next to me on the bus, it'd be a disaster. As long as it's someone who can ignore me, it's fine. But when someone I kinda know notices I'm there and stops chatting with their friends, it makes me feel really bad. It plagues my heart with guilt. So much guilt that I want to apologize for being born, like I'm Dazai or something.

And worst of all, if I got on the bus now, I'd end up going home at the same time as Yuigahama. And you know her. She'd definitely try to strike up a conversation.

—And if people saw us like that…

I always felt bad whenever people saw Yui Yuigahama being friendly with someone from the lowest caste. I didn't want to make her relive the experience of the fireworks show.

I just had to go home before the weather got any worse.

As the wind picked up strength, even the athletic clubs were starting to beat a retreat. Even if we did stay, I doubted anyone would come to consult with us. And just as the thought occurred to me, the door to the clubroom banged open before the sliding noise could even warn us that we had a visitor.

"You kids are still here?" Miss Hiratsuka, the Service Club's teacher-advisor, entered without knocking as she always did. "The other clubs are already finishing up. You all go home early, before the weather worsens."

When Yukinoshita heard that, she closed her book with a snap. "Let's end it here for today." The low-hanging clouds outside darkened everything in the clubroom, even Yukinoshita's expression.

"Right, then… Take care, you all." Miss Hiratsuka seemed concerned for Yukinoshita, but she walked out without saying anything more.

Neither Yuigahama nor I offered any objections. We just packed up our things and left.

"…I'm going to go return the key," said Yukinoshita, and she strode off down the empty hallway without another word. I didn't watch her go; I just headed for the entrance. Yuigahama seemed a bit unsure about what to do, but about three seconds later, she followed after me.

Neither of us said a word until we put on our outdoor shoes. The only sound in the deserted entryway was the plop of my loafers hitting the ground. I stuffed my feet into them and went outside. "I'm taking my bike," I said.

"Okay. Bye." Yui gave a little wave in front of her chest, and we exchanged our short farewells.

The wind was oddly tepid. Must have brought in some humidity from the south.

×　×　×

I frantically pedaled my bicycle into the headwind. I'd been abusing my city bike for over a year now, and it creaked and whined to let me know.

No matter how I pedaled and pedaled, I didn't feel like I was getting anywhere. I was even starting to feel like I was being pushed backward. The wind was so strong, it nearly broke my spirit, but I kept the pedals turning.

Twilight came earlier now, but the sun hadn't completely set yet. However, thick clouds obscured what natural light would have remained. Lampposts stood at regular intervals, shining unreliably, and plastic bags and empty cans tumbled along the road.

I could smell wet earth in the dark, and then black spots began to appear on the asphalt. One by one, the stains increased, each one accompanied by a loud *plip*.

Eventually, the black covered the whole ground. The drops were pouring down in a rush with no concern at all for me, hitting my bare arms so hard it stung a little. The mercilessly pounding raindrops turned my white uniform shirt translucent. Too bad there were no high school girls around.

What a pain in the ass. What the hell, man... I grumbled under my breath, and then I pulled my umbrella off my bicycle and deployed it to shield me.

An instant later, a blast of wind broke it entirely. The ribs snapped and pointed every which way, and the plastic part became a sail. *The wind drags me away, ah, like a yacht.* I lost my balance, panicked, and put my feet on the ground.

...I'd just about fallen on my face. Wiping off the cold sweat and rainwater, I surrendered and folded up my broken umbrella.

This really is a pain in the ass.

The wind was drowning out all the other sounds, and I could hardly keep my eyes open in the driving rain. My drenched clothing was leeching away my body heat, and the added weight from the water made my body feel heavy. My vision was already fogging up.

In the rain, everything just thoughtlessly skims along the surface—tires, words, thoughts.

I could see the Hanami River from my route, spitting out an endless flood of dark water to wash away everything.

Only I was left behind in the storm.

Minami Sagami
aggressively makes a request.

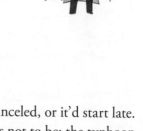

Typhoons meant that either school would be canceled, or it'd start late. Or so I had hoped, once upon a time. But it was not to be; the typhoon passed during the night, and by morning, I was back to my usual daily routine. In the end, the sun was shining bright and perfect in the sky, and I was doing so, so great.

I was not doing great.

I'd thought that at the very least I could use the typhoon as an excuse to be late, so I'd stayed up the previous night. Now I was really tired. With my lack of sleep, I was just about qualified to be the opening song for *Kiteretsu*.

Typhoons these days are so unmotivated. It sucks.

Though I somehow did make it to school on time, exhaustion reared its head the whole way through. Usually, during breaks, I'd put my head down on my desk and pretend to sleep, but that day, I really was asleep.

And not just on breaks, either. I was battling the sandman in class, too. I tried leaning my cheek on my hand, lying my face on my desk, and pillowing my head between my arms, in my desperation to find the best position. I mean, you know, fighting isn't nice after all, so it's best to just settle things peacefully. Yep. I think I'll stay on friendly terms with the sandman.

Meanwhile, class ended.

I concluded that sandwiching my head between my arms, face-down on my desk, was decent. I didn't get sleep marks on my face that way. The problem is that it really hurt my neck, shoulders, and back.

At this rate, I could manage a shallow nap at best, and to make it worse, forcing myself into this uncomfortable position was only ramping up the sleepiness. I had to lie down and get some shut-eye, or I wouldn't feel rested.

Now that it had come to this, there was only one place I could go. I stood up and wobbled over to the rear door of the classroom.

The moment I opened the door...

"Ack!"

"Whoops, sorry," I said. It wasn't like I crashed into the other person with a *kablam!* ☆, but I did feel a slight impact on my chest. I'd bumped into the person coming in right as I was leaving. Hey, who is this person who doesn't watch where he's going and shouldn't get his driver's license of the year?

I glared at whoever it was, until I got a better look and recognized the familiar squirrel-like boy trembling there oh-so-cutely. He was out of breath as he came into the classroom—the one who really should not get that license because I just want him to be in the passenger seat forever while I drive...of the year, Saika Totsuka.

"Oh, Hachiman. Sorry..."

"O-oh, no! I should be apologizing. I was kinda zoning out there." *To be honest, I'm still zoning out now.* Coincidence though it was, I'd ended up catching Totsuka in my arms. *Phew...* That was close. If Totsuka had been holding bread in his mouth, love would have blossomed right there.

Noticing the position we were frozen in, Totsuka gently pulled away from my chest. "Sorry. It's because I was in a rush... Where did you mean to go, Hachiman? It's time for the next class."

"I've just got some stuff." I couldn't simply confess that I was going to skip and sleep in the health room. If you're gonna brag about your crimes like that, do it on Twitter.

Totsuka seemed a bit curious about my answer. "But during the next class, we're going to decide roles for the cultural festival. So maybe you should stay?"

"Oh, is that right?" In the long homeroom the other day, we'd only decided what the class plan was. In the next class, we'd probably be able to move on to discussing the details.

"Well...I'm okay with anything." No matter what I did, it'd all be the same anyway. As usual, I'd be no more than present. A being that just is. Once the prep work got started, the most I could expect to do was stand there like an unusual totem pole. No matter what role I was assigned, my life wouldn't change. I wouldn't have anything to do, so I'd only sort of hover behind someone, peek at what they were doing, and go, "Hmm..." like I knew what I was talking about and mutter to myself as I waited for someone to ask me to do something. Like a martial arts master who specializes in counterattacks.

"You can just shove me in whatever's left at the end," I said.

There was no way for me to know if Totsuka understood what I was thinking, but still, he nodded, his expression a little mystified. "Okay, then."

I waved a hand casually to say my thanks and left the classroom.

✕ ✕ ✕

In the hallway, I heard the bell signaling the start of class as I headed for the nurse's office on the first floor of the special building. As you might expect, there were no students wandering the halls at this hour, and it was silent as I walked along.

It was a little chilly near the nurse's office. I knocked lightly and opened the front door, and the pungent smell of disinfectant hit my nose. Inside, a girl was chatting with the school nurse. Until I came in anyway. The girl whose name I didn't know dropped her eyes to her phone uncomfortably. I kinda felt like I'd done something bad. Sorry, tee-hee. :P

"My, my, you're one of Shizu's," said the school nurse, a young woman in a white coat. She watched me intently.

I dunno about that. Talking like Miss Hiratsuka is my mom is bound to make a person angry, y'know. Miss Hiratsuka, mainly. For the implications about her age.

"I kinda feel like I'm getting a cold." Briefly, I explained the reason I'd come. While I was at it, I also assumed an air of mild exhaustion. Times like these, my acting is flawless. I wouldn't be surprised if they started calling me the Master of the Cold. Oh man, that title sounds so cool. I mean, even the kanji character for the illness comes from putting "wind" and "evil" together. That's a pretty distinctly M-2 naming sensibility, there.

"Amateur diagnoses are dangerous. Show me." But though I'd poured my heart and soul into my performance, the school nurse casually brushed it aside.

Tch. Unsurprisingly, she had a lot of experience dealing with students trying to skip out. This school nurse had seen it all. *So she won't be deceived so easily!*

The nurse's eyes were piercing, as if she were attempting to see through my lies. No, it may be more accurate to say she was leering at me. In the world of Pokémon, my defense would have been reduced. "…You've got a cold, all right."

"That was a fast diagnosis." What the hell was with that lead-up? I shot her a look of annoyance, partly to protest.

She laughed at me pleasantly. "I mean, your eyes are so dull. You're clearly sick."

By that logic, I was sick 24/7. *And what do you mean, "dull" anyway? Even dull-skied London turns to Paris once things brighten up.*

The nurse scribbled something on her clipboard, then turned back to me. "Now, then. What will you do? Get some rest here?" she asked. *And will you equip that right now?* I almost expected her to add.

"Oh, sure."

"The bed at the end," she replied briefly, and I did as I was told.

It was divided off by a curtain, with a neatly folded thin blanket lying on top. I pulled it over my stomach and lay down.

Beyond the pink curtains, the chat resumed again. Only the sound of their voices remained faintly in my ears as I drifted away.

X X X

What…did you say…?

It was just after my break. When I came back to the classroom, I learned that I'd been forced onto the Cultural Festival Committee. On the blackboard was my name, Hikigaya, and underneath it, *committee member. Gyawaa!* This is conspiracy!

Okay, I know I said I was fine with whatever job was left over. It'd be the same no matter what I did, so I was ready to accept any petty job in silence. But do they feel no pangs of conscience for giving me the job nobody wants to do? Standard procedure for this situation is to toss a loner some harmless and inoffensive job, right? It's always been that way, at least for me.

The fabled "you weren't there, so we made you the committee president, lol" method is something popular kids do to each other in good humor, and that's exactly why it's been established as a funny joke among themselves. When you pull that with someone from a different cultural sphere…

That's war…! It doesn't count…! It doesn't count!

Dumbfounded, I was standing there in front of the blackboard when I felt a slap on my shoulder.

"I suppose you need an explanation?" Without even turning around, I knew who it was.

H-here she coooomes. The thirtysomething teacher who wants to get married right now, Shizuka Hiratsukaaaaa.

I accepted her offer and wordlessly asked for an explanation.

Miss Hiratsuka blew a short sigh and glanced at the clock. "It was time for the next period, but the class was still quibbling about who'd be on the committee. So we went with you."

Hold on there, Japanese teacher. You can't use so *in that sentence. There's no causal relationship here.* "What's this about, Miss Hiratsuka?"

"What do you mean?"

"This is crazy! What do you think a loner is?! Forcing one into the middle of a class event will only bring about tragedy!"

These committees exist for the fun and excitement of social groups. My presence would only have them all walking on eggshells! The teacher *could* have tossed me into a position where I wouldn't have much influence, where things would be fine whether I was there or not, where nobody would have had to bother with me, and where we all could have gotten through this comfortably! I'll take Gandhi's nonviolent civil disobedience and raise you nonnegotiable noninterference!

"I thought about checking to see what you wanted, but...you did say you were fine with anything, right?"

Oof..., I thought, expelling a sigh. Looking over to the window, I saw Totsuka putting his hands together apologetically. Cute. Oh, pressing the wrinkles of each hand together is happiness. *Naamuu.*

As I was looking away from Miss Hiratsuka, the wrinkles on each side of her forehead came together. Iron out your wrinkles before you work on mine. *Wriiinkllles.*

"Just sit down. I have to start class. Decide the rest after school."

×   ×   ×

After school, the classroom was chaos.

They were deciding who would be in charge of what for the cultural festival. Typically, they would have made these decisions in the previous class, but it had apparently taken them such a long time to decide who would be the male committee member that Miss Hiratsuka had made the tyrannical decision that it would be me. This is what they call abuse of power...

Ngh! If only I were higher on the ladder! Then I could have forced this onto someone else! Abusing your power all the way down the chain is the core of Japan's hierarchical society. Recently, I'd been thinking,

Man, I'm so Japanese. I'm feeling my Japanese identity rather strongly right now.

So this was why the female committee member had yet to be decided.

The bespectacled class representative was directing the class from the teacher's podium. I didn't know his name. People mostly just called him Class Rep. If he had been a girl, then I'm sure she would have the popularity of a committee president character, but unfortunately, it was a boy. I guess "Class Rep" was enough of a name for him.

"Okay, any girls who want to be on the committee, raise your hands," he said. Obviously, no one was going to react to that. The class rep sighed in resignation. "If we still can't decide on someone, we could do rock-paper-scissors—"

"Huh?" Miura cut him off.

He seemed scared, as he gulped down the rest of his words. Silencing him with a single syllable—*were you born in a temple?* Truly incredible.

After that, there was more sporadic chattering in between the silences, over and over. Many times, I witnessed the same exchange: A conversation would start up somewhere, the class rep would suggest that person, and each time, silence fell again.

"Um…is it really hard?" Yuigahama asked, apparently unable to watch anymore.

The class rep looked clearly relieved. "Normally, I don't think it would be, but…the girl might ultimately end up having a hard time," he said, glancing over at me. That four-eyes. He just indirectly announced I was DFA. That four-eyes. He'd acted so embarrassed about saying it, too, so I couldn't even get mad. I just ended up feeling bad. *Sorry, Glasses Guy. Now, now. Go ahead, Glasses.*

"Hmm…," Yuigahama said with a conflicted glance my way.

The class rep seemed to take that as hesitation, and he pounced on the chance to go on the attack. "Frankly, it'd be a big help if you did it, Yuigahama. You're popular, you'll do a good job bringing the class together, and I think you're qualified."

"Well, I'm not really like…" Yuigahama was replying ever-so-shyly when someone interrupted, cold as ice water.

"Wait, you're gonna do it, Yui?"

"Huh?" Yuigahama turned around to look at the girl. I think her name was…Sagami?

Sagami was in a group with three other girls, some distance away from Yuigahama and her friends. Unlike Miura's clique, which sat by the window at the very rear of the classroom, Sagami's was on the hallway side, partway to the back.

"That's so nice. I'm sure you'll have *lots* of fun planning this event with your *friend*," said Sagami, and her friends giggled scornfully.

Yuigahama replied with a vague smile. "Mmm. It's not really like that, though."

Sagami shot a meaningful look toward me, and the smirk that accompanied it was incredibly ugly. And the giggling whispers she exchanged with the other girls sitting near her were as grating as you could get.

It was completely obvious what their laughter was about. It was just like the day of the fireworks show.

Both of us had to deal with those sneers, scornful but curious. She always from the inside, and me always from the outside. Their snickering lapped at my ears like little wavelets.

"But, like…" A haughty voice cut through the noise like a foot stomping into a thicket, and all the insects went silent. "Yui's gonna be bringing in guests with me, so she can't," Yumiko Miura stated, her attitude decisive and confident.

Sagami's followers must have been overwhelmed by her intensity, as they fell completely silent.

"Oh, really?" said Sagami. "Yeah, that's pretty important, too, huh?"

"Y-yeah, yeah!" Yuigahama echoed. "Bringing in guests is important, too… Wait, when did we decide that's what I'm doing?!" Yuigahama had just been going along with everyone else, so she was caught off guard, too. And I thought only the male committee member had been decided…

For her part, Miura was a little confused by Yuigahama's reaction. "Uh...w-we're not doing that together? A-am I wrong? Was I just assuming?"

"It's okay, Yumiko! You're basically right. It's just who you are!" Ebina stuck out her tongue, winked, and gave a thumbs-up. Yeah, well, it really was very Miura, wasn't it?

"C'mon, Ebina, don't be so...flattering! It's embarrassing!" Unfortunately for Miura, blushing bright red as she gave Ebina a whap, the comment was probably not supposed to be flattery.

Off to the side, Yuigahama's shoulders dropped just a wee bit. "S-so I don't have the right to decide..."

You only just realized that? But relax. Someone like me doesn't get any options at all, since Miss Hiratsuka decided for me in her despotic wisdom, and nobody really wanted me in that position anyway. I'm pretty damn unwanted here.

We hadn't made any progress at all, and the class rep breathed a short sigh. You could feel the grief of middle management in that sigh. "In other words, we're okay as is?"

Hayama had only been watching, but he finally broke his silence, without raising his hand. Naturally, all eyes gathered on him. The class rep's glasses sparkled in anticipation.

"We want help from someone with a knack for leadership. How does that sound?"

Hayama's words were exceedingly respectable, valid, and reasonable. Well, if someone's going to be in charge of something for the cultural festival, leadership is a must, obviously. The only problem in his phrasing was it sounded like he meant I had none of that. Well, he's not wrong. The only kind of ship I've got is me/Totsuka, apparently.

Anyway, he was saying this job should go to someone of the highest caste. But the boys' seat was already occupied by me, and clearly, no one was interested in the girls' seat.

The general sense in such a situation is that if there were no takers from the top caste, then the role would be passed on to the B-group.

Tobe grasped precisely what Hayama was implying. "So why not Sagami?"

"Oh, that might be a good idea. She'd do a good job," said Hayama. This was exactly the conclusion he'd been steering us toward, yet Hayama acted as if Tobe had convinced him.

Tobe, being Tobe, answered with a smug "Right, man?" or something. He's a little cute and very pathetic.

Whereas Sagami, suddenly finding herself at the center of the conversation, was waving her hand in front of her face in a tiny gesture of refusal. "What? Me? Could I even do that? No way." Though her pose said no, she wasn't the least bit sincere. Come on, I'm a first-rate expert in rejection. You can't fool me. When a girl is *actually* turning you down, her face is a mask and her eyes are frigid as she goes, *Um, could you stop, seriously?* The sheer terror makes your heart freeze over as you wish for death.

Hayama clearly understood that much about the inevitable course of events, as he put his hands together in apology as if he were just making doubly sure. "Would it be possible to ask you, Sagami?"

"Well…if there's no one else, I guess I have to. Really? Me…?" But even as Sagami grumbled for the benefit of everyone else, she was clearly happy, and her cheeks were pink. Is this Jigoku no Misawa now? Getting a request from Hayama, or rather, being the person Hayama chose to request, probably didn't feel so bad for her.

"I'll do it, then," Sagami replied with feigned reluctance.

The class rep clouded his glasses with a sigh of relief. "All right. Then we're done for the day," he said, exhausted, and then everyone filtered out of the classroom.

× × ×

The committee meetings began that very day.

It was three forty-five in the afternoon, and I mentally confirmed the schedule.

The most vital ability for maintaining a solo position at school is self-management. I have to have a good general grasp of when we're switching classrooms, which days are holidays, and what the schedule is after school. As for why: because nobody would tell me. I'm an expert in finding out about holidays, especially.

The time of the meeting was looming near, so I started heading to the conference room.

There was a smattering of other people on their way there, too. Some among them were co-ed groups, chatting as they went along. *Good grief, you can't even head to the conference room alone, you lost children in life.*

The room assigned to the Cultural Festival Committee was as big as two normal classrooms, with some fairly legit chairs and tables. It was apparently normally used for staff meetings.

When I entered, I found about half of the committee already assembled. Sagami was among them, too. She'd probably left before me. She was also chatting with two other girls. Either they'd been friends before, or they'd become friends very quickly.

"Like, it's such a relief you're on the committee, too, Yukko. I was wondering what I'd even do here, you know?"

After Sagami got the ball rolling, the other two reacted. "I'm just doing it 'cause I lost at rock-paper-scissors."

"Me too! Oh, Sagami, can I call you Minami?"

"Sure, sure. What should I call you?"

"Haruka is fine!"

"Haruka… Wait, you're on the girls' basketball team with Yukko, aren't you?"

"Yep, yep."

"Nice! Maybe I should've joined a club, too. I've got no luck with my class."

"Ohhh, Class F is the one with Miura and stuff, huh?"

"Yeah…" Even dejected as she was, Sagami was a formidable person, but the girl who immediately named Miura in the context of "class luck" was pretty scary herself.

The frightening thing about the way girls talk is that even when there's nothing nasty about each of their words individually, when you put them all together, it's deadly venom. It's a lot like how the trace amounts of poison in some creatures turn into lethal tetrodotoxin when they're stored inside a puffer fish.

"But you get to be with Hayama, so that's cool."

"I guess. He recommended me for the committee, too. Though it's kind of embarrassing."

Seriously, who are you—Sagamisawa?

Perking up my ears, I listened in on other groups' conversations.

Every new arrival created a little stir. As we approached the starting time, the number of people in the room increased, one by one. Each time the door opened, all eyes would turn to the entrance, but once it became clear it wasn't someone they knew, they'd quietly look away. *I don't like those looks… It's like they're announcing,* It's not you I was waiting for. Boring.

But things were completely different with the next person to come in.

The moment the door opened, the loud chattering stopped instantly. It was like someone had slapped a hand over all their mouths as Yukino Yukinoshita walked in with silent footsteps. Her usual overbearing attitude was muted. Everyone had stopped breathing, as if they were watching snow melt away.

Yukinoshita recognized my presence and paused for a moment. But she quickly jerked her gaze away, took a few steps, reconsidered, then took a few more steps toward a nearby empty chair. Until she sat down, time in the conference room was clearly frozen.

I should have been used to her by then, but even I couldn't help but stare for a moment. Maybe it was seeing her out of her usual context. Or maybe it was because I was surprised to see her here with the Cultural Festival Committee.

Time was already moving again. Though reluctantly, the hushed chatter resumed its ebb and flow. Then right about when the second hand was about to hit the time for the meeting to start, there was a thunder of footsteps, and the door to the conference room clattered open again. A group of students came in holding printouts, with the gym teacher, Atsugi, and Miss Hiratsuka following behind.

Why's Miss Hiratsuka here? I wondered, looking at her. Our eyes met, and she grinned at me. The smile was much younger and cuter than you would expect from someone her age. That is to say, it was malicious.

I knew it. I've been had.

A few of the students gathered at the front of the conference room and looked toward a pleasant sort of girl, who answered with an affirmative nod. At the signal, two apparent first-years began passing out some documents to all of us present. After making sure everyone had their copies, the girl gently rose to her feet. "Now then, let's begin the Cultural Festival Committee meeting."

Her medium-length hair fell to her shoulders, and her bangs were held back with a hair clip. Her smooth, pretty forehead gleamed in the light. She wore her uniform entirely according to regulations, but her embroidered lapel badge and the colorful hair elastics around her wrists gave her a cutesy look. As she beamed around at everyone, her orders were somehow pleasant. All the students sat up straighter.

"Um, I'm Meguri Shiromeguri, the student council president. I'm really glad to have the opportunity to join all of you in running another cultural festival this year... U-um, so...l-let's all do our best! Yeah!" Meguri ended with a simple cheer, and without a moment's delay, the student council applauded for her. The rest of the crowd followed suit.

Meguri gave a couple of pleasant nods in response. "Thank you very much! All right, then let's get straight to selecting a committee chair." The crowd murmured a little.

Well, of course. I'd thought for sure the student council president would also head the committee.

Meguri gave a rather wry smile. "I'm sure many of you already know, but every year, a second-year is selected as chair of the Cultural Festival Committee. I'm, you know, already in third year, so..."

Oh, that makes sense. I mean, you couldn't do something like this

right at the beginning of fall in third year. You'd have to study for entrance exams and stuff.

"Okay then, so do we have any volunteers?"

No hands rose.

No surprise there. I don't think it's that the students weren't into the cultural festival. I think a lot of them were pretty gung ho about it. But wanting to demonstrate your skills, be active, and work hard was a whole 'nother field.

It's natural to want to work together with your own class or your club as much as possible. You want to be with your close friends and enjoy an emotional event together with that certain someone you'd been thinking about.

This was demanding you to work your ass off with a bunch of randos.

"Anyone?" Meguri said with concern, but the conference room maintained its silence.

Then Atsugi, the gym teacher, cleared his throat like a war cry. "*Wagh!* Come on, kids, show a little motivation! You don't have enough ambition! Ambition! Listen up! The cultural festival is *your* event." He was so passionate about this, I thought he might end that sentence with a *See ya, folks!*

Apparently, Atsugi was going to be a teacher-advisor for the cultural festival. Miss Hiratsuka, standing beside him with her arms folded and eyes closed, probably occupied the same role.

Atsugi scanned the conference room, making eye contact with each one of the students, until he came to a halt on Yukinoshita. "Oh... you're Yukinoshita's little sister! We'll be expecting a cultural festival like that old one." There was an implicit message behind his comment: *Of course, you'll be the committee chair, right?*

Meguri seemed to pick up on that, too, and she muttered, "Oh, she's Haru's little sister."

Haruno Yukinoshita strikes again. She must have left quite an impression on both the teachers and her juniors.

"I'll give my utmost as a regular member of the committee,"

Yukinoshita replied very simply, in a manner that wasn't discourteous. But the twitch of her eyebrow hinted at her slight irritation.

Atsugi knew a flat rejection when he saw it and gave a noncommittal, half-hearted *uh-huh* or *sure* and fell silent. That meant it was Meguri's problem now.

She folded her arms exaggeratedly and groaned, sinking deep into reflection. "Hmm… Um, well, being the committee chair can earn you a lot of brownie points. You know, with the teachers. It might help out a lot for anyone looking for a recommendation to a particular university."

Is this girl an idiot? That wasn't going to inspire anyone to volunteer. Now you'd look like you had blatant ulterior motives.

"Um…how about it?" Meguri was still looking at Yukinoshita as she asked.

Whether Yukinoshita noticed or not, she stubbornly refrained from reacting and stared right back.

Yukinoshita doesn't like standing up in front of a crowd. She's not the type to chair a committee. But under Meguri's bright grin, it must have been awkward. Yukinoshita shifted a bit. Perhaps you could call it the pressure of a pure smile. There's nothing nastier than an innocent gaze.

If Meguri works on her a little longer, I think Yukinoshita will fold…

Just as Yukinoshita blew out a deep, resigned sigh, there was an "Um…" The odd sense of tension slackened all at once.

Breaking the silence was a somewhat timid voice. "If nobody else wants to do it, then I wouldn't mind." The source was three seats away from me: Minami Sagami.

Meguri clapped her hands with glee at the offer. "Really? Great! Then can you introduce yourself?" she prompted.

Sagami took a breath. "I'm Minami Sagami, from Class 2-F. I was kinda interested in something like this…and I've been hoping this cultural festival might help me grow as a person, I guess… I'm not really good at being a leader, but… Wait, I shouldn't say that. Then it'd just be like, 'Don't do it,' right? Yeah, that's something about myself I wanna change. And I think this'll be a chance to practice some new skills, so I want to do my best."

Why do we have to help you with your personal growth? I wondered, but it seemed like no one else had any serious objections.

"Yep, yep," said Meguri, "I think it's a good idea, too. New skills are important."

A couple of people clapped, and a smattering of applause continued throughout the classroom. Sagami gave a slightly embarrassed little bob of a bow and then sat in her seat.

Glad they'd found a candidate and settled on her, Meguri muttered a quiet "Yes!" as she stole a marker from the secretary and wrote on the whiteboard *Committee chair: Sumo.*

Uh, those are the wrong characters. She's not E. Honda, you know…

Meguri tossed the marker back to the secretary and then, with a flutter of her skirt, spun around to face the room. "Okay then, now we'll decide everyone's roles. I've written a simple explanation of each section in the meeting overview, so please read those now. I'll take your requests in about five minutes."

As instructed, I glanced over the outline that had been handed out to me.

Publicity and Advertisement, Volunteer Management, Equipment Management, Health and Sanitation, Accounting, Records and Miscellaneous…this was all some fancy-sounding stuff. But still, a cultural festival put on by high school kids couldn't be that complicated. My little sister, Komachi, had been on student council or something back in middle school. It hadn't seemed that hard. It was a school function after all. You just had to walk firmly down the rails laid down for you. Like in *Stand by Me.*

I skimmed over the paper. Which one seemed like the least amount of work?

Publicity and Advertisement. Well, I didn't even have to read the blurb for that one. That was the thing where you went around putting up posters at convenience stores or whatever. You'd have to draw pictures and negotiate with people to get them displayed. The only future I could see for myself there was open humiliation. Pass.

Volunteer Management. You'd be handling the volunteer groups: basically, the people who'd be performing in bands or dancing. Yeah, no. Clearly, you'd have to deal with top-caste people. I have dealt with loan groups, though. No thanks.

Equipment Management. Borrowing the tables the classes would use and managing the transport of electronics, I figured. I couldn't handle carrying tons and tons of stuff. It sounded super-exhausting. I might be able to carry the beat with some castanets, though. *Untan ♪, untan. ♪* Ignore that one.

Health and Sanitation. Oh, that's the one where you have to arrange all the applications for food-related stuff. Maybe I'd have done it if it were health and physical education. Declined.

Accounting. Yeah, yeah, financial matters. Well, if some kind of problem ever did come up, I sure wouldn't be able to handle it, so I'd be in trouble. Money stuff is scary. Firmly refused.

…I think that just now was a little much, even for me.

So then it was looking like the only thing I could do was Records and Miscellaneous. From what I'd gleaned as I skimmed, about all you had to do was take some pictures the day of the event. It wasn't like I had any plans for that day anyway. It should make a perfect excuse for killing some time.

After reaching my conclusion, I stretched lightly with a *hnn*. While I was at it, I looked around the area to see that most of the others had decided as well. They were zoning out, fiddling with their phones, or entertaining themselves with idle chatter.

Some of the loudest among these voices were near me.

"Oh man, I just went and made myself committee chair, didn't I?"

"It'll be okay. You can handle it, Sagamin."

"Maybe. I don't know. But, like, I feel like what I said was super-embarrassing. It wasn't too much?"

"No way; it was nice! Besides, we'll be helping you out, too," Sagami's friend said, turning to the other girl for additional support.

The other girl gave her endorsement. "Yeah, yeah."

"Really? Thanks!"

I heard their whole heartwarming exchange. Wonderful. Just like the sort of beautiful friendship you see before the start of a marathon.

…I felt like I'd seen this exact same exchange a moment ago, too. What is this, déjà vu? Or is it a copypasta? But even if it's not, man, those types always have the same conversation, every time. It's like, the only thing that's different is the topic and the vocabulary, and then at the end, they compliment each other, and it's over. It looked fun.

"Are we all about done?" Meguri's voice was surprisingly audible and clear. I'd call it fluffy-wuffy, or fuzzy-wuzzy, or *wanyaka-pappa yun-pappa*. Maybe that was why it so easily grabbed hold of the fringes of your attention. Unlike how they would've reacted if she had yelled, everyone naturally and calmly turned their heads to face her. Maybe it wasn't a skill she'd cultivated but rather part of her very nature.

"Has everyone basically made up their minds? Then, Sagami, you take it from here."

"Huh? Me?"

"Yep. I think everything from this point on is going to be the job of the committee chair."

"Okay…"

Meguri waved Sagami over, like *Come on, come on!*

Sagami sat down among the student council, almost disappearing into their midst. "W-well then, let's decide…" Her voice was barely above a whisper, but in the silence, we could hear her fine.

But this wasn't a stable sort of quiet.

It was the acute, dangerous silence used to attack a foreign body.

It stung awfully. Even one snicker would be enough to set off a storm of harsh criticism and abuse. Sagami had gone from enjoying herself in conversation to an entirely different person.

An individual cut off is so frail.

"First…then…is there anyone who wants to do Publicity and Advertisement…?" Her voice was wilting gradually. No one raised their hands.

"Okay, so, Publicity and Advertisement. You can go to lots of different places! You might even be able to go on TV and radio, too, you know?" Meguri's inviting remarks swayed my heart for an instant. If we're talking about television in Chiba, then first on the list is Chiba TV, and if we're talking radio, then it's Bay FM. That "Fight! Fight! Chiba!" song that occasionally plays on Chiba TV is so famous, if someone told me I could meet Jaguar at the station, I would have gone for Publicity and Advertisement without a moment's hesitation.

However, I probably wouldn't, so I refrained. By the way, I don't mean the one from *Pyu to Fuku*, but the one who's the hero of Chiba.

I don't know if Meguri's mysterious helping hand worked or not, but her timely assistance finally got the group into motion. A few hands rose, and once we'd checked off the number of people and their names, we moved on to deciding the next roles.

"Th-then...Volunteer Management," said Sagami. The volunteers are the stars of the cultural festival, so maybe that's why hands shot up so fast. Clearly, more than Sagami had predicted. "U-uh..." She was stuck.

Meguri promptly stepped in. "That's too many! Too many! Rock-paper-scissors, okay?" Meguri's forehead was sparkling, glittering with eagerness as the Megu-Megu rock-paper-scissors began.

×   ×   ×

Though her unique brand of enthusiasm didn't really make sense to me, Meguri managed each item on the agenda, one after the other. Either she just had more experience with this, or it was just in her nature, since she managed every bump in the road smoothly.

From first to last, each committee member's role was decided in the same manner. Though Meguri may not have seemed so dependable at first glance, she was the president of the student council after all. Thanks to her abilities, the roles were divided up reasonably. By the way, I was neatly installed in "Records and Miscellaneous."

Perhaps because that category had been decided last, or maybe because everyone had thought the same thing, it was where proactivity went to die.

It was painful when everyone got together with their sections to introduce themselves.

"Um, so what are we going to do?"

"Self-introductions...and stuff?"

"Are we going to do that?"

"Sure."

"..."

"..."

"Um, who'll start?"

"Oh, I'll go, then."

And so it went. The conversation was so sporadic I started wondering if I was in a field of mushrooms.

Yukinoshita was also among us, as if this were the obvious choice.

Once we finished our self-introductions (which only consisted of our names and which class we were in), the long-awaited rock-paper-scissors match to decide section head began. This match was decidedly pessimistic, as whoever lost would be taking up the role, so this tournament had a wholly different vibe than the previous one to narrow down volunteers.

First, we quarreled about whether to throw down a rock before beginning, then we had our match, and thus it was decided that someone-or-other in third year would be the section head before we promptly dispersed.

"Thanks for your hard work." We all said the formal farewell and scattered our separate ways. Yukinoshita took the lead and left first. I inserted myself into the flow out the door, too, but right when I was about to leave the conference room...

Minami Sagami was in the corner of the conference room, dejected. She must have been mulling over how her first task as the committee chair hadn't really gone well. Beside her were her two friends and, for some reason, Miss Hiratsuka and Meguri as well. They must have been discussing future meetings.

When I passed by them, for an instant, Miss Hiratsuka's eyes met with mine. A wink flew at me with a *smack* ☆, and she waved a hand. *Bye-bye.*

…I'm leaving now.

Minami
Sagami

Birthday

June 26

Special skills:

Nothing in particular

Hobbies:

Nothing in particular

How I spend my weekends:

Working at the neighborhood
convenience store, shopping

Hina Ebina's musical is homoerotic, as expected. (Part 2)

It was one month until the cultural festival, and the school was a flurry of activity.

Starting that day, we were allowed to stay behind in the classroom to prepare. In other classrooms, students were carrying in cardboard boxes and setting up paints, and the easily excitable types were bringing in snacks and drinks to start up a party for everyone and get attention for their generosity.

Class 2-F's prep was moving right along, too. Hayama was addressing the room from the teacher's podium. "Okay, let's decide the staff and the cast. Ebina's handling the script, so would anyone else be interested in the other roles?" He wrote down the jobs that needed to be filled on the blackboard.

The results:

Direction: Hina Ebina
Production: Hina Ebina
Script: Hina Ebina

And so the dream staffing was complete. She was probably the only one could manage those anyway... I guess you'd call that "total creative control," or maybe being a super-producer.

But those creative roles aside, the principal staff were decided as follows:

Production Assistant: Yui Yuigahama

Publicity and Advertisement: Yumiko Miura

If the girls weren't going to be cast in the play, obviously they would be doing this sort of work.

All right, now the problems would begin.

A play needs actors, of course, and this play had male leads, too. In fact, it was all guys. It was a stud-studded *Little Prince*. Some benevolent impulse did inspire them to ask for volunteers, but not a single person wanted to star in the play. Well, no wonder, considering that plot.

"Um, you don't have to worry about the character descriptions we saw earlier, okay? We're not going to depict anything blatant." Hayama attempted to salvage the situation, but once that image was in your head, you could never quite get it out again. A strange silence hung over the boys.

"We've got no choice…," said Hina Ebina, her glasses glinting perversely—er, assertively—as she took the stand.

It was the casting board from hell. She ignored the class's clamoring and wrote down names for all the roles—apparently, she was ready to exercise her authority as creative lead to the fullest.

First, Ebina filled in the supporting cast. Chalk clicking, she wrote names in under the roles such as the Rose, the King, and the Vain Man.

"Nooo!" "Anything but the Geographer!" "But my Matterhorn!" Cries of the dying erupted with each and every name. The very lowest levels of the abyss were unfurling before me.

And then she revealed the main cast.

The Prince: Hayama

Hayama froze. He looked a little pale. But you could hear a few girls squeeing. Well, it was a main role, so it made sense to pick someone who would attract an audience.

Now then, as for the other lead…

As I watched Ebina's hands, the white lines there transformed into very familiar shapes.

The Narrator: Hikigaya

"Uh…there's no way." The remark left my mouth the moment I saw my name.

Ebina had been listening eagerly, and she acted scandalized. "Huh?! But Hayama/Hikitani *doujin* is a must-buy! In fact, it's a must-gay!"

What the heck is she talking about?

"The Prince skillfully seduces the sulky pilot with his pure, warm words... That's the whole appeal of this story!"

That is not at all the appeal of this story. You're gonna piss off the French. "I mean...I'm on the committee, though..."

"Th-that's right. Hikitani's helping with the committee for us, and if we're doing a play, we'll need to rehearse and stuff, too. This isn't very realistic."

Thanks for the assist, Hayama.

"Oh...that's too bad," said Ebina.

"Yeah, so maybe we should rethink the whole thing...such as who'll be playing the Prince," Hayama added.

So that's *your ulterior motive.* But before his suggestion was even finished, Ebina had written out new names.

The Prince: Totsuka

The Narrator: Hayama

"It'll be a little less sulky now," said Ebina, "but I guess it'll do."

"So I have to be in this no matter what, huh...?" Hayama's shoulders slumped.

"Ooh, nice brooding!" Ebina gave a thumbs-up in approval at his performance.

I didn't give a damn about Hayama, but Totsuka as the Prince was some pretty good casting. He did indeed strike you as the little prince of the story.

But the boy in question acted puzzled. He must not have considered this possibility. "This seems really hard... Do you think I can really be the prince?"

"Oh," I replied, "I think you fit the role." It seems like Ebina actually had some good eyes in her head—though maybe that just meant they were rotten in a different way from mine...

"Oh...I don't really know a lot about this stuff, so I've got to do some proper research."

"I don't think you need to do any research. In fact, it'd probably be easier if you just read the original book. She's misinterpreting the plot pretty hard." I appreciated his diligent spirit, but there are some things you're better off not knowing. If Totsuka's research led him to that path, I can't say for sure I wouldn't follow him, so I would really prefer it if he didn't.

"Have you read it, Hachiman?"

"…Yeah." It was an okay story. If pressed, I'd even say it's sort of up my alley. But there were a number of things about it that I found unsatisfying, so I couldn't exactly sing its praises without a few caveats. It was a book I simply had trouble judging. "If you want to read it, I can lend it to you."

"Really? Thanks!" Totsuka beamed at me like a blooming flower.

It's a good thing my hobby is reading, I thought, for the first time in my life.

Meanwhile, Totsuka was called to the cast meeting. "See you later, then, Hachiman."

"Yeah." I saw him out and then scanned the cast. They were having their meeting nearby, and a bunch of other meetings were starting all over, too: costuming, advertisement, a mourning party for the cast.

I glanced behind me at them all, then left the classroom.

A loud pitter-patter of footsteps chased after me. Without even turning around, I knew whose they were. I think the only people out there identifiable by their footsteps are Tarao and Yuigahama.

"Are you heading to the clubroom, Hikki?" she called out after me.

Slowing my pace a bit, I replied, "Yeah, there's still some time before the committee meeting. Besides, I probably won't be able to go to club for a while now, so I figured I'd go let her know."

"Oh, that makes sense… I'll go, too," Yuigahama said, coming up alongside me.

I just gave her a glance. "You don't have any work to do?"

"Naw. I think I'll only be busy once things actually get started."

I replied with a brief "Oh" and walked down the hallway to the clubroom.

X   X   X

The committee meeting was set to start at four, so I still had some time until then.

If I stayed in the classroom, I wouldn't be assigned any role in particular, and I figured I'd just be in the way. And since I'd been appointed to the committee, even if I'd wanted to help, I would barely have time to do anything anyway. Then someone would have to take over for me when I left halfway, and that would be time-consuming and leave us prone to mistakes. So clearly, it would be better for me not to bother with any of it from the start. Sometimes, abstaining from work can be beneficial.

...If I'd been put on the committee because they'd foreseen that, all I can say is: I'm impressed. In a way, my classmates might actually understand me the best.

I am an untouchable presence. Phrasing it that way makes me seem kinda cool.

At Soubu High School, only some of the clubs make presentations for the cultural festival. For example, the orchestral club has a concert, and the tea ceremony club holds a formal tea party. Generally, the students participate with their classes, and they can volunteer for additional presentations.

The racket I'd been hearing for a while now had to be a volunteer band practicing. Yet again, a guitar was seizing the spotlight, energetically picking away like *pokasuka-jyan*. The bass was strumming *bom-boko-bom-boko*—what, is this a tanuki battle?

But that was just between the main building and the new building. In all the hustle and bustle, only the hallway leading to the special building maintained its silence. Perhaps because of the shade, the air felt one or two degrees cooler.

The door to the clubroom was already unlocked. I could almost feel the arctic winds seeping out from within.

Putting my hand on the sliding door, I found Yukinoshita there, as always.

"Yahallo!"

Yuigahama's greeting prompted Yukinoshita to slowly raise her head. She squinted at the door and then hesitantly opened her mouth.

"...Hello."

"Hey." I gave my vague reply to her usual greeting and then sat down in my regular seat. "So you're on the committee, too, huh?"

"Huh? Is she really?" asked Yuigahama.

"Yes," Yukinoshita replied briefly, her eyes locked on the paperback in her hands.

"It's surprising you'd do something like that, Yukinon."

"Is it? Well, I suppose so..." Yukinoshita wasn't the type to put herself out there. It wasn't that she lacked initiative. She just hated standing out. That was the Yukinoshita I knew.

"Personally, I found it surprising *you* were on the committee, Hikigaya."

"Oh yeah, right? It's totally not like him," Yuigahama agreed.

"Hey...I was half forced into it. Well, running miscellaneous tasks for the committee is better than being in that musical, so all's well that ends well, though."

"That reason is very like you," said Yukinoshita.

"This isn't like you, though," I quipped. It wasn't really directed at Yukinoshita. It was directed at myself. Again, I had been made uncomfortably aware of how I force my ideals on people.

"..."

"..."

Yukinoshita didn't even dignify my words with a response. She hadn't moved her gaze an inch off her paperback. In the silence, it felt like even time had slowed to a halt. The only sound was the ticking of the worn clock on the wall measuring out time, and its second hand was deafening.

Yuigahama breathed a deep sigh and glanced over at the clock. "Um...you've got a committee meeting today, too, right? I have to go to a discussion in the classroom, so..."

I picked up on what she was about to say. "Oh, that's right. Since I'm on the committee, I won't be able to come to club for a while." Maybe it would have been more accurate to say that I just wouldn't be coming in general.

Yukinoshita closed her eyes for a long moment, as if she were processing this, then closed her book, too. After that, for the first time that day, she looked at me. "...That works out well, then. I was just about to bring that up today. I think we'll have to suspend club meetings for a while, until the cultural festival is over."

"Yeah, makes sense."

"Hmm..." Yuigahama thought for a bit but finally conceded. "All right, that's fair. Since we've got the festival, maybe that's for the best, until it's over."

"Right, well, that's it for today, I guess."

"...Yeah. When you've got some free time, Hikki, be sure to help with the classroom stuff, too," Yuigahama said, and I briefly considered it. Doing work for the class play on top of my work for the committee would be a lot of grief. *Unlimited Double Works...*

"...If I get the time. I'm...gonna head out, then." My reply meant *I'm definitely not going to do it.* Bag in hand, I stood up. Even though it was totally empty, it felt super-heavy.

...Waaah. I don't wanna go.

I wonder why going to work is so painful. Somehow, my stomach started to hurt. Is it like that mind-over-matter stuff where your thoughts affect the real world? What Marble Phantasm.

Oh well. It's work, so I'll do it anyway. But a sigh escaped me. *I just don't want to get a job.*

Right as I put my hand on the door, there came a *knock, knock.* I perked my ears up at the sound and heard some noise on the other side, like giggling.

"Come in," Yukinoshita called out, and the door opened hesitantly. The laughter got louder, like the whispers of wind through the trees.

"Pardon me!" In came a girl I knew: Minami Sagami. She was in my class and on the Cultural Festival Committee with me, and she was serving as its chair. Two other girls were waiting behind her. They all had similar thin smiles on their faces.

When she saw us, Sagami's eyes went wide. "Oh, it's Yukinoshita and Yui!"

Whoops, you missed one, you know? Your classmate? Also on the committee with you?

"Sagamin? What's up?" Yuigahama looked at her curiously.

Sagami didn't reply to her question, giving the clubroom a full-circle scan instead. "Huh! So the Service Club is *you* guys' club!" she said, glancing from me to Yuigahama and back again.

I got cold shivers. Hidden in those eyes was the cunning of a snake. For an eerie moment, her pupils almost appeared vertically slit.

"Did you need something?" Yukinoshita's tone was cold and high-handed, as it always was, even with people she didn't really know. I wondered why it felt even colder in there than usual.

"Oh...I know this is really sudden... I'm sorry." Sagami flinched a little and added an apology at the end. "I came because...I wanted to ask your help with something," she continued. She wouldn't meet Yukinoshita's gaze, instead giving little glances to her friends at her side. "I ended up becoming the committee chair, but, like, I'm just not that confident about it, I guess... So I wanted some help."

That must have been what Sagami had been discussing with Miss Hiratsuka after the meeting the day before. Yet again, the teacher had sent someone with a problem to the Service Club.

Well, I understood what she was trying to say. Anyone would shrink away after taking on a new job, or a role with a heavy responsibility. Not to mention, from what I'd seen of Sagami's manner in class, she didn't seem like the leader type.

But was Sagami someone the club should be helping?

Yukinoshita watched her in thoughtful silence for a while. Under her quiet gaze, Sagami awkwardly averted her eyes.

"It seems to me," said Yukinoshita, "that it would be straying from the goal of personal growth that you were touting, though."

Yukinoshita was right—Sagami had volunteered for this role of her own free will. When she had put her name forward as committee chair, she had claimed to take on that responsibility for the sake of her own personal development.

Sagami seemed momentarily taken aback, but she kept her reaction in check, putting on another thin smile. "Yeah, but…it's just, I really don't want to be causing trouble for the whole team, I guess. And we don't want this to fail, right? Besides, I think cooperating with others to pull it off is a part of that growth. That stuff's important, right?" Yukinoshita just listened in silence as Sagami continued without pause. "Besides, I'm a part of the class, too. I want to, like, help out with the class stuff, too. I'd feel bad if I had to say I wasn't going to show up there at all. Right?" Sagami said, then turned to Yuigahama.

"…Yeah, that's true." Yuigahama paused for just the briefest moment to think, but she agreed with Sagami. "I like doing things together with other people, too."

"Right? I want to take advantage of the opportunity to build closer relationships. So I've really got to make this a success!"

The pair flanking her were vigorously nodding their agreement.

But Yuigahama frowned slightly.

I could understand how she felt, too. Ultimately, Sagami was just asking Yukinoshita to wipe her ass for her, since she'd impulsively jumped into the position. On a fundamental level, it wasn't much different from that time Zaimokuza had gone overboard online and pissed off the UG Club.

All Sagami wanted was the *title* of "chair of the Cultural Festival Committee," not the experience and knowledge that could be gained through that role. If she really wanted to do her job as the committee chair, then she wouldn't have been asking for help from outside the committee. Meguri, for example, was good at getting everyone within the organization to cooperate with her like that. She came off as a little flaky, but she seemed to be managing the organization well by getting the firm support of all the student council members. Perhaps that was because of her personality, or perhaps her unreliable and delicate manner itself created a sense of unity in its own way.

But Sagami was different. It seemed to me like she was trying to gain the help of outsiders because she was embarrassed about showing weakness—trying to put on a bold front. Again, I think that's more or less what Zaimokuza did, not so long ago.

Unfortunately, when you ring up a tab like that, you have to pay it off yourself. Everyone needs to figure out eventually that just screwing up your courage in the heat of the moment generally doesn't lead to anything good. When you feel miserable about it afterward, regret your decision, and are cautioned into never repeating it again, it's its own form of growth. From that angle, it would be best to refuse Sagami's request now.

In fact, if you seriously considered what was best for her, it would be better not to just jump in. I also didn't want any more work.

Yukinoshita had been silent for a while, and perhaps Sagami was anxious about her response. She kept glancing over toward Yukinoshita, but never directly at her.

Noticing that Sagami was waiting for a reply, Yukinoshita slowly opened her mouth, apparently still gathering her thoughts and checking them over. "To summarize...you mean you would like me to be your advisor?"

"Yeah, that's it." Sagami did her best to give a cheerful nod as if to say, *Just what I was thinking!*

But Yukinoshita's expression was as ice-cold as ever. "I see... Then I don't mind. Since I'm on the committee myself, I can help you in that capacity."

"Really?! Thank you!" Sagami clapped her hands in an open expression of joy and took two, three steps up to Yukinoshita.

By contrast, Yuigahama was staring at her with some surprise.

Frankly, I was a little surprised, too. I'd thought Yukinoshita would simply brush off a request like that.

"I'll be counting on you, then!" Sagami thanked her casually and left with her friends in tow. Once it was only the three of us, a little of the gloom returned.

Just as I was stepping out to leave the clubroom—for real this time—Yuigahama planted herself resolutely in front of Yukinoshita. "…I thought we were suspending club." Her tone was a little colder than I was used to hearing from her.

The change was not lost on Yukinoshita, and her shoulders twitched. She lifted her head for just an instant, then quickly looked away again. "…I'm taking it on personally. You two don't have to worry about it."

"But we always—"

"It's the same… Nothing's any different." Yukinoshita cut her off before she could persist.

Yuigahama breathed a faint, resigned sigh in the face of Yukinoshita's determination. "But…we could all do it together."

"That's unnecessary. I realize it would be rather selfish to ask you to deal with committee matters. It's more efficient for me to handle it by myself," said Yukinoshita.

"Efficient? Well, yeah, maybe it is, but…" Yuigahama faltered.

Still cold, Yukinoshita focused on the cover of her closed paperback, as if to put an end to the discussion.

Having seen Yukino Yukinoshita's skills up close, I understood full well that she would indeed manage on her own.

"But…I don't think it's right," Yuigahama said, then spun around and started to leave. No one called after her. "I'm going back to the classroom." With that, she walked off. I was taken aback by the whole exchange, but I soon snapped out of it and shouldered my bag again to follow Yuigahama out of the room. As I closed the door, I turned back.

Yukinoshita was all alone in there.

She was so beautiful, it was terrifying. Like sunlight gently flowing down on a ruin after the destruction of the world—full of sorrow.

X X X

A pair of indoor shoes smacked lightly against the linoleum tile. For someone who seemed rather slow, her feet sure were quick. "Agh, man! This is so... It's so...so, *so*—!"

"Hey, hold on a second and calm down," I called out to stop Yuigahama in front of me.

Then the smacks on the floor stopped, and her shoes squeaked as she turned around. "What?" Her face formed a sullen frown. She was clearly in a bad mood.

Huh, I don't usually see her like this, I thought. "What's with you, all of a sudden?"

"I don't know! I just...ragh."

Don't growl. Are you a dog?

Yuigahama stomped on the ground as she sorted out her feelings and put the words together bit by bit. "It's like... This is different from usual... Like, Yukinon doesn't usually do that."

"Well, that's..."

"And you too, Hikki," she added accusingly.

"..."

Even I could tell. I'd been trying my best to act the same as I always did. But the fact that I was even consciously trying to do that was different from usual. Once you're aware things are weird, any attempt to rectify the situation makes it even more awkward. I was well and truly stuck in that particular spiral.

So it was obvious after all.

Whether she took my silence as an affirmation or as guilt, Yuigahama didn't press me any further. I was pretty grateful for that.

"Also, like..." As I waited for Yuigahama to continue, she twisted around as if she found this hard to say. "...Listen. Can I say something a little mean?"

"Huh?" Unsure what she was getting at, I gave her a vague answer.

Yuigahama looked up at me uneasily and checked one more time. "Don't...hate me for this?"

"I can't make any promises."

"Huh? I'm stuck, then..." Yuigahama stopped on the spot.

It's not like she only lets you see her good side anyway, be that out of stupidity or something else. She'll reveal her feminine calculating side when you least expect it, which makes her more than I can handle.

But still, at this rate, this conversation was not going anywhere. Well, no matter what she told me at this point, I doubted it would change anything.

To fill up the silence, I scratched my head roughly. "...Agh, it'll be fine. I have a lot of experience hating people. Some petty little comment won't be enough."

"That's kind of a sad reason."

That was genuine pity there...

"Whatever, right? So what is this mean thing?" I prompted her to continue.

Yuigahama quietly took a deep breath and opened her mouth. "Yeah... Listen, I...don't really like...Sagamin..."

"Uh-huh. And the mean part?"

"I—I just said it..."

"What?" Automatically, my eyes went as wide as a Furby's. Pet me! "Huh? What? Was that supposed to be mean?"

"Um, we just can't get along. Or I guess you'd call this a squabble between us girls or something. I know that isn't very nice, but..."

Was that all? I guess so, if you thought about it normally. I'm sure it wouldn't make her seem nice.

However she took my silence, Yuigahama folded her hands small in front of her chest and made an inverse triangle with her fingers. "I... didn't want to show you that side of me, though," she said, focusing on a corner of the hallway.

"You're dumb." I had to snicker. *You think things would change now just because of that? Idiot.* "I mean, I don't like her, either."

"Yeah, but it's a little different. I don't like her. I guess, I probably just dislike her. But we're friends, so..."

"O-okay...but you're still friends..."

"Yeah, I do try to be friends with her."

Still don't understand girls' definition of friend.

"But maybe she doesn't feel that way. I kinda feel like she hates me."

"Yeah, I bet. You can tell just by looking." I'm sure it wasn't quite that Yuigahama hated her, but I could sense antagonism or hostility in some form. I was going to elaborate, but then I noticed Yuigahama had frozen.

"…Huh? Y-you're looking?"

"Stop. Cancel. I'm not, actually. Not at all. I can just tell."

"Um, though…you're totally…allowed to look, you know…," Yuigahama replied, finger-combing her hair.

But, um, sorry. I'm kind of really looking at you a little bit a lot. I'm sorry for lying.

As I was repenting and apologizing in my head, Yuigahama suddenly got this faraway look in her eyes. "In first year, me and Sagamin were in the same class."

"Huh. Were you close?"

"Fairly close, I guess." Yuigahama's expression was complicated, halfway between worrying and contemplating.

"…In other words, you weren't."

"Hey, what makes you think that?!"

"Were you close?"

"Hmm, well, close enough." Another hard-to-read expression…

"In other words, you weren't," I said.

Yuigahama gave a resigned sigh. "…Fine, let's go with that."

It wasn't "Let's go with that" at all; it was exactly that. The world of women is complicated and mysterious.

"Back then, we were part of a pretty prominent clique. And I guess that kinda gave her a lot of confidence."

Sagami and Yuigahama. Well, I'm sure there would have been others, but it's easy to imagine them as central figures in the class. Yuigahama had the looks, the social skills, and the knack for putting others at ease. So I'm sure she could fit herself in well with a popular A-group atmosphere. Sagami, on the other hand, was the type who could aim for such a position and find a fair degree of success, depending on the combination of people there, I think. In the cultural committee, she'd immediately found herself some friends and people to hang out with, and she turned them into a clique as one with interpersonal skills and a knack for self-promotion.

But once they hit second year, their positions changed. What was the source of this difference between Yuigahama and Sagami? Pride, and a different environment...

The greatest reason had to be Miura. The moment Miura came into Class 2-F, the position of number one was set in stone. And then, at the team selection stage, Miura chose the members of her clique based on her rather cruel standard of "cuteness."

...She really was something. She ignored the existing social hierarchy and just picked the people she wanted to be with. For good or for ill, she really was a queen.

And Miura and Sagami didn't really get along. I don't know if it's right to put it this way, but it was easy to understand why Sagami was the leader of the B-group. For Sagami, conscious as she was of social caste, it had to be humiliating. Maybe she couldn't do anything about getting booted from the top caste, but the fact that her former peer was still there must have driven her nuts.

Naturally, everything Sagami had done so far fell into place.

"So that's why I kinda don't really like what she's doing... Asking Yukinon this favor, trying to be friends with her, too..." Yuigahama tilted her head, puzzled by what she'd just said. Then she gave a little nod of understanding. "...Maybe I like Yukinon more than I realized."

"What are you talking about, all of a sudden?" *YuruYuri is one thing, but if it's full-blown* yuri, *I can't entirely back you up there.*

"No! I don't mean it like that! I... I dunno if I like other girls being friends with Yukinon... I'm acting like a little kid." She must have been embarrassed. Her cheeks were red, and she was petting her bun attentively.

That desire to monopolize someone was a bit childish. I'm sure it's fairly common among young girls. I think even my little sister Komachi was like that at some point. Humans, at their core, are not that different. We just train ourselves to repress our feelings until, occasionally, they peek out anyway.

"Girls are a lot of trouble… There's all this stuff."

It was kinda funny how seriously she was taking this, and I couldn't help but smile. "Hey, hey, boys are a pain in the ass, too. We have cliques and social groups. Girls aren't so special."

"Really?"

"Pretty much."

"Huh… People in general are a pain, huh?" Yuigahama gave her characteristic *ta-ha-ha*.

They really are. Humans are such a pain in the butt. I hate it, and that's why I gave up on them a long time ago. When they put in so much effort to keep up appearances, you know they're not real.

"Promise." The word left her mouth so suddenly, I didn't understand what she meant. I replied with silence and a head tilt.

Yuigahama stopped in place, gave me a firm look in the eye, and continued, "That if Yukinon is in trouble, you'll help her out."

I do recall Yuigahama saying something like that on the way back from the fireworks show. Just as then, she was so earnest, her uncompromising attitude overwhelmed me. So I answered as honestly and accurately as I could. "I'll do what I can."

"Okay. It's a relief to hear you say that," Yuigahama said, grinning. The unconditional trust made me uncomfortable.

It seems when you keep your argument short, it's much more effective. When people tack on a bunch of extra reasons, you can pick out the self-interest or contradictions, but when they just finish it off with a smile, there's nothing you can find there to argue with.

"I'm going back to the classroom, then. Good luck with the committee." She gave a casual wave and trotted off. I replied with a raised hand, then started walking again.

X   X   X

I parted ways with Yuigahama and continued on down the hallway to the conference room. It was past a left turn in the hallway, right on the corner. If you went straight forward, the hall would lead to the stairs on the third floor, where our second-year classrooms were.

There was a figure on the far end of the shadowed hallway, blocking the way to the staircase. It looked familiar; even though it was still a little hot out, the figure was wearing a trench coat and fingerless gloves on his hands as he crossed his arms. I ignored him and passed on by.

Suddenly, he pulled out his cell phone and started to make a call.

A moment later, my cell phone started vibrating.

It irritated me that he would go to the trouble of calling my phone even though we'd both recognized each other. Then he began a little act that made it even worse. "Herm. I cannot quite seem to get ahold of that fellow! Could it be he's otherwise engaged? …Ha-ha-ha! That could never be! Not for Hachiman! Is that not so, Hachiman?"

"I don't want to hear that from you." Now that he'd dissed me, I really couldn't keep my mouth shut. If it had been anyone else, I would've been able to snort and ignore them, but my stupid pride would not allow Yoshiteru Zaimokuza to run his mouth at me. "So what're you doing here? Stair-climbing diet?"

"Heh, how nostalgic. Once, I did engage in such training. But in long times past, I got water on the knee. Besides…my old wounds ache. Aye, I mean my chub rub."

I-is that right? I think you should take care of your health.

Zaimokuza ignored my concern and pulled out a stack of paper from parts unknown. "Of more import, Hachiman, is this. Observe! What do you think?"

"What? If it's your light novel, I'm not reading it." Usually, I'd be a bit nicer, but I didn't have much time. I was supposed to be heading to a meeting right then, and I didn't have the patience, time, energy, or goodwill to deal with him.

"Nay! Not a light novel!" His denial was pointlessly emphatic, which made me mildly curious. If it wasn't his light novel, then what the hell were those papers?

Seeing that my eyes were on his stack of paper, Zaimokuza smirked and struck a pose. "Listen with amazement! Prostrate yourself with rapt attention! And…apologize with your death… Did you know my class is putting on a play?"

"I don't care. And why do I have to apologize with my death anyway—hey, wait, wait, stop, don't say any more…"

"For a play, what do you need? A script…"

"Enough. No. Cut it out."

But Zaimokuza plunged ahead despite my attempts to restrain him. He lifted a fist high up in the air and proclaimed everything he wanted me to know. Honestly, it was really obnoxious. "Oh, 'tis no great matter. They were whimpering about how they didn't want a regular play. They wished for an original script."

"Hey, stop this. Please." I knew what came next. I knew exactly how this was going to end. As for why, because I've gone down that road once before, in middle school.

Writing an original script and playing with a scenario is only permissible up until the end of elementary school. Oh, it actually is an option for elementary school kids. You're allowed to write comic skit–style scripts for school arts festivals and farewell parties. In fact, people will love it. But the moment you start middle school, the act makes you a target for contempt.

"Heh." I laughed weakly.

"Hmm? What is it, Hachiman?" he asked.

I gazed up at the sky through the window. "Oh…just thinking about how adulthood hits so fast."

"Heh, what a curious fellow… I actually have no idea what you were talking about. That was super-weird. But no matter: Your issues are insignificant. So as for my original script…"

I got the feeling he'd taken advantage of the confusion to hurl an insult at me. I couldn't know for sure that they weren't still using my old script now…

While I hate to say it, this guy is basically an acquaintance of mine. My conscience wouldn't let me say nothing and let him walk into certain disaster. From the kindness of my heart, I decided to warn him. "Okay, I understand what you're talking about. Just don't make the heroine the girl you like. It's way too awkward. And don't give yourself the lead role in the first place."

"Ge-gerk! Hachiman, do you have ESP?!"

"No. Listen, I warned you, okay?" I don't have ESP. This was just experience talking. Ever since that day, I have sworn solemnly in my heart to never show anyone anything of that nature ever again.

"Hrr-pum, I see, I see. In other words, what you're trying to say is this…" Zaimokuza assumed his most serious expression and cleared his throat. "The recent trend is to make the villain or rival the protagonist rather than the standard hero, so that would be cooler and more popular?"

"You completely missed the point."

"Herm? Is some part of that mistaken?"

"Oh, your line of argument isn't really wrong. I mean, even for Pre-Cure, they made the one in black the main character for the first generation. I think that's probably what they were going for there, establishing character based on color scheme. The *problem* is everything about you." I wanted to emphasize that very last part, but Zaimokuza's ears function at an incredible level that allows them to filter out everything he doesn't want to hear, so he just made his weird listening noises. *Mfun, mfun.*

"I see. You do indeed have a point. This 'Rule of Cure Black' you subscribe to…may just be it. Herm, as expected of the authority of PreCure-ology."

"Hey, stop it. Don't you set me up as an authority. I'm not worthy. Besides, I'm a Cure White stan." Seriously, *authority* is too lofty for me. I'm just someone who just watches it 'cause I like it. I'm a casual. I can't even tell at a glance who drew the key frames, and I just have the old-edition DVD box sets and Blu-rays. In fact, it would be presumptuous and inexcusable to call myself a true fan. I'd want to kill myself if I did.

"Herm, that reaction… He's the real deal…" Zaimokuza drew back.

"Whatever, I don't care anymore. I hope you suffer and regret it." It was no use, no matter what I said. So then he had no choice but to learn the hard way and carve those wounds deep into his heart. Love, friendship, and courage aren't what changes people. My wish was that the people of Class C would give Zaimokuza an extralarge fatal wound.

"By the way, are you going to the October film?" he asked.

"Don't be stupid. Someone like me going would scare the families and the little girls. It'd be inexcusable of me... I'll buy the Blu-ray."

"Hng! You must want to see it forthwith, and yet, you restrain yourself...a man among men!" For some reason, he burst into manly tears for me.

I'm the one who wants to cry. I'm about to go off to work right now. Why do I have to have a discussion with this guy here? I shook off Zaimokuza's gaze and headed to the conference room. My feet felt even heavier than usual.

Suddenly,
Haruno Yukinoshita attacks.

A few days after Sagami's visit to the Service Club room, the committee was notified that Yukinoshita would be assuming the office of vice-chair. Sagami made the announcement at the beginning of the meeting the day after that, and she seemed chipper about it.

The reaction from the cultural committee was generally positive. Atsugi had been for it from the start, and Meguri had acknowledged Yukinoshita's talents already, so of course they were on board. You could say that people had high expectations for her, and her entrance had come at the right time.

This meant one member was being discharged from my own section, Records and Miscellaneous, but there wasn't a whole lot of work for us to do in the first place. It was determined that it wouldn't be a big issue. *Maybe I didn't have to come...* The thought crossed my mind for an instant. But it was thanks to being shunted aside that I was able to avoid participating in the class play. I couldn't get greedy here.

Once appointed, Yukinoshita went straight to work. She revamped the schedule, disseminated that information to the committee, and arranged for each section to present a daily progress report while she checked over their work. Business was moving along smoothly.

In the east, Publicity and Advertisement worried about where to put posters, but Yukinoshita calculated the lines and volume of pedestrian traffic on a map and gave them instructions. In the west, Volunteer

Management was in trouble because they didn't have enough volunteers, so she made the performances a contest with a prize.

A minion like me wouldn't know much about the affairs of the executive ranks, but I could tell that Yukinoshita was working at an incredible pace.

Anyway, though the official notices were going out under the name of the committee chair, Minami Sagami, it was easy to see that Yukinoshita was doing nearly everything.

It seemed all of it was moving along smoothly.

Meanwhile, we were going through tons of meetings.

Four in the afternoon, right on time.

Sagami looked out over the members of the cultural committee in the conference room and got things started. "Well then, let's begin the meeting."

Everyone said the formal greeting in chorus and bowed.

First, we began with the reports from each section.

"Okay, Publicity and Advertisement, go ahead," said Sagami.

The section head stood up to give their progress report. "So far, we've posted notices on about seventy percent of the bulletin boards we had planned, and about fifty percent of the posters are done, too."

"Really? That's sounding good." Sagami nodded in satisfaction.

But her warm reply was followed by a much colder one. "No. It's a little slow." The unexpected remark brought up a stir of murmurs in the room. But despite this, Yukino Yukinoshita ignored the reactions and continued, somewhat accusatory. "The cultural festival is in three weeks. If you take into account the time it takes for the guests to adjust their schedules, it needs to have been done by now. Have you already negotiated the placement on each bulletin board and uploaded a notice to the school's website?"

"Not yet…"

"Please hurry. Prospective students from middle schools and their guardians do check the website frequently."

"O-okay." The head of the advertisement section sank back down, overwhelmed.

Silence fell upon the conference room. Sagami, off to the side, didn't appear to have grasped what had even just happened. She gaped at Yukinoshita.

"Go on, Sagami," Yukinoshita prompted, and at last, the meeting resumed.

"Oh, right. Then, Volunteer Management, go ahead."

"…Right. Right now, we have ten volunteer groups participating," the group leader announced hesitantly.

Sagami was a little awkward, but she nodded. "More have applied, huh? That must be because of the prize we're offering now. Next…"

"Are those volunteers only from within the school? Have you sounded out other local groups? Look into the records from previous years and try contacting them, please. If our promotional line every year is our strong regional ties, then we have to keep the participation from regional groups high. Also, have you scheduled all the stages yet? How big do you predict the audience will be? Do you know the staff you'll need during the performances? Please come up with a timetable and submit it to me."

The moment Sagami had attempted to move on, Yukinoshita pressed the section severely. They weren't going to half-ass anything on her watch.

Things went on like that the whole time, as the meeting moved on to Health and Sanitation and then Accounting. Each time, Yukinoshita hurled demands for details and orders left and right.

"Next, Records and Miscellaneous." Before you knew it, she was the one taking control of the meeting.

"Nothing in particular," the boy in charge of Records and Miscellaneous briefly stated. Most of our work in this section was actually just archiving the day of the festival, so at this stage, there wasn't that much work to do.

Sagami, the chair, understood this, too, and she nodded and then glanced around, attempting to end the meeting. "Then that should be it for today…"

"Records, submit a schedule for the day of the event and the applications for equipment. Keep in mind that we only have access to a limited amount of video recording equipment, so if volunteer groups also intend to film, there may be schedule conflicts. Consult with them about equipment delivery, please."

"Okay…"

Even though the section head was a third-year and her elder, Yukinoshita didn't hold back. It was a little tense.

But that had to be over now. The reports from each section were done. Everyone was breathing sighs of relief and exhaustion, but the vice-chair was not ending the meeting. "Also…can the student council manage guests?"

"Yes, we can handle that," Meguri replied instantly. She was still fully attentive.

"All right then, please do. It would also be helpful if you could update the guest list from last year and bring it to me. Also, reception of general guests is Health and Sanitation's job. Please hand in the guest list beforehand."

"All right. Roger!" Meguri nodded agreeably. Then she expressed her impression of the situation in brief. "Wow, you're amazing, Yukinoshita… Just what you'd expect from Haru's sister," she added appreciatively.

Yukinoshita responded with a display of modesty. "…No, it's really nothing much."

It was true—Yukinoshita really knew her stuff. I thought she was pretty amazing, too. But the way she was going about this was dangerous.

Now that the issues had been exposed in the reports, there was some conferring about how to deal with them, and then we shared information about the schedule moving forward. Most of what had to be discussed that day was done. Once we could sense that it was over, the atmosphere relaxed. A few people stretched and groaned.

Yukinoshita seemed to notice she'd stolen the role of directing the meeting partway through and turned to Sagami. "Well then, Chair."

"Oh yeah. Um, we'll be counting on you again tomorrow, too. Good work, everyone."

Now dismissed, the cultural committee members all said their farewells and left their seats. I could hear them all chatting among themselves: *Oh man, oh man, I'm tired, so tired, but wasn't that something, oh yes, really for real, I really feel like we worked our asses off.*

They were all applauding Yukinoshita's talents. She was so powerful, so striking, that some tactless rumormonger even commented that they couldn't tell which one was the chair. Some members of the student council, in particular, even mentioned her as a candidate for the next student council president. As expected of Yukino Yukinoshita.

The one in the toughest position here was undoubtedly Sagami.

They were similar enough to be compared. Both girls were second-years, but one of them had just taken control of the meeting. One of them was falling behind, while the other had shown that she could even compensate for the first.

If Yukinoshita had been exercising her abilities independently, it would have been another story. But now that Sagami and Yukinoshita were in comparable positions, the differences between the two were thrown into relief. It was clear to everyone, and complimenting Yukinoshita was a form of disdain for Sagami.

As Yukinoshita stayed behind to handle some tasks, I saw Sagami practically fleeing with her two buddies.

Now that the direction of the cultural committee was established, operations were sure to become more efficient. Yukinoshita's working methods were worthy of commendation.

But had Yukinoshita realized…she wasn't saving anyone or anything?

× × ×

After school on the day after Yukinoshita went on her rampage—er, performed wonderfully at the cultural committee meeting, Hina

Ebina was performing wonderfully—er, going on a rampage in the 2-F classroom.

"Nooo! When you take off a businessman's necktie, you've got to be more seductive about it! Just what do you think a suit is for?!"

What do you *think that suit is for?*

Ebina's passionate acting coaching was leaving the boys in tears.

But not all the boys were wallowing in misery. Some of them were receiving rather fine treatment.

"Um, isn't this enough already?" Hayama said, an embarrassed edge to his voice as girls surrounded him.

"Not by a long shot!"

"We're just getting started!" The cluster of girls shot him down with glee.

The cast was practicing makeup through a ton of trial and error in preparation for the show. I could see Sagami among them, too... Well, there was still some time until the committee meeting after all.

Totsuka also had three girls assigned to him for hair and makeup, and he was utterly terrified.

"Totsuka, your skin is so pretty!"

"Yeah, it's perfect for makeup."

"U-um...this is just rehearsal, so you don't have to put on so much..." Totsuka attempted to refuse them very mildly, but his cuteness backfired.

"We've got to practice, too!"

"That's right!" It seemed to only stoke the girls' enthusiasm.

He shrank into himself even more. "Y-yeah... I—I get it. Practice is important...huh?"

I felt a little sorry for Totsuka as he wilted, but the thought of him getting even cuter weakened my resolve, and I just couldn't bring myself to stop them.

But still, the makeup team was treating certain people very differently than others. Tobe and Ooka had been finished off in just five minutes. And nobody had been willing to handle the class rep at all, so he'd mostly done it himself. To make matters worse, he'd done a decent job, which made the girls wonder suspiciously how he knew so much about it...

I was not the only one observing the goings-on. Miura was watching Hayama and the others when she seemed to have an idea. "So, like, what're we doing about the photos? We need posters, right?"

Ebina overheard her muttering and came to give her an enthusiastic thumbs-up. "Nice, Yumiko! Yes! When you're putting on a heartthrob musical, uploading character shots generates the most buzz. It's important to carefully disseminate cast information. We're deviating quite a bit from the source material with *Hoshimyu,* so we're pushing star power instead!"

What the hell is with that Hoshimyu *abbreviation? And wait, just what business are you in here?*

Miura and Ebina's conversation led the class to another topic. "What about the costumes? Are we renting them?"

"But if we rent, we might get them dirty..." The girls were *hmm*ing in indecision.

Yet again, Ebina jumped in. "No, no. At the very least, the Prince has a very specific image, so we can't use some other costume. For the others... Well, we can borrow those."

"What's the problem? Plenty of people have never seen the pictures before."

"Are you underestimating the fans of the original work?! Do you want to get trolled into oblivion?!" Ebina screeched dramatically.

This time, a voice rose up from a different direction. "Hmm, I dunno if we can rent costumes. We barely have any budget. Honestly, I kinda want to spend the money on other things..." Yuigahama scratched her head with a ballpoint pen as she punched some numbers into her calculator and scribbled something in her notebook. *You kinda look like a housewife there.*

"Why don't we just make them?" The queen pointed to a needle.

And so the commoners began considering the idea. "Do we have anyone who can sew?"

"I've only ever done it in class, though..."

Huh. There's a good balance to how they're handling this. I was standing by the window admiring the sight when I noticed a bluish ponytail in my field of vision.

It was Kawagoe...I think her name was. Kawashima had been glancing inquisitively over at the other girls' conversation. That was somewhat surprising. Shimazaki was the last person I'd expect to be interested in this. Curious, I looked at Okazaki more closely. She seemed to be reacting to words like *make*, *clothing*, and *sewing*. *That's not much like Okajima*, I thought before I called out to her.

Unable to just stand there and watch, I said, "Hey, if you want to do it, I think you can just say so."

"Wh-what are you talking about?! It's not like I want to do it!" Kawasaki bounded out of her chair.

...Right. The correct answer was Kawasaki. Okajima was way off, wasn't it?

It was good that I got the right answer, but no matter what I said, I'm sure she would have been determined to deny it. So then it would be best to approach this in a roundabout way.

"Hey, Yuigahama," I called out.

"Ack! Hold on!" Kawasaki was yanking at my sleeve, pleading me to stop. She probably should have stopped for her own good, though; a reaction like that tends to pique my sadistic streak.

"What?" Yuigahama tucked her red pen behind her ear and came over.

Are you some middle-aged man at the racetrack? Come on. "Kawasaki says she wants to do it."

"Wh-what?! Wh-what're you talking about?! I can't! There's no way I could do something that fancy! I've never done any clothes or anything yet... Um, I'd just cause trouble..."

So does she mean she's made something else?

Yuigahama gave Kawasaki a long, appraising look as she considered the possibility. Uncomfortable, Kawasaki twisted her tall, slim frame around in an attempt to become as small as possible. Yuigahama's eyes locked on a single point. "Hey, is that scrunchie handmade?" she asked.

Kawasaki nodded.

"Could you let me see for a sec?" No sooner had Yuigahama said it than she'd reached out to Kawasaki's ponytail. Her hair fluttered down and fanned out across her shoulders. Yuigahama observed the scrunchie in her hand and *ohhh*'d appreciatively. The little ball of fabric was kind of reminiscent of lingerie. It made my heart race a bit.

"Hina. Come over here a sec," Yuigahama called.

"Coming!" Ebina bounded over and examined the scrunchie with deep interest.

"That one is...hand sewn... But I've made some with a sewing machine, too," Kawasaki said, and she pulled another scrunchie out of her pocket. It was also kinda lingerie-like.

"Hmm, hmm... The stitches are neat, and the colors are cute... and you can sew by hand and use a machine... I like it! Kawasaki-san, I choose you! We're counting on you for those costumes!"

"Huh? Hey, you can't just..." As Kawasaki tied up her hair again, she looked uneasy and embarrassed at Ebina's super-casual request.

Yuigahama intervened. "Hey, hey, Hina is being serious about this, Kawasaki. You've altered your uniform, haven't you, like the blouse and stuff? I think she's probably picked you because she knows that."

...As expected of Yuigahama. She's so attentive to people.

"Oh yeah, huh?" Kawasaki answered vaguely, blushing and a little nonplussed. She was probably surprised and flattered that they'd picked up on such minor details.

"Exactly! There's an ideology and an art to using limited resources to the greatest effect. That's why I think we can let you handle this. If anything happens, I'll take responsibility!" Ebina smacked her chest as if to say, *Leave it to me!* It's disconcerting how normal Ebina can be, in her own way. Sometimes, I suspect she just hides her shrewdness and puts on that act most of the time.

"If that's what you mean, then...I'll do it..." Kawasaki's bright-red face was pointed toward the floor.

Ebina grabbed her firmly by the shoulders. "Yep, I'll be counting on you. Oh, and do some alterations on the Narrator's costume, too.

Make it kinda dirty. Make some stains—the kind that don't disappear."
There wasn't a shred of shrewdness in that.

Actually, I just don't get her after all.

I noticed that the costuming-related stuff was getting started, and
now there was even less real work for me to do. Everyone was engaged in
their respective roles.

I did have a part to play, more or less, the one that no one wanted to
do: the sacrifice to the cultural committee. *So let's go get that done.*

Yuigahama noticed I was about to head out of the classroom, so she
looked around and called out to Sagami. "Sagamin, you don't have to
go to the committee?"

"Huh? Yeah, it's okay."

"But…"

"Oh…I can't really help much, and I think I'd just get in the way
instead, you know?"

"That's not true. It seems like they've got a lot of work to do, so it
might be a good idea to relieve some of the burden."

"It's fine, it's fine. Yukinoshita's super-reliable. Besides, part of my
job is writing up the event proposal for the class."

I quietly closed the door on the conversation behind me.

Right after leaving the classroom, I bumped into Hayama. "Going
to the cultural committee now?" he asked. He was scrubbing his face
with a towelette for removing makeup. He must have gone to the bath-
room to wash it off.

"…Yeah."

"All right. I guess I'll go with you."

"…?" I asked with my expression alone. *Why? What the hell are you
talking about? I mean, it's fine if you come, but we don't have to go together,
right? I mean, you don't have to go at all. Just explain, okay?*

Hayama smiled. "I'm applying with a volunteer group. I'm going to
get the documents."

"Oh, I gotcha." That was a very Hayama-like reason. He was acutely
aware of how much attention he would draw. Of course, as that kind of

person, he would be in demand for this cultural festival, too, and he was trying to meet those expectations as best he could.

Hayama didn't ask any more or say anything else as we walked away from the classroom. I felt like someone was glaring at my back, but that was probably just my imagination. Right, Ebina?

X   X   X

I left the classroom and headed for the conference room. There was no meeting, but to my dismay, I did have Records and Miscellaneous work to do.

Even more dismaying was the fact that I was with Hayama.

"..."

"..."

Neither of us really said much.

He'd probably picked up on my "don't talk to me" aura, and this was his way of accommodating me. I glanced at him out of the corner of my eye, but he wasn't acting bored or awkward. He seemed very normal. He was humming casually, as if he wasn't that concerned about me at all. Remarkably unfazed.

As for me, I was pretty unsettled.

Now very aware of how I was alone with Hayama, I was reminded of that summer camp in Chiba Village, and his cold remark from that night in the dark cabin. Thinking about how Hayato Hayama had feelings like that gave me the shivers. It wasn't that I was scared of him. What scared me was that even he lives with those emotions. Even perfect, successful Hayama, loved by all as the undisputed good guy.

Silent the entire time, we turned a corner in the hallway.

When we reached the door to the conference room, I could see a few people inside. Was there an incident or something? But incidents don't happen in conference rooms. They happen at the scene.

"What's up?" Hayama asked casually.

A girl turned around with some annoyance, but when she saw it was Hayama, she began her explanation with an anxious "Um…" *Hey. Why are you blushing?*

At the rate this shy girl was beginning to talk, it seemed like we'd be here for a while. It'd be a lot faster for me to go look myself rather than listen to her. I touched the door handle, and the people around let me pass through.

As soon as the door was open, I instantly regretted it. It really is best to go along with the assessment of the masses.

The conference room was practically humming with tension. A few people had shifted over to the corners to form the gallery. There were three people standing in the middle:

Yukino Yukinoshita.

Meguri Shiromeguri.

Haruno Yukinoshita.

Yukinoshita and Haruno were standing about three steps apart, facing each other. Meguri was fidgeting behind Haruno, flustered.

"What have you come here for, Haruno?" Yukinoshita demanded like a lawyer cross-examining her sister.

"Aw, I came as an OG from the school orchestra, since I got a notice that you're looking for volunteer groups."

OG… For a minute, I thought she was talking about super robots, but that probably wasn't it. So then I thought she might be revealing her history with gangs, but that couldn't be it, either. I think it stands for *Old Girl*? Hey, stop slandering Miss Hiratsuka!

That was when Meguri intervened. "S-sorry, I'm the one who called her. I just happened to run into her in town, and then, you know, we hadn't seen each other in so long, so we talked about a lot of things, and we didn't have enough volunteer groups, so I was wondering if maybe…"

Nothing ever just "happened" with Haruno Yukinoshita. She only made it seem that way, which was why she was terrifying.

"You weren't in this school yet, Yukinoshita, so you might not know, but when Haru was in her third year, she volunteered with a band. It was really amazing! So I was hoping maybe…" Meguri gave Yukinoshita a tentative, beseeching look. *Maybe?*

"I know…because I saw it. But…" Yukinoshita gritted her teeth hard and looked down at the floor. A silence fell as she ignored Meguri's silent plea.

Then Haruno cut in with an embarrassed laugh. "Ah-ha-ha! Oh, no, Meguri, that was just for fun. But this year, I plan to do something more serious. I was hoping you could let us practice at the school a little… So that's fine, right, Yukino-chan? If you don't have enough volunteers." Haruno slung her arm around Yukinoshita's shoulders for good measure. "I just want to do what I can for my adorable little sister!"

"Don't give me that… First of all, you—" Yukinoshita swiped Haruno's hand away, taking a step back with a glare.

"I what?" Haruno stared back, not averting her gaze. She had a sweet smile on her face, but for some reason, just the sight of her made my knees feel weak.

"You're…doing it again…" Yukinoshita bit her lip in frustration as she gently looked away. Her eyes happened to meet mine.

"…" We both silently looked down. We were probably both focused on the same spot on the floor.

"Huh? It's Hikigaya! Yahallooo!" Noticing me, Haruno greeted me with vigorous cheer that really did not fit the mood.

What the hell is with that greeting? Is it the end of the century?

"Haruno…" Hayama followed me into the room and stood beside me.

"Heya, Hayato."

Haruno raised a casual hand, and Hayama answered with a casual nod.

"What's going on?"

"I've been thinking about performing with a volunteer orchestra. I figured it would be interesting to get a bunch of alumni together for it. Doesn't that sound fun?"

"Just jumping right in again, Haruno?" Hayama sighed. I'd known

they were acquainted, but this was weird. It was probably because of the way he was talking to her. *First-name basis, huh...?*

I looked between the two of them, until Haruno noticed and smirked. "Hmm? Oh, Hayato is practically like a little brother to me. We've known each other for a long time. If you like, you can speak to me informally, too, Hikigaya. How about I call you Hachiman instead?"

"Ah-ha-ha." I refused with a dry laugh. I'd absolutely love it if she would not. The only people allowed to call me Hachiman are my parents and Totsuka.

That little bit of teasing must have satisfied her, as she returned her gaze to Yukinoshita. "Hey, Yukino-chan, I can perform, right?"

"Do whatever you like... Besides, it's not my decision."

"Huh? It's not? I thought for sure you'd be the chair. Nobody recommended you for it?" She'd been recommended hard for it, and being Haruno Yukinoshita's little sister was part of the reason, too. Haruno chuckled as if she saw through everything. Yukinoshita was looking away.

"So then who is the committee chair? Meguri...is a third-year, so it's not her. Hikigaya?"

If that's supposed to be a joke, I'm not laughing. I shrugged, and my attitude made the answer clear.

The atmosphere was oddly tense when someone flung open the door to the conference room with abandon. "Sooorry! I went to check on the classroom but ended up running late!" Minami Sagami didn't seem even the slightest bit concerned.

Well, there wasn't a status meeting today, and most of the work was proceeding ahead of schedule. I could understand why she was letting things relax.

"Haru, this is the committee chair," said Meguri, and Haruno's eyes focused on Sagami.

That look again. That penetrating, cold, evil eye, like she's measuring your worth.

"...Oh, I'm Minami Sagami." Her voice wilted, overwhelmed by Haruno's flashing eyes.

"Hmm…" Haruno didn't seem to be interested in her at all, but she gave a small sigh and inched a step closer. "The Cultural Festival Committee chair is late? Because she was checking on her class? Huh…" Her tone was frightening. It was like that low, dictatorial sound was welling up from the core of her body, and it permeated every inch of Sagami. Just a moment ago, Haruno had been acting so cheerfully, so her ice-cold looks were all the nastier. This was what made Haruno scarier than Yukinoshita, and the most frightening part of all was how she didn't hide her dark feelings. That attitude told you that as long as you were submissive to her, she would approach you amicably, but if you were to defy her, she would mercilessly slaughter you with her bare hands.

"Uh, um…" While Sagami was desperately searching for an excuse, Haruno suddenly burst into a smile.

"That's what you need in a chair after all! You have to enjoy the cultural festival to the utmost! I like you! I *like* you! Um, it was something-mi, right? Amagami? Well, whatever. I'll call you Chair."

"Th-thank you very much…" Sagami kept her expression cheerful, even though she was baffled by Haruno's about-face. This was probably the first time she'd gotten approval since she'd come here.

As Sagami blushed, Haruno continued. "So I've got a request for you, Chair. You know, I'd like to join in on this event, too, with a volunteer group. I tried asking Yukino-chan, but she didn't seem into it. She doesn't like me much…" She sniffled pathetically. She was being so obvious it was downright pushy, but also cute at the same time. I just couldn't bring myself to be critical of her for it.

"Huh…?" Sagami looked over at Yukinoshita. Yukinoshita's indignant expression held firm. She didn't look at Sagami, either.

"…Sure," said Sagami. "We don't have enough, and if we get some alumni participating, we can emphasize regional ties? And stuff." I got the feeling she was just parroting what she'd already heard, but Sagami acted like it was her own idea.

"Yeeek! Thanks!" Haruno gave Sagami a quick and forced-looking hug. But she backed off right away and then muttered with a faraway look in her eyes, "Yeah, yeah, it's wonderful to have an alma mater you can return to, even after graduation. I've got to tell all my friends, too. They'll all be jealous."

"Really?"

"Yeah. Sometimes, you really want to come back…and this goes for me, too," said Haruno.

For a moment, Sagami adopted a pensive pose as Hayama and Yukinoshita breathed short, resigned sighs. If Sagami noticed, she gave no indication that she did as she clapped her hands. "…Really? Oh, then why don't those friends join in, too?"

"Oh, good idea! Should I contact them right away, then?"

"Go ahead, go ahead," Sagami said, and instantly, Haruno cheerily began punching in a number on her cell phone, one-handed.

Looking panicked, Yukinoshita came in to stop her. "Hold on, Sagami."

But Sagami innocently asked, "Why not? We're actually short on volunteer groups. And this covers that 'regional ties' thing, right?" Sagami was basking in her victory. But had she realized that it was Haruno Yukinoshita who had led her to just about every element of that plan?

"Besides, I don't know what happened with you and your sister, but that has nothing to do with this, does it?"

"…"

Anyone who had seen that exchange between Yukinoshita and Haruno could tell they didn't get along. Sagami had made that remark with full knowledge of that, leaving Yukinoshita without anything to say. Sagami smiled triumphantly, having gotten the upper hand with Yukinoshita for the first time.

"Saw that coming…," Hayama said briefly.

His all-knowing comment made me a little curious. I silently glanced at him for details, but whether deliberately or not, Hayama didn't touch on it further.

"I'm going to take these documents and go." And just like that, Hayama left the conference room.

The only foreign body left among the cultural committee was

Haruno Yukinoshita. Once she was done with her phone call, she took a set of volunteer application papers and then started a deep conversation with Meguri, Sagami, and their friends.

Haruno wasn't technically getting in the way, but since she stood out so much, her presence made the cultural committee restless. Naturally, they were all watching her every move. Yukinoshita was the only one stubbornly refusing to look at her.

Sagami and her friends were chattering excitedly about something. I watched them, curious, to see our chairperson having a good time chatting with her friends and Meguri nodding pleasantly. Then there was Haruno Yukinoshita. She glanced my way and then stood up.

Haruno walked over and deliberately plopped down right next to me. "Are you doing a proper job, young man?"

"…Yeah, I guess so."

"This is a little surprising. I didn't think you were the type to do something like this."

"Agh. Neither did I."

"Hmm… Shizuka-chan twisted your arm?" Haruno nodded as if that made sense to her. Though there was another committee member whose presence was more inexplicable than mine.

"If we're talking about surprises, isn't your sister the odd one out?"

"You think? I thought she would do it."

Not convinced, I tilted my head.

Haruno examined my face and then added, "I mean, her club is a little uncomfortable now, and her older sister acted as committee chair way back when. That's enough to make her want to do it."

Though I sensed some condescension in the way she said it, I considered the meaning of each part of her argument. It was true that club was getting kind of unpleasant. And most of all, I felt like I'd come to understand just a bit what Haruno was to Yukinoshita.

"Well, it looks like the former is more of an issue," she added, as if she'd just seen something humorous.

The relationship between these sisters was more complicated than it seemed from the outside.

Be they brothers or sisters, siblings are bound to be compared. Often, one is seen as superior. I have a little sister myself. But maybe it's because she's a girl and I'm a boy, or perhaps because we were raised to complement each other's shortcomings, I've got no sense that we get compared like that.

But with the Yukinoshita sisters, they're as similar as twins: the extraordinary older sister, and the equally talented but nonetheless inferior younger sister. If one of them were stupid, at least, then the two of them would probably not have gotten so contrary. One of them may have ended up with a twisted personality, though.

Yukinoshita was constantly battling with the illusion of her sister; she felt she could almost win but always fell short. It would be a lot easier for her if she would just run away from everything Haruno had done. But it seemed her pride, or some other strong emotion, would not let her do that.

If Haruno knew, if she understood, then couldn't she do something about it? Couldn't she find some other way to interact with her little sister?

"Um...what are you thinking?" I asked her frankly.

The scary part about Haruno was, first and foremost, that you didn't know what was going on in her head. It may be strange for me to say this, but I've been observing humans for a long time (in the worst sort of way), and if even I'm having difficulty understanding her, she's very good at what she does.

"What would I have to say for you to believe me?" she replied.

"..." I wouldn't believe anything. My impression of Haruno Yukinoshita was already set in stone. She could tell me some profound reasoning or grand ideal, but I'd still disregard it.

Apparently, my silence got the meaning across just fine. "Then don't ask." Her voice was frosty. I think that was probably genuine. No pretending, no fabrication.

After that, she didn't say anything. Haruno had a cheerful persona, but when she was like this, she reminded me a lot of Yukinoshita.

Now that Haruno had gone silent, all the sounds around us

suddenly seemed louder to me. That meant I could easily hear everyone else chattering, too. Sagami's group seemed particularly engrossed in their talking and giggling.

Apparently encouraged now, Sagami called out to the room in a loud voice, "Everyone, do you all have a minute?" For a moment, the noise in the conference room died down.

When I looked at her, Sagami had stood and was surveying the room. She cleared her throat gently to ready herself and nervously began to speak. "I've been thinking a bit…and I think that maybe the cultural committee really should have a good time with the festival. Like, if we don't have fun ourselves, we can't make it fun for other people, I think…"

I've heard that somewhere before…

"I think the classroom side of things is important, too, so we can enjoy the cultural festival to the fullest. Everything is going smoothly and according to schedule, so how about we slow down the pace a little?"

There was a pause as everyone seemed to consider Sagami's proposal for a moment. Things weren't actually going so badly. Yukinoshita had been fielding concerns one after another, so you could say our progress was decent.

But Yukinoshita objected. "Sagami, I don't really think that's a good idea. We should keep an aggressive schedule to maintain a buffer…"

She was rudely interrupted by a cheerful voice. "Oh! That's a great idea. Back in my day, everyone put in a lot of work with their classes!" said Haruno, acting nostalgic for the good old days. Yukinoshita shot her an accusatory look.

But that attitude just egged Sagami on. "See? There's precedent. Besides…the festival that year was really exciting, right?" Sagami appeared to be seeking confirmation, but Yukinoshita didn't reply. Sagami took that as a yes anyway and kept going. "We should emulate the things they did right after all. I mean, we've gotta learn from the wisdom of our predecessors. Don't bring *personal feelings* into it. Let's consider everyone, now."

Meguri seemed conflicted as she watched the exchange.

Meanwhile, the cultural committee members were exchanging looks, but some scattered clapping suggested a few were already on board with Sagami's proposal. Apparently, this plan had been approved.

As a result, by order of Minami Sagami, the Decree of Return to Class Groups was passed (not the Decree of Return to Farming).

If everyone was going to go along with it, then Yukinoshita could not overturn the decision alone, no matter how much she argued. Sagami smiled in satisfaction, while Yukinoshita returned to her work wearing an incredibly cold expression. The way Sagami saw it, she must have felt like she'd finally managed an act befitting the committee chair.

"I just love the cut of her jib. Right, Hikigaya?" Haruno, sitting right beside me, said to me.

I'm sure it was unkind of me to suspect that this, too, was part of some kind of plot, but...

Yeah, I don't really like her.

×   ×   ×

The changes happened immediately.

Within just a few days of Haruno Yukinoshita's arrival, people started to skip committee meetings here and there. Apparently, Sagami's comments had spread to all the members of the committee. Still, they were just coming in thirty minutes late or being absent with notice. We weren't that affected. Everyone's burden increased slightly, but with rotating breaks, we created a sort of shift schedule.

But as the number of volunteer groups increased and a proportionate number of places became willing to put up signs for Publicity and Advertisement, it created some fairly heavy recalculation of the budget, and the workload started to get lopsided. Both Health and Sanitation's and Records and Miscellaneous's workloads were concentrated on the days of the cultural festival, so it caused no problems if more of these people were to slack off. But there was an undeniable feeling that the volunteer management, advertisement, and accounting sections were a bit short on man power.

In those cases, the executives ended up shouldering the burden, mainly the student council and Yukinoshita. Yukinoshita's intervention was a big help, but still, the work had begun to pile up, and those piles just wouldn't go away.

As a member of Records and Miscellaneous, I was getting more miscellaneous-type work. Strange...I'd heard there wasn't much work here...

"Um...do you have a minute?" The head of our section addressed me.

The fact that he had asked "Do you have a minute?" rather than just "Hey" or something was abnormal. My alarm bells were ringing.

But it was for just such an occasion that I'd thought up some excellent methods for dealing with attempts to pass unnecessary work on to me. I've titled them *Four Strategies for Dealing with Attempts to Pass Unnecessary Work On to You.*

"Um, can I ask you to do this?"

Strategy One: As long as they haven't addressed you by name, just ignore them.

"Are you listening?" He *tap-tap*ped me on the shoulder. *Tch. Failure, huh?*

"Oh, me? Eh-heh."

"I'd like to ask you to do this."

Strategy Two: If you're asked to do something, just give them a look of reluctance.

But the section head must have had a fairly strong heart, as he scowled right back at me. "...Please do it." The look he was giving me expressed even more reluctance than mine, so I was outmaneuvered. Damn it, even that was no good?! Now that it had come to this, it was on to the next method.

"*Haaah... Haaaaaah...*"

Strategy Three: Constantly sigh while you're working!

It's so obnoxious, not only will they never give you any more work again, they'll even roll out their last resort: saying *If you don't want to do this, then just go.* This was so effective for me that back when I had a part-time job, I even used this to leave on the spot and never come back. Tried and true.

But the section head was not bothered at all. In fact, he just pushed up his glasses and came to talk to me. "Are you done?"

There was no way I could have finished it in such a short period of time... *If I were that good, I wouldn't be working for you.*

Finally, I used my ultimate technique.

Strategy Four: Clack away annoyingly hard on the keyboard in the hope that he will leave.

The student council had temporarily loaned the cultural committee a number of computers. They not only made writing work significantly more efficient, they also helped me execute my grumpy typing stratagem.

Taka, taka, taka. TAAAN! How do you like that?! This much emphasis on how I don't want to work has to make him want to give up...

"See you, then. I'm heading home first. Once you're done, you can go. If you have any questions, ask the executives."

"'Tchabye." (Translation: *Oh, I understand. See you later.*)

Heh-heh, I did a wonderful job of dodging work... Now my workload is the absolute minimum! With the piles of work atop my desk before me, I was triumphant... *Wait, whaaaaaaaaat?!*

I clearly have work here! In fact, all I'd managed to do was give that guy a bad impression! I just acted like a jerk! What's more, "You can go once you're done" means "Don't you dare leave until you're done," doesn't it?! Nooo!

The life of an employee is rough. This was far beyond my expectations...

To make it worse, the title of "miscellaneous" must have led to some misunderstandings. Now even the extra work of others was all getting passed to me.

"Um...you're Records and Miscellaneous, right? Can I ask you to do this, too?"

"Agh, but..."

"The cultural festival is a group project! That's how it goes! We have to help one another out!" they declared quite emphatically.

Come on, copying posters definitely isn't my job. And besides, how are you *helping* me *here?* But since it was an older student talking, I couldn't refuse. Never more have I cursed the slumbering Japanese instincts inside me: the tradition of seniority by length of service.

Some people were even refusing to look at me and holding cups toward me. "Tea."

"Agh…" *Why me? Hey, do they think they can just talk to me however they want, since I'm just a lackey? Maybe you've forgotten, but lackeys are humans, too, you know? Come on. If I keep working like this, I'll end up becoming a full-fledged employee.* I Can Be a Corporate Slave!

Oh, damn…I should've taken a break earlier.

With projects like this, frankly, the more diligent you are, the more you get the short end of the stick. There was already a ton of work piled up in front of me, and more than I could muddle through in a day or two, as far as I could tell.

Reflexively, I sighed.

Right then, at almost exactly the same moment, I heard another deep, deep sigh. Looking toward it, I saw Yukinoshita with her hand to her temple, her eyes closed. Did she have a headache or something?

The apparent cause was right in her line of sight.

Nearby, Haruno Yukinoshita was chatting genially with Meguri as she spun a pen in her hand. It had to be her.

Having assembled a bunch of alumni for her volunteer group, she often came to the school to practice for her thing or whatever. On the way, she would often pop in at the cultural committee. She'd entirely settled in. In fact, she was a real regular.

"Hikigaya, some tea for me, too!" she called to me.

"Um, that isn't the miscellaneous section's job, though, I don't think…" I wasn't really sure, so my sentence got timid at the end. What's more, I was making her tea even as I complained. I was a tragic corporate slave by nature. I was pouring the pleasantly burbling tea out of the teapot when I heard Yukinoshita quietly putting her ballpoint pen down.

Her calmness had its own kind of awful impact.

"Haruno, if you're going to be in the way, then leave."

That might work on someone else, but not Haruno. Like a joker against an ace, Haruno was not at all perturbed. "Don't be so crabby. I'll help you out."

"It's fine. Get going, now."

But Haruno ignored that and snatched up some nearby printouts, slurping at her teacup. "Let me see. I suppose I'll give you a hand with your work, as thanks for the tea."

"Hey, stop, don't just—"

Faster than Yukinoshita could stop her, Haruno took a calculator in one hand and briskly began operations. She scratched away something with a red pen with finality and tossed the paper toward Yukinoshita. "Your income and expenditures don't match up."

"…I was planning to check that afterward." Yukinoshita narrowed her eyes in displeasure, but she still took it.

"You haven't changed, Haru." Meguri gazed over at the Yukinoshita sisters with a pleasant smile, gently soothing the tension. The effect she had even made me feel cozy.

"Well, it's not much. I'm used to it. Should I scribble off a few more?" Haruno said, starting in on a few nearby documents.

This time, Yukinoshita didn't stop her. She just pulled her lips tight and dispassionately did her work.

Meguri Shiromeguri is pleasantly trifled with.

What's something that never decreases in amount, no matter how much of it you do?

Work.

Such thoughts lingered in my brain as I faced the PC with empty eyes.

Even writing up the minutes for the meeting had become my job now. When the hell did that happen? I could've sworn the Records and Miscellaneous section head, some third year, was supposed to be the one doing it.

"Records and Miscellaneous, you have yet to submit the record of the proceedings from last week." It had all begun with that one line from Madam Vice-Chair of the Committee.

Who was the one responsible for it? Absent, huh? So then who was next in line? They were off, too. Then next after that? After that? After that...

After that was me.

When I was informed that I would do it, I literally snorted.

Of course there was no way I'd remember a meeting from a week earlier. Half of it was completely fabricated, a string of vague words that sounded appropriate: *proceeding in earnest refer to progress report on attached sheet, suitable adjustments,* and *general compilation planned.* It was fine. The responsible parties would take care of it. That's why they're the responsible parties.

I finished up when it was basically good enough and guzzled down some tea I'd poured for myself.

It's quieter than usual, so I've gotten a lot done, I thought. Looking around the conference room, there were fewer than twenty people working like me. Five of the people there were from student council. Originally, there should have been two kids from each class in the cultural committee, but at this point, not even half of them were there.

The one most aggressively plowing through the work was Yukinoshita. Perhaps because Haruno wasn't around that day, she was able to calmly get things done. She seemed to be working more and longer than she had before. Maybe the cause was her rivalry with Haruno.

There was also that the work volume had simply increased.

The arrival of Haruno's volunteer group must have triggered this new wave of groups, which meant we were flooded with adjustments to make.

We wouldn't have been able to manage it all with our diminished numbers if it weren't for the efforts of the executives and the student council, Yukinoshita's talents, and Haruno's help. She would occasionally float in to handle a few things when she was here for practice with her volunteer group. Somehow, we had been scraping by.

On my break, I checked up on how everyone else was doing and found someone else taking a breather.

It was Meguri. When her eyes met mine, she tried to talk to me. "Uh, um..." It seemed like she was trying to remember my name. I sensed she was about to pleasantly ask me, *Sorry, what was your name again?* And that would make me sad, so I decided to beat her to the punch.

"Working hard, huh?"

"Yeah. So have you." Meguri smiled. I could see a touch of exhaustion in her expression. The way things were going, the burden on all personnel was increasing. You could say there was no way around it, though, and you'd be right.

"So…," I began, "our numbers are kinda dwindling, huh?"

"Yeah…it looks like everyone is pretty busy." The conference room was so empty, it felt even larger than usual. "B-but I'm sure we'll get more tomorrow!" said Meguri. That probably wasn't going to happen.

In fact, more and more people were bound to drop out from that point on. Once this idea that it was okay to skip out had taken root, the attendance rate would plummet faster and faster.

There's something called the "broken windows theory."

Let's say there's a broken window on a building in a certain town. If you leave it be, it becomes a sign of apathy, and that apathy invites the erosion of morality, which leads to crime. The theory born from this string of causation is the "broken windows theory."

Fundamentally speaking, people are soft on themselves.

Not all members of the cultural committee had volunteered to join up. Some, like me, would have been forced into it. But they'd still do the work anyway because they believed everyone else was working hard, and the guilt would drive them forward. If you remove that general perception or compulsion that prevents people from slacking off, it all collapses. It's axiomatic.

It's a lot easier to look for reasons to not try than it is to do the opposite. I'm sure everyone has felt it before, be it when studying or dieting. You use the weather, the temperature, your mood—anything as a reason to skip out.

At some point, we wouldn't be able to handle things anymore. Meguri must have understood that, too. But nobody knew what to do or how to get out of this. Anyhow, the chair herself wasn't around, and the vice-chair was so remarkably talented, she could more than make up for the people who were skipping out.

Meguri and I both sipped at our tea in silence. I was enjoying my peaceful moment with her (though neither of us said anything), but we couldn't rest for long. As we got closer to the festival, things were getting more intense, and with that intensity would come more work.

Now there was yet another *knock, knock* on the door of the conference room.

Speaking of which, I've heard that the well-known *dun dun dun duuun* of Beethoven's "Fate" is the sound of destiny knocking on the door. If that's true, destiny sure has nice manners.

I wondered if the person knocking on the door right then would be the bearer of more work. In other words, fate means work, and I, in my attempts to live without toil, am he who struggles against fate. I think they really should turn my life into a game with the Characteristic Genre Name "RPG to struggle against the fate of work." I hope I can use the royalties to feed myself without getting a job.

"Come in," Meguri called out, since nobody had replied yet.

Someone stepped in, saying, "Pardon me." The identity of the one knocking on heaven's door was Hayato Hayama.

×   ×   ×

"I've come to submit my volunteer application...," Hayama said to Yukinoshita when he noticed her.

"Applications are to the right, at the rear," she responded, hands still flying across the keyboard. She would get zero points in customer service for that, but, well, this was Yukinoshita, so there was no helping that.

It seemed Hayama understood that well enough, as he headed over to apply with a smooth "Thank you."

Now Hayama had done what he came to do, but strangely, he was still here. In fact, he came right up to me. "...Are you down some people?"

Oh, that. "Yeah, kinda."

"Hmm..." He combed up the hair on the back of his neck in thought.

Hey, if your hair is irritating you, then cut it off. Actually, what was weirdly irritating was his presence, although that was nothing new. "So...did you want something?" I asked, unable to take it any longer, and he grinned at me.

"Oh, not really. I'm just waiting for my documents to be evaluated. She said she was going to look and see if there was anything missing."

Is that all? So why is he standing right next to me? I wondered, but then I remembered he was just like that. I don't know why, but these types form groups even when they have no real reason to. I guess when they see a face they know, they're just unable to keep themselves from approaching it. It's less uncomfortable if you just think of the habit as something a puppy would do.

Meanwhile, we got another guest, and yet another.

The volunteer groups weren't the only ones who needed to fill out applications for their presentations; classes and clubs did, too. For volunteers, we also had to keep the stage situation and equipment issues in mind, which was part of Volunteer Management's jurisdiction, but the executives handled all other applications. For anything regarding foodstuffs, Health and Sanitation would be sent to handle that, and they would be the ones to evaluate and approve it.

The due date for applications was coming up, and this contributed to the particularly large number of visitors that day. But this rush was poorly timed, and there weren't enough people at each counter, so things were starting to get chaotic. That was when we started getting some applicants who didn't know where to go.

One confused-looking girl, probably in first year, didn't know what to do and came over to talk. To Hayama...to Hayama. "Um...I'm volunteering..."

"Applications for volunteer groups go over there." He helped her so naturally, it was like he was on the committee himself. Obviously, that invited some misunderstandings, so all the people who had come in with their applications were going, *Oh, you ask Hayama, you ask Hayama!*

"I don't know how to fill this out... Could you help me with this?"

"Oh, if you don't mind getting help from me."

I think that girl is probably asking because *it's you, Hayama.*

While Hayama was explaining it to her in-depth, a line formed behind her.

"Come give me a hand," Hayama said to me.

"Ah, hey—" Before I knew it, I'd been roped into this, too. Did the girls who were turned over to me look disappointed for a moment? Well, yeah.

Hayama and I both had our hands full, and we processed the line as best we could. Meguri hurried in, too, and the three of us managed the crowd until the application rush had passed.

"Sorry. Thank you!" When things had finally settled down for the time being, Meguri poured some tea. For Hayama...for Hayama. Well, she must have felt awkward for making a nonmember like him help out. *It's just, um, I was doing work outside my jurisdiction, too, though...*sniffle.

Hayama thanked Meguri as he sipped his drink and then asked, "Do you have enough help?"

"I don't know the whole situation," I said. "Us underlings have our hands full with our own responsibilities."

"So what are you in charge of?"

"Records and Miscellaneous," I replied.

"Ah." Apparently, that made sense to him. "That's very you."

You trying to start a fight here?

Having seen the situation firsthand, Hayama seemed to have a general grasp on what was happening. He nodded with a know-it-all look. "I see. Must be rough, then."

"...Oh, not really." There wasn't really any problem. Exactly the opposite: The problem was that there were no problems.

Yukinoshita was dealing with just about everything herself. She had the skills, she had a certain degree of authority as the vice-chair, and what's more, without any work to do for her club or her class, she had nothing but time. Even with about half the committee skipping out, she managed to cover for them all.

"But from what I can see, Yukinoshita is doing just about everything." Hayama turned around and tried to get Yukinoshita's attention.

Yukinoshita had been silent for a while, but she couldn't resist Hayama's warm gaze. It was like he was waiting for a reply. So she said, "...Yes, this is most effective."

"But you'll burn out soon." It was an unusually harsh way to put it for a guy like Hayato Hayama.

Meguri reacted to the change in mood with anxiety.

The only sound in the room was the *clickity-clack* of the keyboard.

"..."

That was true. Yukinoshita couldn't argue that.

"You should really start relying on other people before it's too late," said Hayama.

"You think so? Actually, I disagree," I said, and Hayama gave me a hard look in the eye, waiting for me to continue. "A lot of things really do go faster when Yukinoshita does it on her own. Fewer losses, and that's a plus, right? Most of all, trusting people with responsibility is exhausting. And when you're so much more capable than they are, that goes double." We—or at least I—can't trust people to handle stuff.

If things don't go well for you and you alone, you have only yourself to blame, and you don't get the urge to pawn off responsibility. You can't bring yourself to resent someone else for it. And not out of kindness or a sense of accountability. It's because when it's you, you can let it go, but when someone else has done it to you, you can't. Living your life thinking *If she'd only done this then* or *If he'd just done his job* is oppressive, painful, and miserable.

So it's better to do it yourself.

Because when it's only your own regret, all you have to do is mourn.

Hayama narrowed his eyes just slightly and then gave a short, slightly pitying sigh. "...Will it work out if you do it that way?"

"Hmm?"

"If things go well, that's fine, but right now, you're not managing everything, and it won't be long before it all falls apart. The most important thing is to make this work, right? If so, you should change the way you do things."

"Ngh..." *Just gonna* sail on *in here with your perfect arguments, huh, Hayama? Wait, wasn't that a place famous for making black tea? He's argued me down with assam real flair.*

While I was moaning, I heard a quiet "You're...right." It seemed his remark had hit Yukinoshita where it hurt, too. Her hands had gone still over the keyboard.

But Yukinoshita had no one to rely on. If Yuigahama were around, things probably would have been different, though.

"So…I'll help out," said Hayama.

"But you're not on the committee…" Meguri attempted to refuse him.

Hayama smiled in reply. "No, I'll just handle the coordination of the volunteer groups. As their representative."

His proposal was attractive. Unlike the classes and clubs, which had clear representatives and systems for giving them directions, the volunteer groups and their presentations varied in composition and content, and dealing with each one appropriately would get very complicated. If the groups could do that for themselves, then the burden on Volunteer Management—the burden on Yukinoshita, to be blunt—could be significantly reduced. Furthermore, it did make its own sort of sense for the volunteer participants to coordinate independently.

Meguri wavered for a moment, but then she raised her head and smiled shyly. "If that's all it is, all right. It would be great if we could ask you to do it."

"How about it?" Hayama asked Yukinoshita.

She put her hand to her chin and considered for a while. "…"

"Relying on other people is important, too, Yukinoshita," Meguri admonished her kindly.

Hayama and Meguri were not wholly wrong. It was wonderful. Touching. What a lovely expression of fellowship.

That was all well and good for people accustomed to getting help. They can rely on people without hesitation. To cooperate and work together: What truly wonderful things those must be.

But I wasn't going to praise those acts with blind conviction. I mean, that's what they were doing, right?

If participating with the group is wonderful, if it's such a good thing, then is working by yourself a bad thing? Why do you have to reject people who work hard alone?

I couldn't allow that.

"…I'm sure it's important to rely on others, but right now, we've got nothing but reliers. Relying by itself is fine, but some of these people are *using*." It came out more aggressive than I'd expected. When I noticed Meguri had gone pale, I played it off as a joke. I didn't want the guilt of freaking out such a pleasant and comforting beauty. "Specifically, you know, um… Oh! Yeah, like the people dumping off work on me. Man, that's some pretty heinous stuff. I can't avoid getting off my ass this time around…but that means no one else gets to take it easy, either!"

"You really are the worst, aren't you?" Meguri shot back cheerfully. She must have taken it as a joke, then.

"I'll help you out, too." Hayama smiled wryly.

Yukinoshita sighed very quietly. "It's true—it does seem that much of the burden has been shifted to the miscellaneous section, so I'll reconsider the assignments. Since Meguri has judged it appropriate as well, I'll accept your proposal. I'm grateful… I'm sorry." Her eyes never left her computer the whole time. It wasn't even clear who she had apologized to.

I'm sure a blithe interpretation was that Yukinoshita was being considerate for my sake, but I hadn't really been sticking up for her. There was no reason for her to apologize to me, either. I really just can't stand people who dump their work off on others so they can take it easy.

I hate it when people who are putting in a diligent effort get the short end of the stick. I can't turn a blind eye when the people who are seriously tackling the matters at hand are stuck doing the dirty work.

That's all.

I mean, it's not like I'd helped at all anyway. In fact, I'd created a new task: redistributing the workload. I was about as useless as you could get.

"Guess I'm on the team, then,"

"Tomorrow, I'll try contacting the people I can get ahold of, too."

Hayama smiled broadly, and Meguri gave an encouraging nod.

X X X

"We're really short on people…"

A week later at a committee meeting, there were even fewer attendees than before. It wasn't even worth comparing. Aside from Yukinoshita, I could only see a handful of the executives around.

Meguri groaned helplessly. "I did contact people. Maybe I should have said upfront that Sagami's proposal was no good…," she said, apologetic.

She must have been referring to Sagami's earlier claim that the classes were important, too.

Yukinoshita's hand stopped flipping through documents. "It's no problem. I will handle the review and approval of applications from each section myself. I believe we'll be able to proceed without issue to finalization." Things seemed to be moving along smoothly, perhaps because of the reallocation of labor.

Maybe I got this from some manga or anime, but they say that only 20 percent of ants work seriously. Another 20 percent of them don't work at all. As for the remaining 60 percent, they sometimes work and sometimes don't. It seems this is also true of humans.

The point is that 60 percent are reading the vibe to determine which group to side with. Or possibly, they court both groups just enough to avoid causing discord.

The way things were headed with the cultural committee right then, the odds weren't looking good for the hardworking ants. It wasn't like people were deliberately not attending. But an unspoken rule was brewing: *You don't have to go.*

Everyone gets vaguely more at ease when they have numbers on their side. It's true; you feel like *If everyone else is doing it, then I guess I'm good, too.* So in a manner of speaking, working hard wasn't the trend for the cultural committee.

I'd become part of the minority—again. At this point, it even felt like destiny.

But even among those remaining few, some people were actually giving it their all. As you'd expect, the student council had a strong sense of responsibility and unity. They were playing an active part in both their regular duties as student council members and also as executives of the cultural committee.

Perhaps they accomplished this feat due to the natural virtues of their leader, Meguri. That day, like every day, the student council members were working together to support their pleasant but still somewhat featherbrained president.

Meguri was trying hard to respond in turn, too. She went around addressing all the executives and each person in attendance. "We don't have a big crowd, but we do have regular attendees, so there's nothing for it but to give it our best. I'm counting on you, okay?"

"Ha-ha-ha, thanks, I guess...," I replied. She'd even come to talk to me, too. *Phew...* If she'd skipped me and no one else, I really might not have shown up the next day.

I put down my bag and checked my tasks for the day. Recently, we'd been chipping away at the work, so quite a lot of progress had been made. At this rate, if I worked hard, it wouldn't be long before I was done.

I was slowly muddling through my work when I felt a couple of taps on my shoulder.

When I turned around, there was Hayama carrying a bunch of files. Even though hardly any others were showing up, Hayama still came in now and then. In fact, he was going out of his way to come and work. Of course, it wasn't every day, but it seemed like he was making the effort when he had the time.

Hayama was a good guy.

"Sorry to get you in the middle of work," he said. "Help me consolidate these equipment applications. It'll just be thirty minutes."

"O-okay..." Not only had he given me a fixed timeline, he'd also clearly described what we were doing, so I couldn't find any reason to refuse. Not a bad way of roping a guy into something.

He was the ideal manager. And now, I was undeniably working under him. *Ahhh, I want to die.*

We were silently chugging along when someone opened the door with a big rattle. The conference room was a desolate wasteland, so it sounded especially loud.

All eyes gathered on Miss Hiratsuka, who was standing in front of the door and beckoning with her hand. "Yukinoshita, do you have a minute?"

Yukinoshita poked her head around the monitor on her desk. "Miss Hiratsuka...I can't really leave my work right now. If you don't mind, you can tell me here," she said.

Miss Hiratsuka seemed to consider for a moment. "Hmm... Well, it's not like we need to be formal about it..." She strode into the conference room and stood quietly beside Yukinoshita. "It seems you haven't decided on your curriculum stream yet," she said.

"...I'm sorry. I'm a little busy right now." Yukinoshita looked down, embarrassed. Her hands had left the keyboard to lie on her lap.

"I see... I understand that the committee is a lot of work, but don't push yourself too hard."

"I understand."

Miss Hiratsuka smiled kindly in admonishment, and Yukinoshita's reply was brief.

"Hmm... Well, you can do it after the cultural festival is over. Since you're in the international curriculum, your choice won't have an impact on class arrangements. You still have time. Really, it's just an attitude survey. Nothing you need to think too deeply about." Miss Hiratsuka patted Yukinoshita's head lightly, almost stroking her hair, then left the conference with a casual raised hand. A scowl on her face, Yukinoshita rearranged her hair as she watched the teacher go.

I was a little surprised that *the* Yukinoshita had failed to submit something like that. Apparently, I wasn't alone, as Hayama was giving Yukinoshita a doubtful look, too. Both Hayama and I had paused in our work.

"Hey...are we done yet?" I asked. It's hard to say that when the other guy has his nose to the grindstone, but now that our task had been interrupted, I could say it! I wanted to be free!

Hayama snapped out of it and smiled at me. "Yeah, sorry. Let's get started again."

That's not what I meant... I'd been trying to ask, *Can we stop doing this task now?* It wasn't a request to start again. But now that Hayama had interpreted my comment in good faith and even given me his Hayama smile, I couldn't tell him he had the wrong idea. More significantly, the thirty minutes I'd been promised weren't up yet. Yeah... I wasn't getting out of this.

I was typing the information from the applications into Excel and making them all into a list when Meguri, who had been doing her own work nearby, struck up a conversation with Yukinoshita. "So which are you going for, Yukinoshita, arts or sciences?"

"I haven't quite made up my mind yet."

"Of course! Yep, yep. I understand how hard it is to make a decision! I had a difficult time, too. So then which subjects are you better at? Sciences?"

"...Not necessarily..." Yukinoshita didn't seem angry, exactly, but her answer was very chilly. Meguri didn't know quite how to reply.

Hayama's hands paused in their task, and he lifted his head from his computer screen. "You're good at arts subjects too, huh, Yukinoshita?"

"Oh, she is?" said Meguri, relieved at having Hayama join in on the conversation.

Come to think of it, I'd had a vague sense that Yukinoshita was good at arts subjects, too. At our grade level, I'm third in Japanese, while Hayama is second, and Yukinoshita is number one. We're locked in at the top three, and if we all were to select the arts stream, we'd probably be ranked at the top there as well. Anyway, Yukinoshita reads a lot, too, and I think she has plenty of artistic inclinations, at least as far as I can tell on the surface.

"I'm in arts, you know," said Meguri. "If you're unsure of what to choose, ask me anything!"

"Agh... Thank you. I'm grateful for your concern." I thought for sure Yukinoshita was going for a polite response, but then she went in to refuse Meguri in a super-roundabout way.

But Meguri didn't seem to have noticed that. She continued to babble on with some excitement. "Yep, yep! Oh! I don't know much about the sciences stream, so I can't answer things about that, though. But Haru was in sciences, so I guess you can ask her."

"I…suppose…I could." Suddenly, a shadow fell over Yukinoshita's face.

I doubted Yukinoshita would ever ask Haruno, though.

Yukinoshita hadn't been very talkative before, but after that, she didn't say a word. The atmosphere called for silence, so Meguri naturally stopped talking, too. After that, the only sounds in the room were taps of typing and the rustle of documents, like badly done Morse code.

In the silence, even an *ahem* draws your attention. No matter who the source or how quiet it was, anyone clearing their throat to speak pulled your eyes toward them.

"…The rep for 2-F? Your plan application documents have yet to be submitted." Papers in hand, Yukinoshita breathed a short sigh.

There were still people who hadn't turned those in? Good grief. Who was it? …It was meee! My sense of affiliation with the class was so weak, I forgot entirely.

Wait, didn't Sagami say she'd take care of it? Well, she hadn't been attending the committee meetings lately, so I couldn't check with her.

"…Sorry, I'll write it up." I could have waited, but the documents might never be handed in otherwise, so I'd just write whatever myself.

"All right…then submit that today."

I accepted the documents from Yukinoshita and immediately began writing.

Number of people, name of representative, registration name, equipment required, name of homeroom teacher… *Come on, why are they even making me draw a diagram? Throwing down the gauntlet, are we? I took Art 2…*

I skimmed over the other items for entry.

Ah-ha… I have no idea.

My commitment to nonparticipation in class activities had borne fruit. Not only did I not know their group registration name, I didn't even know the number of people in my own class.

But it was for times like this that *he* was around. In fact, it was the only time I needed him around. "Hayama, what do I put on this thing?" I asked him.

He seemed to think a bit. "Sorry, I don't really know everything about it."

"That's fine. I'll just make something up for the rest."

"Uh, you can't do that."

"...I can hear you." Yukinoshita's eyes remained locked on her monitor, but her voice was enough of a warning.

Hayama gave a wry smile. "I think it would be faster for you to ask someone who's been with the class."

"Okay, then." I gathered up the papers and left for 2-F.

X   X   X

The classroom was abuzz with activity after school in preparation for the festival. The noise from the large number of participants in the middle of their preparation showed how much they were enjoying the project.

When a girl and a boy are conversing together, the number of times he succeeds in making her laugh is equal to one youth hit (yH), each hour engaged in the undertaking is expressed as one youth hour (yH), and the product of these two values is his youth hero degree (yH), which they compete over. It's pretty hard to understand 'cause all the units are the same.

And as for 2-F, the yH value was fairly high. There was the play, so they were putting tables together to build a stage. In one corner, they were sewing the costumes, while in another, the actors were rehearsing their parts.

"Geez, guys, do it right!" Sagami was yelling at a number of boys, including Ooka.

So Sagami was out here, huh?

Well, even if Sagami had been with us, she wouldn't have been very useful, so it didn't really matter. Sometimes, it can be cruel when someone outclasses you so thoroughly.

I don't know if I should tell her to actually come or not, I thought.

But if I did, she'd just talk about it behind my back: *Like, so Hikitani was complaining about me. Ew. This is basically harassment. Actually, he's so creepy, that makes it sexual harassment, right? lol. Lawsuit, lol! But actually, like, he's not even the boss of me or anything, lol. Who is he, seriously? LOL... Wait, actually, who is that guy?* And that would be the punch line. The vision rose so vividly in my mind, I started to wonder if my powers of clairvoyance hadn't spontaneously awoken before an impending super-powered battle.

Scanning the classroom, I saw that my classmates were not in their regular uniforms.

It has been done...

Those fearsome, soul-destroying weapons: class T-shirts.

Class T-shirts. Basically, the T-shirts that each class makes for the cultural festival. Exactly what it says on the tin. That explanation was a waste of time.

I think these shirts are supposed to emphasize class unity, camaraderie, and excitement for the cultural festival. I also get the sense it's a memento of the event, concrete proof of their youth.

With class T-shirts, you usually see everyone in the class's nicknames printed on the backs for whatever reason, at least in my own experience.

These shirts had everyone's nicknames written on them, too, while I was the only one with my real name written on it, as *Hikigaya*. Since the majority of the nicknames were written in phonetic katakana or hiragana letters, the formal kanji characters stuck out like a sore thumb. What's more, they even added a friendly little *kun* honorific in katakana in an attempt to somehow make me sound more like part of the group. That misdirected kindness even made me feel kinda bad.

Back in first year, this sort of thing would have hit me rather hard, but now, I'm like, *Just bring it on.* I wouldn't even care if they wrote my full name in kanji. Ha-ha-ha! Once the cultural festival was over, I'd immediately use this shirt as a rag. It wasn't very high quality, so it wouldn't make good pj's.

I searched for Yuigahama's figure in the classroom. *Hmm... Gahama, Gahama...*

And that was when a lovely figure suddenly entered my field of vision.

The androgynous being emanated a delicate charm. The baggy, overlong coat sleeves covered everything but the fingertips of Totsuka in his Little Prince costume. It looked like he was currently in the process of having the pants hemmed. His rolled-up cuffs had pins stuck in them.

He seemed bored until he noticed me, and the hands peeking out of his sleeves waved at me. "Oh, Hachiman. Welcome back."

"...Yeah. I'm back." As embarrassing as it was, I had returned! I very nearly bowed on reflex. If Totsuka would welcome me back with those words, I'd love to come home to him every day.

"Oh yeah!" Totsuka pattered off as if he'd just remembered something. He pulled that something out of his bag and then rushed back. On his way, he tripped on the hem of his coat and fell right into my chest...! Or rather, I briefly fantasized about it. Things did not actually go that well. Reality is always cruel.

"Thanks for this." Totsuka was holding out a book to me.

It was the paperback copy of *The Little Prince* that I'd lent him a while earlier. I'd read it countless times now, so the corners of the cover were worn, and the book was a little dirty, too. I sort of regretted that now, thinking it wasn't the sort of thing I should have been lending out.

"So I've been thinking about how I could say thanks for it..." Totsuka nodded firmly as if he were trying to psych himself up a little, then looked up to gaze straight into my eyes. "Um...is there anything you like, Hachiman?"

You, Totsuka.

I was inches from just blurting it out. In fact, the *y* had already left my mouth. "Y... Yeah, not much that I can think of, really," I replied, somehow managing to cover up my slip.

Totsuka folded his arms small and began to seriously ponder the matter. "Hmm…really…? Th-then how about you tell me any foods or books you like, or…snacks? Anything you want."

You, Totsuka.

Yet again, I just about blurted it out. In fact, I even got as far as the *you*. "U… Usually can't think of anything on the spot. Well, if I have to come up with something, then I like sweet stuff." Like MAX Coffee. Also, miso peanuts, malt jelly, and the soft-serve ice cream from Chiba's own Mother Farm, and the peanut pies at Orandaya.

"Sweet stuff… Okay, I'll get you something soon!" Totsuka said with a smile, but then a voice called out to him. It sounded like they were ready to do the hemming. Totsuka answered the call before turning back to me. "Well, I'm off."

"I'll see you later," I replied, watching him go as he left with a raised hand. …*I like this. I want to see Totsuka off from my house every morning.* But for some reason, having Totsuka be the one supporting me seemed sorta perverse. It made me feel guilty.

Now alone, once again I scanned the classroom. Totsuka was so cute, I'd completely forgotten my original goal.

Um, Gahama…

Oh, there she is.

"Yuigahama."

The ice cream bar she was biting into suggested she had been out doing some shopping, and she was holding a piece of paper as she participated in a meeting of some sort. Just then, she lifted her head and ran toward me. "Huh? Are you done with your work, Hikki?"

"You can stop doing work, but that doesn't mean it's over."

"What are you talking about?" she said, looking at me like I was an idiot.

Tch, *people blessed with good work environments…* I considered kindly explaining the terror and tragedy of corporate slavery to her, but I really didn't have the time. Silently locking away my loathing of labor in my heart, I figured I'd get this over with quickly. "I'm still working. Sorry, but could you tell me what goes here? I have to submit this today."

"You're in a hurry? Oh, wait, is Hayato over there, too?" She must have meant with the cultural committee.

"Yeah."

"Then let's do it over there, since there's so much noise here. I was thinking about calling for a stage meeting soon anyway."

As we were conversing, Sagami piped up behind us. "Oh, I've got to head off to the committee, too. Sorry, guys. Once I've finished this, I'll get going."

×   ×   ×

I returned to the conference room, and Yuigahama gave me the rundown on their plans.

Aside from the practical side of things, like necessary equipment, number of people involved, and detailed budget, I also had to fill in some pretty abstract stuff, like project intention and a general overview. I would have been able to fake something if it had just been in writing, but I even had to draw a diagram of the structures, too.

This was a real pain in the butt.

"I'm telling you, that's not right!" Yuigahama was saying. "It's gotta be more like, *bam!* It'll have fancy decorations!"

"I don't get it…" The pain in the butt was less the drawing itself and more understanding Yuigahama. Why were her explanations so intuition based? She was frighteningly enigmatic.

"Also, the number of people assigned to this is wrong."

"This is humiliating… To think that Yuigahama would ever teach me a lesson…"

"What was that?! Just redo it already!" She was surprisingly strict.

I sketched out some lines and somehow managed to survive the task.

Seeing other students diligently occupied must have encouraged the executives as well. Meguri had a smile on her face as she did her work. As time passed, the conference room wasn't mildly tense like it usually was but peaceful and calm.

Just then, a metallic squeak cut through the atmosphere. "Sorry I'm laaaate! Oh, here you are, Hayama!"

Behind Sagami followed her two usual friends. This was the first time she'd come to work in a while. After addressing Hayama, she was about to approach him when Yukinoshita stepped in front of her instead. Sagami seemed nonplussed at the sudden hindrance, but Yukinoshita didn't give her the time to be surprised. She just shoved some documents and a stamp at Sagami. "Sagami, your approval stamp on these. There should be no issues with the review of these documents, since I've personally amended any inadequacies."

"...Really? Thanks."

The conversation went straight to business, with no room for any small talk.

Perhaps because her conversation with Hayama had been interrupted, or perhaps unhappy about being forced into a sudden business conversation, Sagami was expressionless for a few moments. Still, she quickly accepted the documents with a smile in an attempt to hide any displeasure.

Sagami went over the documents with her stamp, *bam, bam, bam,* hardly looking at the papers at all. Meanwhile, Yukinoshita was off to the side, accepting them back and giving them one more check before she filed them. This arrangement wasn't anything new, but there were quite a few problems with it.

This was something I could sense, being on the inside, but I did wonder how it would look to an outsider. With that question in my mind, I glanced at Yuigahama and saw her lips pressed shut and her gaze pointed at the floor. Well, she must have had her opinions about this. With club on pause, she and Yukinoshita were oddly distant, and now she was personally witnessing this exchange between Yukinoshita and Sagami. And it wasn't pleasant, either.

On the other hand, the other outsider, Hayama, wore the same unfaltering smile. He even called out to Sagami. "Hey. Were you in the classroom, Sagami?"

Hearing his voice, Sagami twisted around like a weasel toward Hayama. "Oh, uh-huh."

"I see… So how are things going?"

"Pretty well, I guess," Sagami replied.

Hayama paused for a few seconds. The glaring pause before it gave his next comment extra impact. "Oh, I didn't mean that. I meant with the committee. It looks like Yumiko is doing a good job handling the class stuff." There was just the slightest trace of venom in his words, be it conscious or not. If Hayama had chosen that turn of phrase deliberately, that meant there was something else behind his words. Translated loosely, I think it'd be something like, *It looks like you're skipping out on the committee… Should you be doing that?*

But apparently, Sagami was immune to such venom, as she continued unfazed. "Ohhh…Miura. She's really psyched about this, huh? I hardly recognize her. Like, she's really got this covered." (Translation: *That bitch is even more grating than usual. It's so obnoxious how she keeps butting in.*)

"Ha-ha-ha. Well, she's a big help, so it's all good, right? It's not a bad thing." (Translation: *Stop talking, okay?*)

I was reading so much into their words, I must have eaten a translation jelly or something.

It wasn't like I really cared. I think it was just because Sagami's poorly chosen phrasing had flipped some weird switch in me. I could even sense hidden implications in Hayama's words, and he was supposed to be a good guy. My brain processed this information and projected it across my field of vision as subtitles. I was following along with them until there was a loud clap in front of my face.

"Hey, hurry it up. I wanna go back," said Yuigahama.

"But, like, this wasn't even my job in the first place…" Yeah, wasn't this something Sagami said she was going to do? Why was I the one stuck with it in the end? *I can't understand what's going on here. I don't understand, Masked Niyander.*

"…You're being loud," Yukinoshita muttered quietly at our discussion.

Yuigahama and I shut our mouths automatically, but Sagami must not have heard her, and her fun little chat with Hayama continued. "Y'know, I wish I could be more like her! The way she leads everyone is so inspiring." (Translation: *I want to crush her and take her place.*)

"You have your own strengths. You're fine the way you are, don't you think?" (Translation: *I told you to stop talking, didn't I? Know your place—for your own sake.*)

"Huh? But I don't really have a lot of strengths." (Translation: *Here, now I'm being self-deprecating! Compliment me, compliment me! Hayama, compliment me!*)

"Everyone's different. Maybe they don't seem like strengths to you, but other people can see them." (Translation: *Sorry, I don't know you well enough to give you a compliment, so here's the standard placation.*)

The whole time, I was reading the surprisingly liberally translated subtitles that you sometimes see on American films, and it was really distracting. Dubs are the way to go for foreign films.

The sound of a cell phone snapping shut broke off my train of thought. "Hikki, you stopped working. I put the stage meeting off until evening, so we're going to do this thing right."

"It's twenty minutes until it's time to go home," said Yukinoshita.

They were all pressuring me...

"Hey, he hasn't been in the classroom, so it's inevitable that it'll take him more time, right?" Unable to just watch, Hayama swooped in to support me. What a good guy.

Well, if you'd just filled me in on the project outline, this never would've happened, though. Still, if this is part of the cultural committee's job, there's no getting around it, I thought, biding my time.

Sagami said, "Since I'm chairing the committee, I do have to leave some things to you. Thanks!" (Translation: *Do it right, minion. Nyeh.*)

I just bided my time... *After two turns, I'll give it back to you double.* But that's not really biding much, is it?

Anyway, somehow or other, after what seemed like an eternity, I cobbled together the application form. "It's over..."

"Done, huh?" Yuigahama replied, exhausted.

"Sorry. But thanks. You've been a big help."

"Huh? Oh yeah. No problem. You don't ask me for stuff often anyway."

"Yeah. I never thought this day would come, either."

"Just how dumb do you think I am?!"

I let Yuigahama's complaint roll off me as I submitted the documents. Yukinoshita accepted them without a word, checking the first and second sheet, and when she was done reading them, she *tap-tapp*ed their edges on the desk to align them. "Accepted. Good work." Without a single glance my way, she put the papers with the approved documents and filed them away.

"Don't you need to get them stamped?" I asked.

"...Oh." With a short "Of course," Yukinoshita pulled out the papers once more.

It was nothing. A thoughtless error.

And that was exactly what made it so incredibly out of place.

"Your stamp here, Sagami," said Yukinoshita.

Sagami interrupted her discussion to accept the documents. "Oh, sure. Actually, I'll just give you my stamp, so you can sign off on them, okay?"

"I'm not so sure that's a good idea, Sagami," Meguri advised frankly, unable to let that one slide.

But Sagami wasn't shy at all about what she was doing. "Huh? But the way we're doing things now isn't efficient, is it? I think substance is more important than formality. You know, delegation?"

Out of context, the words would sound like a wonderful explosion of sound logic. Still, from a purely pragmatic perspective, it would indeed be more effective to leave the stamping to Yukinoshita rather than to wait for Sagami's approval.

Meguri must have been thinking the same thing, as she was *hmm*ing uncertainly. "If Yukinoshita doesn't mind, then..." She gave Yukinoshita a searching glance.

For her part, Yukinoshita didn't seem bothered. She nodded. "I don't. From here on out, I will be making approvals."

Sagami entrusted Yukinoshita with the stamp, and Yukinoshita immediately stamped my documents.

Now today's operations were over. Right then, the bell rang.

"Right, I guess that's it for today. I'll lock the door, so all of you can leave before I do. Executives, please handle all the end-of-day checks." Meguri gave her directions, and the student council swiftly scattered. The cultural committee was in charge of handling dismissal, so we couldn't ignore Meguri and stay late. We quickly cleaned up and packed our things away, then left the conference room.

On the way to the front entrance, I saw Sagami having a friendly chat with her friends, and then she called out to us, too. "Hey, why don't we all go out to eat after this? Hmm?" As she said it, she was really only looking at Hayama.

Hayama's and Yuigahama's eyes moved, apparently checking to see how everyone else was taking this. Yukinoshita noticed Yuigahama's gaze flicking over to her, and she coolly replied, "I still have work to do." I'm sure it wasn't just an excuse, and she actually did have work. To say nothing of the additional task Sagami had just delegated to her. Her responsibilities and workload had increased along with that, too.

"Oh, of course, yeah, I got it," said Sagami. "There's no helping that." (Translation: *Listen, I was never inviting you in the first place.*)

Apparently, my subtitles had yet to be disabled, as I could see right through to her underlying intentions. Don't underestimate the power of the Jagan eye…

After Yukinoshita, I refused, too. "I'm going home."

"Yeah, I gotcha." (Translation: *There's no seat for your ass anyway!*)

I'd known full well I wasn't invited, but I'd figured it would be the right thing to do to give her a proper refusal. 'Cause I mean, look, forcing someone to say, *U-um, so…what about you? You don't have to come if you really don't want to* at the end is pretty harsh. So is hearing it. That wouldn't make anyone happy. And why do I have to be roped into parties after work in the first place?

The ones Sagami was inviting were not me or Yukinoshita but the other two.

Perhaps because Yuigahama had already come to her decision, she hesitated as she spoke. "T-today isn't so good for me, either... I have to go to a meeting for the play..."

"What? You're not coming, Yui? Let's gooo!" (Translation: *Hey, if you don't come, then Hayama won't, either, will he? Eh?*)

Whoops, one of those reactions was not like the others, was it? It was so brazen I started wondering if she'd been taking metalworking classes.

"Oh, there's a stage meeting? I'll go, too." (Translation: *I'm gonna jump at this chance, thanks.*) Hayama gallantly took advantage of the opportunity to refuse Sagami's offer.

And so Sagami reluctantly withdrew her suggestion. "Hmm... I gotcha... You've all got plans, huh? Another time, then." (Translation: *If Hayama isn't coming, then I really don't care.*)

Though I was aware that reading between the lines was really no fun, I couldn't help how it came across to me. To have a nature *this* rotten was a unique ability.

Sagami's subtitles just didn't want to disappear, right up until we all parted ways at the school entrance. Sagami wanted to walk some of the way home with Hayama, and even once we were outside, she dragged the conversation out.

Following after her and the others, I shoved on my shoes, too, and went outside.

The sunset was already long past, and the darkness of night had spread across the sky.

"Bye." Yukinoshita bid her brief farewell and swiftly marched away. Her bag must have been heavy with all the papers she would have to take care of at home, as she was repeatedly adjusting it on her shoulder.

"Well, see you tomorrow, Hikki." Yuigahama gave my shoulder a light pat and then dashed off. I guess she was going to her meeting. She had a lot on her plate, too.

I began pedaling my bicycle out of the sparsely populated parking lot.

The street lights were horribly overbright. I'd abused my eyes a lot that day. Subtitles really strain your eyes.

As my head filled with trivial thoughts, one more crossed my mind.

Oh yeah. For some people, those weird subtitles don't show up at all, huh?

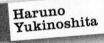

Haruno Yukinoshita

Meguri Shiromeguri

Birthday

July 7

Birthday

January 21

Special skills:

Cooking, laundry, cleaning, household chores in general, aikido

Special skills:

Playing musical instruments, napping

Hobbies:

Reading, horseback riding

Hobbies:

Napping

How I spend my weekends:

Taking trips to nowhere

How I spend my weekends:

Studying for entrance exams, napping

Unusually, **Yui Yuigahama** is indignant.

What never gets easier, no matter how much work is put into it?

My life.

It's so bad, even the famously overworked poet Takuboku Ishikawa would have to admit it. I bet it's even worse for a pleb like me. My hands paused in their task, without my telling them to. I gave them a nasty glare. That made them stop again as the whole situation became more and more agonizing. What is with this downward spiral?

To solve the mystery of why the hell I was so busy, I looked around. First of all, we were shorthanded.

The executives were being hounded left and right in a chaotic mess, and their helper Haruno had not come that day. Hayama was working with us, having single-handedly undertaken the volunteer-related tasks, but even he could get tired, it seemed. His usual smile was a little strained.

Not so long ago, we'd kept on top of the work, even with a smaller group. The difference this time was that Yukinoshita wasn't there: Yukinoshita, who would normally come to the conference room earliest and stay the latest. That day, she was nowhere to be seen.

"What's happened to Yukinoshita today?" Meguri asked.

I had no answer. "Dunno…" And I wasn't the only one without answers—I doubt anyone on the committee had any, either.

The door to the conference room creaked open. Forgetting to knock was a bad habit of Miss Hiratsuka's. "Hikigaya."

"Yes?" I replied.

She walked up to me, her expression very gentle. "About Yukinoshita—she isn't feeling well today, so she's taking the day off. She's contacted the school, but I figured the cultural committee hadn't been notified." Evidently, we hadn't. No one here would have been able to receive a message from her in the first place.

But still, she was sick? I knew she didn't have much in the way of endurance, but I thought she could take care of her health better than that. Well, she had seemed busy lately, and she'd also made that little slipup the other day. She must have been exhausted.

Is she okay? She lives alone, too, I thought.

Hayama lifted his head, as if the same thought had just hit him as well. "Yukinoshita lives by herself, so someone should go check on her."

"Oh, really? Well, will one of you go check and see how she's doing, then? I can handle things here," Meguri said to the two of us.

"Will you all be okay without the help?" Hayama asked her.

Meguri made a rather complicated expression, but then it changed to her usual bubbly, pleasant smile. "Hmm... Yeah. I think anything I can understand, we should be able to manage." Her tone indicated she was a little unsure, but her smile was trustworthy.

Then it would probably be best to leave the work to them while we took care of visiting Yukinoshita. It would be much better for the student council president to stay than someone from Records and Miscellaneous or the volunteer manager. Meguri was the only one with an eye on the whole picture. "Thanks," she said to us, starting to go back to work.

"President!" The door to the conference room banged open, and someone from the student council marched in.

"What's wrong?!" asked Meguri.

"Actually, there's been an inquiry about the slogan..."

"Ack! Now?!" Sounded like a major problem had surfaced

immediately. Meguri rushed out of the conference room to go handle it. Unable to call after her to ask what had gotten her into such a flurry, we were left behind.

"All right…so what do we do?" Hayama asked me. "I don't mind going myself." The confrontational phrasing bothered me.

I… No, even if I did go, it wasn't like there was anything I could have said to her. If Hayama went to see her, then I would stick around. Conversely, if he didn't go, then I probably would instead. "Well… shouldn't you be the one to go? It'd be best for her to get the considerate and useful one," I said.

Hayama blinked. "…Didn't expect to hear that from you."

"You're doing all this work for us. That's worth a compliment."

Hayama smiled wryly and turned back to me. "I see. But if that's your rationale, then shouldn't the considerate and useful one stay here?"

That was true. Since we didn't have enough people, the standard tactic would be to leave behind someone who could handle the situation well. When your party was down a few players, it was best to rely on a high-level hero. "Oh… Well, if you put it that way, I guess so," I replied, scratching my head roughly.

Hayama looked me straight in the eye. "Just so you know, I don't think you're incompetent. You've been doing the jobs of the entire miscellaneous section. Nobody can call you useless."

…*Now you're the one surprising me. I never thought you'd say something like that.*

"So what are you going to do?" Hayama asked again.

Hachiman Hikigaya could not beat Hayato Hayama. Anyone would say so. And I think they'd be right, too. I doubt I could beat him in any arena.

But it's funny. The more talented and kind someone is, the more constrained they are in life. Someone's always relying on them, they have to live up to those expectations, and before long, the whole dynamic gets normalized. Not only that, guys like him will even reach out a hand to guys out on the fringes, like yours truly.

"…I'll go," I said. "Anyone would say you're the superior one here. Everyone needs you."

"I don't mind hearing that…if you actually mean it." Hayama's smile held a trace of melancholy. He was a good guy, but his kindness meant he couldn't prioritize anyone or anything over anything else. Everything was important to him. That suddenly seemed to me like a terribly cruel thing.

"All right…so then, I'm stepping out for a bit," I said to Miss Hiratsuka.

She smiled. "Okay. Go ahead. I can't give you another student's address, though…"

"Oh, that's fine." I didn't know Yukinoshita's address, but I did know someone who knew. Someone who would probably rush out in a second if I told her about this.

I quickly gathered my things, and when I stood up, my eyes met with Hayama's. They glinted sharply as they narrowed suddenly. "I'll let you handle that, then," he said. "And I'll tell Haruno, just in case, too."

"Oh…that'll be a help. Thanks." I gave him a brief show of gratitude, adjusted my bag on my shoulder, and left the conference room.

As I walked to the front door, I pulled out my phone and made a call. One ring, two rings, three rings… After a full seven rings, right when I was about to hang up, she answered. "Wh-what is it? This is so random…"

"Did you know that Yukinoshita didn't come to school today?" I asked.

"…Huh? I…didn't know."

"I heard she's sick."

I could hear Yuigahama gulping on the other end. It's not like a little illness is anything serious. But considering how busy Yukinoshita had been lately, plus the fact that she lived on her own, Yuigahama had to be uneasy.

Yuigahama took a determined little breath. "I'm gonna go check up on her real quick now."

I'd figured she'd say that. "I'm going, too. Wanna meet in front of the school gates?"

"Yeah."

We ended the brief call, and I stuffed my cell phone into my pocket.

It was still bright outside, but the sun was beginning to sink. We'd probably reach Yukinoshita's place at just about sunset.

X   X   X

Neither I nor Yuigahama talked much on the way.

The moment she'd first seen me, she'd launched into question after question about Yukinoshita, but I hadn't had many answers for her.

Yukinoshita lived in an apartment tower that was known in the area for being very fancy, and with that classy status came high security. You couldn't get in so easily.

We rang Yukinoshita's room from the entrance. Yuigahama pushed the buzzer. She had already called and texted Yukinoshita beforehand, but she had gotten no response. I'd wondered if we wouldn't even manage to get in touch with her in person. But Yuigahama rang the bell two, three times anyway.

Not coming out, huh…? "Pretending she's not home?" I suggested.

"That would be fine, then, but if she's actually so sick that she can't answer the bell…" The idea seemed a little extreme to me, but I couldn't bring myself to laugh her off.

Yuigahama paused, then rang the bell one more time.

Then static crackled through the speaker. "…Hello?" a voice responded, vanishingly quiet.

Yuigahama practically jumped on the sound as she replied, "Yukinon?! This is Yui. Are you okay?"

"…Yes, I'm all right, so."

So. So what? Did she mean to say, *So leave?* "Just open the door," I said.

"…Why are you here?" She must have assumed Yuigahama had come alone. She seemed a bit startled to hear my voice out of the blue.

"I came to talk."

"…Could you wait for just ten minutes?"

"Fine," I replied.

As requested, we waited for ten minutes, on the sofa by the entrance. I guess nice apartment buildings have sofas at the entrance…

Yuigahama was glaring at her cell phone the entire time. Her fingers didn't even so much as twitch. She must have been just staring at the clock, frozen.

I was zoning out when Yuigahama stood up from beside me and buzzed Yukinoshita again.

"Yes…"

"It's been ten minutes."

"…Come in," Yukinoshita told us, and the automatic door opened.

Yuigahama marched in with sure footsteps. I followed after her, and when we reached the elevator, Yuigahama pushed the fifteenth-floor button. The elevator rose faster than I'd imagined it would. The floor numbers on the display flashed by, and before long, it said 15.

Once we were off the elevator, Yuigahama and I walked down to one of the many doors along the hall, an apartment with no nameplate. Yuigahama clenched her fists for a moment to steady herself, then reached out a finger, ready to push the doorbell.

I don't know if it was just high quality or what, but it didn't make a mechanical bell sound. It sounded kind of like a fine musical instrument. Yuigahama rang the bell once and then waited for a while. The walls here seemed to be nice and soundproof, as we couldn't hear anything from within. But after waiting for a few seconds, there was a sudden hard rattling sound of the locks being undone, and it was a few more seconds before all the multiple locks were open.

We waited in front of the door until it opened smoothly and soundlessly. Yukinoshita poked only her face out of the crack. "Come in."

Entering her apartment, there was a faint waft of soap smell.

Yukinoshita seemed different from usual. She wore a finely textured knit sweater a little big for her thin stature. Her hands were entirely lost in the sleeves, and her collarbone was peeking out of the neck. Her black hair was tied into a ponytail that hung over her chest to hide the deep neckline. Her long skirt went down to her feet.

From the entrance, I could see a number of doors—three of them clearly led to bedrooms. Aside from those, there were doors on the side of the hallway that most likely led to the bath and toilet. Down at the end, the living-dining room was indirectly illuminated. I'd only heard of apartments this big in rumors.

Yukinoshita was living alone in this enormous apartment.

She guided us down the hallway and through to the living room, where I could see a balcony. Beyond the window was a completely dark sky and the nightscape of the new downtown core. The afterglow of the western sky seemed terribly forlorn.

On top of a small glass table was a closed laptop, and beside it were documents in file folders. Yukinoshita must have been working that night, too.

She must not usually have visitors, judging from the Spartan living room. It was minimally furnished like a business hotel, with functional and simple furniture. The only source of warmth to it was the upholstered, cream-colored sofa.

In front of the sofa was a tiny chest. It was a little surprising to see a big TV in the room, too, but the shelf underneath it was full of Destiny movies like *Ginnie the Grue*. She didn't buy that sweet TV just for those, did she…?

"Take a seat over there." Yukinoshita offered us the two-seater couch, and Yuigahama and I obediently sat down.

I wondered what Yukinoshita would do, but she just leaned against the wall.

"Why don't you sit down?" Yuigahama said, but Yukinoshita quietly shook her head.

"So what was it you wanted to talk about?" Yukinoshita was turned our way, but her gaze was fixed on a point below our faces. The normally overwhelming light in her eyes was muted, calm like the surface of a lake.

When I failed to reply to the question, Yuigahama searched for a response instead. "Uh, um… We heard you were missing school today, so we were wondering if you were okay."

"I'm fine. This is too much fuss over one day off. And I did call in."

"You live on your own," I replied. "People are going to worry about you."

"Besides, aren't you really tired? You're still pale," added Yuigahama.

Yukinoshita quietly lowered her head, as if to hide her complexion. "I was a little tired, but that was all. It's not a problem."

"...Isn't *that* the problem here?" said Yuigahama.

Yukinoshita fell silent. Oh, that had hit her where it hurt. If everything was hunky-dory, she wouldn't have been away from school in the first place.

Yukinoshita's gloom made her seem especially frail.

"You don't have to manage this stuff all alone, Yukinon. There were other people there."

"I understand that. That's why I made sure to divide the work up properly to reduce the burden—"

"But it's not reduced!" Yuigahama cut her off. Yuigahama was quiet and calm, but her voice still betrayed her fervent anxiety. The words hung in the air even after the sound had faded. "I'm kinda mad about this, you know."

Yukinoshita's shoulders twitched in response. I understood Yuigahama's anger, too. Yukinoshita's refusal to accept help and determination to handle everything herself had resulted in her exhaustion.

I breathed a small sigh, and Yuigahama's gaze jumped over to me. "I'm mad at you, too, Hikki. I said to help her out if she was in trouble..."

So that was why she was silent the whole way there. Well, I had no excuse for that. I'd been quite admittedly useless. My shoulders sank apologetically.

"...I never expected anything from him beyond his role with Records and Miscellaneous," said Yukinoshita. "He's fulfilled that role just fine, and that's enough."

"But—"

"It's all right. We still have time, and I've been getting work done at home as well, so we won't get significantly behind. You don't need to worry about anything, Yuigahama."

"That's not right!"

"Oh…isn't it?" Yukinoshita's eyes were still riveted to the flooring. "…What do you think?" It took me a little while to realize her question was for me. The wall Yukinoshita leaned against led to the kitchen, and with the lights off, I couldn't read her expression.

I should tell her that the way she's going about this is wrong.

I couldn't make a moral argument like Hayama. I couldn't say the things he does.

And this wasn't out of kindness, like Yuigahama. I don't have any of that stuff.

But I know when she's screwing up.

"Generally speaking, talking about leaning on someone, how everyone'll help and support each other—that's the right thing to do. That's the standard answer."

"Oh…" Her reply was dry and disinterested. But her arms fell limply from their folded position.

"But that's just an ideal. That's not what makes the world go round. Someone always draws the short straw, and some people get stuck with the job. Someone's always going to pick up the slack. That's reality. So I'm not into saying you should rely on others and cooperate with everyone or anything."

I could hear Yukinoshita gently exhaling. I couldn't tell if it was like a sigh or not.

"But you're going about this the wrong way," I said.

"…Then…do you know the right way?" Her voice was shaking.

"No. But the way you've been doing it is wrong."

"…"

Thus far, Yukinoshita had always had a consistent style. When someone asked her for help, she wouldn't assist them thoughtlessly. Though she would lend a hand, in the end, she would always leave things up to the person in question.

But this time, it was different. Yukinoshita was handling everything from A to Z, and most likely, as she'd just said, she would somehow muddle through. This was bound to end up a fairly legitimate cultural festival—even if it wouldn't necessarily leave everyone happy.

But that wasn't the ideal Yukinoshita had always touted.

Yukinoshita didn't reply.

Silence fell.

"…"

"…"

The room was cold. The thermometer was probably reading a temperature much higher than what we were feeling.

Choo! Yuigahama sneezed. The way she sniffled almost sounded like she was crying.

Yukinoshita must have noticed the rising chill in the room, as she softly stood up from the wall. "I'm sorry. I didn't even get you tea…"

"Th-that's fine!" Yuigahama stuttered. "You don't need to do that… I—I can handle it."

"Don't worry yourself over my health. I feel much better after resting a day."

"About your health, huh?" I muttered. Her throwaway remark stuck with me.

Yuigahama opened her mouth with an "Um…" as if she was struggling to say something. But even after a pause for breath, she said nothing. Eventually, she slowly began talking. "Listen… I've done…a little thinking. Yukinon, you should rely on me and Hikki. Not 'someone' or 'everyone'… Just let us help, okay? I, um… It's not like I can really do anything. But…Hikki—"

"…Are you fine with black tea?" Yukinoshita turned away and disappeared into the kitchen without listening to the rest of what Yuigahama had to say. Yuigahama's voice no longer reached into the gloom.

They were constantly talking past each other. This lofty high-rise was the Tower of Babel, and neither of them could reach the other with words.

Yukinoshita brought in a set of cups and a pot of black tea. No conversation accompanied our teatime.

Holding her cup in both hands, Yuigahama blew on her drink to cool it. Still standing, Yukinoshita cradled hers as she gazed outside. Without a word, I put mine to my lips, and it was soon gone.

There was nothing more to talk about.

I put my cup down and stood up. "I'll get going, then."

"Huh? Th-then I'll go, too…" Yuigahama stood up after me and headed for the door. Yukinoshita didn't stop her.

But still, Yukinoshita did see us off, wobbling a little as she came to the front door. She gently touched Yuigahama's neck as she was putting on her shoes. "Yuigahama."

"Y-yes?!" The sudden touch on her neck made Yuigahama yelp in surprise. She was about to turn around when Yukinoshita gently held her in check. "Um…it's a little difficult to…right away. But I'm sure eventually, I'll come to rely on you. So…thank you…"

"Yukinon…"

The smile Yukinoshita gave her was fragile; still, there was a faint blush in her cheeks. "But I want to think a little longer…"

"Yeah…" Without looking back, Yuigahama gently rested her own hand on top of the hand on her neck.

"I'll leave this to you, Yuigahama," I said.

"Huh? Wait—"

I cut her off, quietly closing the door. *Sorry, but the rest is up to you.*

Yuigahama did what had to be done in the way that only she could. But it wouldn't resolve this.

I'd handle that problem.

It's not true that time solves everything. It just shoves it all away into distant oblivion, erasing any significance or meaning it might have had, bleaching away the problem itself.

It's also a lie that the world changes when you do. It's bunk. The world is always eroding you, pigeonholing you and sanding down all the parts that stick out. It's just that eventually, you stop thinking about it. The world and your environment force you into believing it. You're brainwashed. Neither emotional arguments, nor the belief that "you can just do it if you try!" nor idealism will change the world, your environment, or the group.

I'll show you what changing the world really is.

X   X   X

There was a quibble over the cultural festival slogan. I did seem to recall hearing something about this.

Fun! So fun! Listening to the sound of the sea breeze at the Soubu High School cultural festival~!

…That was no good. I mean, it was basically the Juumangoku Manjuu slogan, and that's Saitama. It was a little hard to accept for a Chiba event.

Well, leaving aside any prefectural disparities, we ended up discussing whether we should appropriate someone else's slogan wholesale, and ultimately, we came to the decision that it wasn't a good idea. We then hastily convened a meeting to resolve this issue.

Haruno and Hayama, who had lately been coming in to observe often, were also in attendance. This in and of itself was the most significant piece of evidence that the cultural committee was falling apart.

The executives (mainly the student council and Yukinoshita) were entirely exhausted. Since they'd barely been managing the declining attendance so far, this new crisis was like hitting them while they were down. It could even be the finishing blow.

At this rate, it was doubtful the meeting would ever start. Murmurs and chatter were rippling across the whole conference room, and Sagami, the one who should have been in charge, was hanging out in front of the whiteboard and chatting with the friend she'd designated as clerk.

Unable to just stand by and watch, Meguri got her attention. "Sagami, Yukinoshita. Everyone is here," she said.

Sagami cut off her chat and looked toward Yukinoshita. All eyes gathered on the vice-chair. But her eyes were glazed over, staring at the record of proceedings.

"Yukinoshita?" Sagami said to her, and Yukinoshita's head jerked up.

"Huh?" She paused for the briefest moment, but then immediately grasped the situation. "Now then, let's begin the meeting. Just as President Shiromeguri has informed you, on the agenda for today is the cultural festival slogan." Once she'd pulled herself together, Yukinoshita began to direct the meeting in an orderly fashion.

First, she solicited ideas, but the group's passivity made that difficult. Nobody was motivated. To them, even a serious meeting was just another topic for casual conversation later.

Hayama, sitting beside me, couldn't take it anymore and raised his hand. "I'm sure it's difficult for us to present a slogan to the group so suddenly. Why don't we have people write their ideas down? Then we can have everyone explain their suggestions afterward."

"All right... Then we'll take a little time for that," said Yukinoshita.

Blank sheets were handed out. Though everyone had gotten one, only a handful of people were actually writing on them. Most of the room was just giggling and gleefully showing each other jokes. What's more, when the time came to submit, they didn't hand those ideas in.

Even in a group of slackers, there was always a certain number of diligent types—those who would actually do the work but didn't want to make a show of it. If you just removed the barrier created by presenting to an audience, some people would actually participate. The support of such people had gotten us this far, and it seemed those people would be carrying us again.

Once the papers had been collected, the slogans on them were copied onto the whiteboard.

Friendship / Effort / Victory

Yeah, they were all basically along those lines. The really random one was *Hakkou Ichiu. Eugh, I think I have an idea of who would write this...*

One other slogan, written in English, caught everyone's attention: *ONE FOR ALL.*

When that one appeared on the board, Hayama made a quiet

ohhh. "I kinda like that sort of thing." Apparently, that one was to his taste.

Yeah, I get the feeling you'd be into that. I mean, it was English. I replied with a snort that said, *Oh, really?*

At that, Hayama shrugged. "One person working for everyone's sake. I like that idea a lot."

"Oh, is that all? That's simple stuff."

"Huh?"

Ha! It seems that even the great Hayama hasn't quite grasped the concept here. So be it, good sir; then I shall humbly explain this for thee.

"Injure one person and shun them. One for all. Happens all the time."

—Like what you guys are doing, right this minute.

"Hikigaya…hey…" Hayama reacted like he'd been struck, then gradually bristled. He turned his whole body toward me, squaring off. Anyone who saw us must have figured we were glaring at each other.

Instantly, the chatter around us stopped.

We'd been talking pretty quietly, so maybe that was why the others were only whispering about us. The silent standoff between me and Hayama ended after only a few seconds—because I looked away first. Oh, it's not like I was scared. It was because everyone's attention had shifted up to the front of the room.

Sagami consulted with her clerk friend and then stood up. "Right then, last one. We're suggesting *Bonds: helping one another in our cultural festival.*" Sagami announced the slogan they'd come up with and began writing it on the board.

"Eugh…" The noise slipped out of me as soon as the suggestion left her mouth. What's it like inside her head? Is it a farm with fields of flowers? Is she making caramel sweets in there?

My reaction set off a wave of murmurs. The scornful timbre of the commotion rubbed Sagami the wrong way. And since I had both caused this commotion and occupied a weak social position, it was no surprise that the brunt of her ire would fall on me.

"...What? Something weird about that?" Sagami was managing to keep up appearances with a smile, but her cheeks were twitching. She still looked pretty upset.

"Oh, it's nothing, really...," I began, and then I left it there, indicating I actually did have a complaint. I knew beyond a shadow of a doubt that this response would piss her off the most. Take it from me, someone who has done it unconsciously and lost friends tons of times.

What I'd done was communicate something you can't say with words. I know how to get my intentions across when words aren't enough—because I barely ever actually use them. Like when I pretend to sleep during breaks, or adopt a reluctant expression when I'm asked to do something, or sigh when I'm working. I've always expressed myself extralinguistically.

I know how to communicate this stuff. Well...I'm only good at using the skill for nefarious purposes, though.

"Don't you have something to say?" Sagami demanded.

"Oh, no. Not really."

She gave me a mildly displeased glare and said, "Hmph. All right. If you don't like it, you make a suggestion."

So then I was like: "How about *People: Take a good look, and you'll find* some *of them are enjoying this cultural festival* or something?"

Boom!

...I thought maybe the world had stopped.

Nobody said anything. Sagami, Meguri, and Hayama were all overcome with surprise. I guess this was what it meant to be truly dumbfounded.

The committee went dead silent. Even Yukinoshita's mouth was hanging open.

Then laughter broke the silence. "Ah-ha-ha-ha-ha-ha-ha! We've got an idiot here! Right over there! That's just great! Hee, ee-hee! Ahhh, I can't, my stomach hurts!" Haruno roared with laughter, while Miss Hiratsuka shot me a sour look. I was scared. Double scared.

Miss Hiratsuka jabbed Haruno with her elbow. "…Haruno, you're laughing too hard."

"Ah-ha-ha-ha-ha, ha… Hmm, ahem." Haruno must have noticed the icy atmosphere as she cleared her throat quietly and smothered her laughter. "Oh, I do like that one. Anything funny sounds good to me."

"Hikigaya…explain yourself." Half-exasperated, Miss Hiratsuka demanded an explanation from me.

"Well, they say the character for 'person' is two people leaning on each other," I said, "but one side is leaning harder than the other, right? I think the idea behind 'people' is accepting that someone is going to be the sacrifice. So I think the idea might be appropriate for *this* cultural festival and *this* committee."

"What do you mean by *sacrifice*, exactly?" The exasperation had disappeared from Miss Hiratsuka's expression.

"Like me? I'm totally getting the short end of the stick here. I've got tons of work, or rather, other people are pushing their work onto me. Wait, is this the 'cooperation' the committee chair was referring to? I haven't benefited from any of that, so I wouldn't really know."

All eyes gathered on Sagami.

She was trembling like a leaf. Everyone looked at the person next to them.

A buzz of whispers ran around the room, from one neighbor to the next. They washed up close to me and then back to the center of the room, like the tide rolling in and receding. And there, they ended.

Sitting in the center of the room were the executives of the Cultural Festival Committee and its vice-chair: Yukino Yukinoshita. Not a single person said a word. The expectant gazes gathered on Yukinoshita, the ice queen who had thus far mercilessly and unapologetically persisted in her autocratic rule. How would she punish this prank?

The meeting agenda in Yukinoshita's hands rustled as she lifted it up to hide her face. Her shoulders were trembling. Her face descended to the table, and her hunched back shook.

All I could do was watch the strange reaction. The painful silence went on for some time.

After a while, Yukinoshita gave a short puff of a sigh and lifted her head. "Hikigaya." She looked me straight in the eye. I got the feeling it had been a long time since I'd heard my name in her voice or seen her clear, blue-tinged eyes.

Her cheeks were faintly flushed.

Her mouth was split in a broad smile.

Her pink, full lips moved gently.

And then, quite cheerfully, with a smile like a warm flower in full bloom, she told me, "Your suggestion is declined." Her serious expression returned, and then she gently straightened up and cleared her throat. "Sagami, let's end it here for today. I doubt we'll get any decent suggestions anyway."

"Huh? But…"

"It would be foolish to waste the whole day over this. Everyone, consider it on your own time, and we'll make the decision tomorrow. And regarding our upcoming tasks, if all of us participate every day, then we'll be able to regain lost ground," Yukinoshita said. She surveyed the conference room quietly, but nobody would dare argue with her now. "No objections?" She was so intense, complaining was out of the question. In just one moment, they'd all been compelled into attending starting the next day.

Even Sagami was no exception. "All…right, then. Then we'll be counting on you again tomorrow. Thank you for your hard work." After that dismissal, everyone left their seats on their own time in groups of threes and fours.

Hayama stood without looking at me and marched straight out of the conference room. As everyone shuffled after him, their piercing looks stung. Some people were even blatantly whispering as they went. "What's with him?"

Yeah, what's with that guy? Oh. They mean me.

Once most of the cultural committee had left, the only ones

remaining were the executives, who always stayed behind. The atmosphere was relaxed, and just one person in the room had a long face. It was Meguri.

She quietly stood from her seat. When she came up to me, she didn't have her usual pleasant, reassuring smile on her face.

"It's too bad… I thought you were more serious than that…"

"…"

She sounded sad, but I had nothing to say in reply.

I mean, I didn't want to work. If people got these expectations that I would give it my all and do everything right, then they were bound to catch me tripping soon enough, and in the end, I'd just let them down. I washed away my regret with a sigh.

With a *hup* of effort, I stood up.

Right when I was about to leave the conference room, I found Yukinoshita in front of the door. "You're all right with this?" she asked.

"With what?" I asked back at her, but she didn't reply.

"I think it would be best if you corrected the misunderstanding."

"That's not gonna happen. Everyone's already got their answers, so the issue's over and done. There's nothing more to resolve." Whether it was right or wrong, it was the final answer. You can't take back mistakes. Once a brand has been seared into you, it can't be erased.

Yukinoshita narrowed her eyes in a brief glare. "…You always make excuses when it doesn't matter, but when it's important, you don't. I think that's a little unfair. Then no one else can make excuses, either."

"There's no point. The more important something is, the more selfish people are with their decisions."

"…Yes, maybe that's true. Excuses are meaningless," Yukinoshita mused.

Once you've come up with an answer, there's no reversing it. What's done is done. A broken egg can't be unbroken. Even with all the king's horses and all the king's men, you can't put it back together again. No matter what you say, you can't scrub out a bad impression.

Even though the reverse is so simple. A single word from someone can ruin your perception of them, and a single act from you can create a bad impression.

That's why excuses are meaningless. Even the excuse will damage your image.

Yukinoshita was standing there, her arms wrapped around herself. But she didn't lean on the wall. Just like always, she straightened her posture and slowly raised her head.

"So then…there's nothing for it but to ask the question again."

An almost combative force of will was shining powerfully in her eyes, beautiful like blazing stars.

I got the feeling they were telling me something: *I won't make excuses. So watch me.* Then that determination melted into something just a bit warmer. "Anyway, what was that just now?" she asked.

"What?"

"That hopeless slogan. It was entirely tasteless."

"It was better than yours. Come on, are you a thesaurus?" I said.

Yukinoshita breathed a long, deliberate-sounding sigh. "You never change… It's exasperating."

"People don't really change."

"And you were especially weird to begin with."

"Hey, that was unnecessary."

Yukinoshita chuckled. "When I look at you, forcing you to change starts to seem foolish." Before she even finished her remark, she was spinning away from me. She trotted over to grab her bag from the table and gently pointed outside. Apparently, that was the signal to leave.

The two of us left the conference room, and she locked up. "All right, I'm going to go return this key."

"Yeah, see you."

"Yes, good-bye."

Though we'd said our farewells, Yukinoshita put her hand to her chin in thought and hesitated just slightly. Then she added, "...See you tomorrow." Her hand moved down in front of her chest, hovering uncertainly, and gave a little half-open wave.

"...See you tomorrow."

We both turned away from each other and began home. After a few steps, I got the urge to look back at her, but I didn't get the sense that she would stop. So I didn't have to, either.

Would I be able to keep myself from looking back?

Would I be able to ask that question one more time?

There are no take-backs in life. When you get the wrong answer, you're bound to be stuck with it. If you're going to turn it around, you have to come up with a new answer.

So I'd ask the question one more time.

I would learn the right answers.

× × ×

At the committee meeting the next day, we decided on a slogan. Revitalized, the committee went from heated discussion to heated discussion, and after a long period of debate, we somehow managed to come together on a single idea. The slogan for that year's cultural festival would be this:

Chiba's famous for dancing and festivals! So if you're an idiot like me, then you've got to dance! Sing a song!

Was that really the best idea?

I did feel a little uneasy about it, but this was the conclusion we'd agreed on. Well, I didn't hate it, though. "Chiba Ondo" is a famous song after all.

The meeting had yet to cool down, and the committee was still in discussion. Seizing the chance to channel that motivation into work, Yukinoshita whispered quietly into Sagami's ear. "Sagami, we should focus on slogan replacement next."

"Oh yeah... Then please replace all instances of the old slogan with the new one," Sagami instructed. The committee resumed action, more or less under her direction.

Deciding on a slogan must have served to unify the group, as everyone was brimming with enthusiasm.

"You! Remake the posters!" howled Publicity and Advertisement.

"Hold on a minute! We haven't come up with a budget estimate yet!" the accounting section snarled back at them.

"You moron! Fiddle with your abaci later! My time is now!"

"More importantly, if you're replacing the posters, be sure to bring back the thumbtacks! We're counting those, too!" Man, even Equipment Management started butting in. Every section was actively exchanging opinions. It didn't even seem like the same committee anymore.

As for me, people were saying all sorts of nasty stuff behind my back. I was being ignored, avoided, and ostracized. But it wasn't bullying. There's no bullying at our school.

Even when they gave me work to do, they didn't talk to me. They just stacked it in front of me silently. Even in this situation, they were still trying to make me work. Managers sure are impressive.

I was buckling down to write up a record of the day's meeting in Word when a good-humored voice descended upon me from on high. "Yo, yo! Working hard, I hope?" Haruno had come down to the conference room during a break in her practice. She probably had nothing else to do now that the committee members were actually doing their jobs, as she took the time to come all the way over and pat me on the head.

"...Just look at me," I replied.

She popped in from behind to sneak a peek at my PC. *Um, that's a little close. What is that, perfume? It smells kinda nice, though, so please stop...*

"Oh...looks like you're not really working hard."

Why? I've got my nose to the grindstone here. I shot her a rotten glare.

Haruno feigned shock. "Oh my, so grumpy! But I mean, your accomplishments aren't in the meeting records, are they?"

"..." I fell silent, and Haruno gave me a broad smirk.

"Pop quiz, Hikigaya. Who is it that most unifies a group?"

"A ruthless mentor?"

"Oh, you! But I know you really do know the right answer. Although I kinda like yours, too." She still smiled, but her expression cooled. "The correct answer…is the presence of *a clear enemy*." I understood the implication of that chilly smile.

Long ago, someone once said, "The greatest leader to bring together the masses is the enemy." Well, everyone's not going to change all at once just because they have someone to hate. But once you get four or five together, they multiply like bunnies. The greater numbers you have, the faster the idea gains traction.

They say humans are empathetic by nature. It's like how when you see someone yawning, you catch the yawn, too. Enthusiasm, fanaticism, and hatred are especially contagious. It's the foundation of solicitations for pyramid schemes or religion. Everyone wants to be a part of something. You just have to propagate the shared perception that it's cool to work your ass off, just like any dogma or sermon.

Social pressure is a numbers game.

Popularity is a numbers game.

War is a numbers game.

If you can create a mood that herds those numbers onto the bandwagon, you've basically won. These days, it's fads that make the world go round. Victory or defeat is not determined by the charismatic dictator but by the absolute majority—or the promise that will win that majority.

So the rest is easy.

If you've got your absolute loser *hikitanikun@not-trying*, then public opinion will naturally trend in the opposite direction. The people working hard are the cool ones. Hikitani's the one slacking off. As long as you've got those labels, everyone will buckle down, even if that's not what they want.

Haruno chuckled and looked down at me. "Well, their enemy is a *bit* of a small fry, though."

Leave me alone.

"But they're showing some excitement for the festival now."

"That's just making more work for me, though." The unspoken

meaning was *So I'd rather you not interfere*, but she playfully ignored my drift.

"That's fine. A villain like you actually working will make them want to challenge you. Besides, you'll never grow without a proper enemy. Conflict just stimulates growth!" Haruno closed her eyes and swung her finger around as she began her commentary. Eugh. It was mildly obnoxious.

But halfway through her playful gesture, her eyes opened and her gaze slid toward Yukinoshita.

A groundless, ridiculous idea occurred to me at that. "Um, so does that mean…?"

Her soft fingertip kept the words from passing my lips. "I hate perceptive kids, you know?"

If the fastest way for a person to grow was for them to have an enemy… *Then maybe Haruno is acting like this so she can stay her enemy*, I thought, although I had no proof at all of that.

Her finger still gently pressed to my lips, Haruno smiled. "Just kidding." Her smile was perfect and flawless. For a moment there, I almost fell for it.

I was frozen speechless when behind me someone snapped, "Miscellaneous, stay on task." *Thump, thump, thump*, and now there were stacks of documents in front of me. When I raised my head, I saw Yukinoshita and an icy glare. "Dispose of these. They're all related to the slogan revision. And the meeting records…you're working on now, I see…" Yukinoshita brought a hand to her mouth and raised her head. "Then…send an e-mail notifying all parties about the slogan change."

"Hey, hold on, you clearly just came up with that." She totally just said, "Then…" What else could that mean? Was she about to say "thenceforth" instead?

"I do sometimes get spur-of-the-moment ideas. The ability to make organic connections is the foundation of intelligence after all. Oh, and while you're at it, integrate the plan application documents and upload them to the server."

Hey, that didn't really make sense. What a crappy excuse. And wait, she just tossed more on my pile, didn't she? Doesn't "while you're at it" indicate the new task is related to what you're already doing? Am I crazy?

I shot her a dubious look, but her glare won. "Anyway, please do that by the end of the day."

"There's no way…"

Dealing with Yukinoshita now made me suspect that my previous work environment point had been on the mild side. In fact, if this were a part-time job, this would be about the time I'd flake out. I'd turn off my cell phone and tell my mom we could afford to leave the landline unplugged for a while.

But it was school, so I couldn't quit…

As I was busy despairing, Haruno raised a hand and waved broadly for her sister's attention. "Should I work on that, too?"

"You can leave and get out of our way."

The point-blank barb made Haruno's eyes water. "Ouch! That's so mean, Yukino-chan! …Well, I have the time, so I'll do it anyway. Give me half, Hikigaya." Haruno reached out for a stack of paper.

Yukinoshita put her hand to her temple and breathed a deep sigh. "…Agh. I'm going to review the budget, so if you absolutely must do something, then make that your task."

"Hmm? Heh-heh… Okay! ♪" Just for an instant, Haruno smiled an ominous smile, but she immediately turned on the energy again, prodding Yukinoshita's back. They must have been going to start up the budget meeting.

Haruno was flitting from task to task, too. Doubtless, she was busy with all sorts of things, but she would show up fairly frequently, and I suspected it was for more than practice with her group. I highly doubted she had that much free time. Though I didn't even have to wonder about her ulterior motive. Rather, it was more constructive to think about tackling the work in front of me.

Heh-heh. They're called corporate slaves because they don't disobey…

X   X   X

With every day closer to the cultural festival, Soubu High school was heating up despite the falling temperature. Class 2-F was abuzz straight from morning. The festival was tomorrow, and we'd spent the whole day preparing.

We'd put the desks together in rows to make a stage. Under the direction of the class rep, Oda or Tahara or somebody put together the plywood-and-cardboard set. Then the trio of Tobe, Yamato, and Ooka the Virgin heaved and hoed and hauled in an airplane set piece constructed with a hell of a lot of heart and soul.

Headphones on, Kawasaki poked the costumes here and there to adjust them, while Miura and Yuigahama decorated with red artificial flowers, chatting all the while. As they started running low, the girls began making more. You know what I'm talking about—the ones you make by folding up five sheets of tissue paper in layers, then tying them off with a rubber band and peeling out the petals one by one. Those things. They always have them at cultural festivals.

Totsuka and Hayama were practicing their lines together.

As for me, I had nothing in particular to do, so I was sitting at the corner of the stage in an empty daze.

"Tonight…you can't come," said the delicate Prince.

The Narrator encouraged him, revealing his true emotions. "We'll always be together."

Even though I knew it was just a play, my teeth were grating and grinding… *Damn it, if I'd known I'd feel like this, I would've starred in that play.* Ngh, I couldn't stand to look straight at them…

I tore my eyes away and found Ebina, the super-producer. The smile on her face was frighteningly greasy. "Get on out there, you!"

Are you from a certain Somebody & Associates? Please don't create an Ebina & Associates… "Uh, I have the festival committee, so…," I replied.

Ebina bopped me on the shoulder with a rolled-up script. "Oh, that's too bad. I think you as the Narrator and Hayato as the Prince would've made a good ship, though. Watching their practice just now from the wings has stoked your flames of jealousy… Ah! Are you going to swoop in and steal him away?! Hnghhlerk!" Blood shot out of her nose then in a disgusting arc.

You're scaring me, seriously.

"Aw, she's started up again. Come on, Ebina, blow. Blow your nose." Miura noticed the outburst and came over with some of the tissue paper for the fake flowers, holding it up to Ebina's face. *I've heard you shouldn't do that when you have a nosebleed, though.*

I observed the class for a while, then stood up and left.

All the classrooms along my way were filled with activity.

It would no doubt be less than comfortable for a loner. If the school day were over, nobody would have noticed if I slipped away—or at least they would have pretended so. But since we'd started up first thing in the morning, I wouldn't be able to just vanish.

I could either inconspicuously wait for instructions or just stare off into space. Usually, I would have done exactly that, but this year, I was on the Cultural Festival Committee.

I descended the staircase, turned the hallway, and continued down the already familiar route.

The classrooms weren't the only sources of building energy. It was the same with the cultural committee. When I arrived at the conference room, it was a hive of activity, too, and everyone seemed to be in a hurry. The door was usually kept shut, but that day, it seemed to be open the whole time.

Inside was Yukinoshita, briskly managing one thing or another. Sagami was beside her, too, sitting like a doll. Haruno was spinning around in a chair during a discussion with Meguri. Haruno really had too much time on her hands. Not that I cared.

I went into the conference room to check the shift schedule for my sector for the next two days as an endless stream of people burst in.

"Vice-chair. The test upload on the website is complete."

"Understood. Sagami, your approval," Yukinoshita said, but even as she did, she was checking it herself.

"Yeah, it's okay," said Sagami.

"All right, then please upload it onto the live server." With each item checked off the list, another was added.

"Yukinoshita, there isn't enough equipment for the volunteers!"

"Volunteer Management, negotiate with the volunteer representative. Please defer to the judgment of the equipment managers for the loans and just send the report back to me," Yukinoshita instructed immediately, before remembering the girl sitting beside her. "Sagami, if there are no particular issues, I think we can move this along."

"Oh yeah. I think that's fine."

Some things proceeded smoothly, while others hit a few bumps in the road. But Yukinoshita fielded each and every matter regardless, and the gears of the Cultural Festival Committee were spinning smoothly. Largely due to her.

"The volunteers' rehearsals are running late, so we'll be shifting their rehearsal time until after the opening ceremony. Keep that in mind." She took a pause for breath after giving the instructions.

Haruno had crept up behind her and swept her up in a tight hug. "That's my Yukino-chan!"

"Get off me, get away from me, and get out." Yukinoshita brushed her off and turned to her computer.

Haruno pulled away from Yukinoshita and gently put a hand on her shoulder. "You really are doing so well, Yuki. It's just like back when I was committee chair."

"Yes, it really is. It's thanks to you, Yukinoshita," Meguri said, singing her praises, too.

"I'm really not doing all that much..." Yukinoshita began typing louder, perhaps to hide her embarrassment.

"That's not true. Your presence here has been such a big help," said Meguri, and every one of the executives there nodded in agreement. When times had gotten toughest, they'd all been the ones pulling this event together. They must have felt the impact of Yukinoshita's work particularly keenly.

But one of the administrators seemed a little tense. Sagami was unable to speak, and her smile was a mask.

"This really is what a cultural committee should be! Man, I hope you guys feel accomplished!" said Haruno, and everyone nodded. They were filled with satisfaction, aware that they were living up to their duty as members of the Cultural Festival Committee.

That was why nobody sensed the additional implications. She was repudiating what the cultural committee had been until recently, as well as criticizing Sagami as a leader. Most likely, the only people to notice would be the mean-spirited types and those who felt guilty.

Sagami crumpled a printout on the table into a ball.

Beside her, Haruno was smiling. "Looking forward to tomorrow! ...Right?" For just an instant, Haruno's gaze flicked toward me. I still couldn't divine what future those dark eyes saw.

It wouldn't be long before the curtain rose on the carnival of unbridled enthusiasm, youth, lies, and pretense. Finally, the cultural festival was about to arrive.

One day in the Hikigaya household,

before the cultural festival

Whatcha doin' on the computer, Bro?

Oh, not much. We're coming up with a slogan for the cultural festival, so I'm brainstorming ideas.

Huh. Sooo...by the way, after you search something, you have to erase it with "Delete History." A little while ago, Mom was restoring the deleted history and poking through it, y'know?

What the hell was she doing? Come on, can't she leave well enough alone...?

She was pretty steamed. Said she found some weird stuff.

That's a false accusation! It wasn't me! In fact, Dad's the only one who would look that up. A long time ago, we got a bill for some mysterious international calls. Mom was about to blow a gasket.

I could've gone without knowing that... So wait, how could you say for sure that it wasn't you?

Wanna hide your search history from your family? Get a smartphone today!

Yikes, your ad sucks...

This is the moment **Soubu High School** is festivaling hardest.

The commotion of the entire student body filled the darkness. Each individual word held meaning, but the multitude of overlapping voices made them all gibberish.

The gym had been meticulously weather-stripped so as to prevent any gaps in the blackout curtains. The only sources of light were weak ones like cell phones and the emergency exit sign, and they only illuminated the palm of your hand at most.

It was pitch-black, and everything was dim.

In the darkness of that moment, we were all one.

Under the sun, the light shines on your differences, underscoring what hopelessly divergent creatures you are. You can't help but notice. Now, the blurred outlines of the crowd made the line between self and other ambiguous.

Of course. It makes sense why they lower the lights before events. Rending the darkness asunder by turning the spotlight to an individual is to imply that one person is distinct from the rest of the crowd. Therefore, the one standing there should be special.

One by one, the students' voices fell silent.

The clock in my hand said it was 9:57.

It was just about time. I pushed the button on my headset to connect it. There would be a bit of lag until the mike picked up my voice, so I waited about two seconds, then began talking. "—Three minutes to curtain rise. Three minutes to curtain rise."

Not even a few seconds later, a burst of static crackled through the earphones. "—This is Yukinoshita. Notifying all personnel. Proceeding on time. If there are any issues, inform me immediately," she finished, her voice calm, and then the communication cut off with another crackle.

Bursts of noise ran through the line, one after another. "—Lighting here. No issues."

"—This is the PA, and no problems here."

"—Backstage, the cast is a little behind with prep. But it looks like they'll make it to stage on time."

The various departments made contact. Frankly, I couldn't keep track of it all.

I wasn't even sure about my own role. Records and Miscellaneous had been assigned a lot of work during the festival. Stage-related odd jobs during the opening and ending ceremonies were also a part of that category. My job there that day was essentially to keep time, simply telling the stage crew when it was time to do something and when they were a little ahead of schedule. If it's the higher-ups giving orders, you can't refuse after all.

Yukinoshita, the control tower, synthesized the information coming in from each section. "—Roger. All stand by until the cue."

In the stage wings, I was having a staring contest with the clock. With each second that ticked by, the silence swelled.

I knew if I peeked through the tiny window into the gym, there would be a crowd of students there. But it was so dark, it just seemed like a single massive creature squirming around. For comparison, think Nyarlathotep. The grotesque god with a thousand faces... Wait, that's not right. Was it Mil Máscaras who had a thousand faces? Well, whatever.

At one minute left to curtain rise, the gym became a sea of silence. Everyone forgot to whisper or murmur, lost in the same moment.

I pressed the button on my headset. "—Ten more seconds." I kept my finger on the button.

"Nine." My eyes were fixed on the clock.

"Eight." I stopped inhaling.

"Seven." Between moments, I exhaled.

"Six."

Then in the instant before I took a breath—

"Five more seconds."

—someone stole my countdown.

"Four." The voice was incredibly calm. Cold, even.

"Three."

Then the voice counting down went silent, and all that remained was someone marking "two" with their fingers.

Yukinoshita was on the second floor above the stage wings, watching us from the PA room window.

And then, in the deafening silence, I mentally finished the count with a *one*. That moment, light burst out on the stage bright enough to blind me.

"Are you all getting cultural?!" Meguri suddenly appeared on stage.

The audience replied with a roar. "YEAAAAAAH!"

"Chiba is famous for dancing and...?"

"FESTIVAAAAALS!"

The slogan actually caught on?

"So if you're an idiot like me, you've got to dance..."

"SING A SONG!" Meguri's baffling call-and-response whipped up all the students into a frenzy. An instant later, dance music was blaring.

The opening act had begun, a collaboration between the dance association and the cheerleading team. The audience was still riding the wave of enthusiasm after Meguri's intro, raising their hands in a semi-joking dance.

...Eugh. Our school is so dumb. What the hell is "getting cultural"? I'm not doing that.

But I couldn't just zone out and watch. *Work, work...*

"—This is the PA. Now finishing up the song" came in the communication from the PA.

"—Roger. Chair Sagami, stand by," Yukinoshita notified us as the supervisor.

The cue must have reached Meguri during her presentation as well. The dance team exited stage right into the wings, and Meguri stood at stage left. "Next is a message from our Cultural Festival Committee chair."

Sagami stepped toward center stage, obviously tense. Over a thousand pairs of eyes were focused on her. Before she had even reached the tape indicating the middle of the stage, she had stopped. Her hands were shaking around the wireless mike. Her stiff arms finally rose, and she started to speak.

Right then…

…a sharp screech of feedback pierced our ears. The timing was so perfect, the audience burst into uproarious laughter.

From the outside, you could tell the reaction wasn't malicious. I mean, I've been on the receiving end of scornful laughter pretty much my whole life, so I can distinguish types of laughter based on experience. But I doubt Sagami, frozen alone on stage, enduring the anxiety and isolation, would be able to tell that. Even once the ringing had faded, she was still silent.

This probably made Meguri nervous, as she picked up a mike and came in as backup. "…Well then, let's try that again! Committee Chair, go right ahead!"

The sound of Meguri's voice seemed to reboot Sagami. She opened up the cue cards she'd been tightly gripping the whole time. Her flustered fingers tangled, and the rustle of a falling card invited more laughter from the crowd. Burning crimson, Sagami picked it up, and a few members of the audience tossed encouraging remarks her way: "You can do it!" They probably didn't mean anything bad by it. But I doubted it would do much to help. When someone is that miserable, there's nothing you can say to them. All they want is for you to be as inconspicuous and silent as an inanimate object. They want to be left alone, like a rock by the roadside.

Though Sagami's opening remarks were all written on the cue cards, of course, she fumbled and stuttered.

Since this was already taking more time than planned, as the time-keeper, I was spinning my arm in an attempt to move things along. But Sagami was so freaked out, she didn't even notice.

"—Hikigaya, give her the sign to finish early." With a crackle of noise, Yukinoshita's voice reached me through the earphones. I glanced up at the PA room on the second floor to see her looking down at me, arms folded.

"—I've been giving it. It looks like she can't see, though."

"—I see… I suppose it's my mistake for selecting you."

"—Are you making fun of me for being hard to notice?"

"—Oh, no, that's not what I'm saying at all. Anyway, where have you been all this time? Are you in the audience?"

"You're definitely mocking me. Come on, I know you can see me." I interrupted the tail end of her remark with my reply. The headset might not have picked up the first part of my reply.

"—Um, Vice-chair. We can all hear you…," someone hesitantly reminded us over the headset.

…Oh yeah. Everyone could hear everyone else on the headsets. I was just a little mortified.

After one of the other cultural committee members had pointed that out, there were a few seconds of silence before another burst of crackling. "—We're advancing the schedule. All of you, move things ahead," Yukinoshita said, and then communication cut off.

Finally, the committee chair finished her comments for the opening ceremony, and we moved on to the next event.

With a start like that, I could see a bumpy road ahead of us.

X   X   X

Once the opening ceremony was done, the cultural festival finally got started for real. It was a two-day event, but it was only open to the public on the second day. The first day was just for the school.

This would be my second festival experience here, and I think it was an extremely typical one, with nothing special worth mentioning.

Each class had some sort of presentation, the arts clubs held recitals or exhibitions, and those who wanted to volunteer put together bands. Perhaps it was a symptom of the times, but we weren't allowed to do any real cooking for food and drinks, so only ready-made items were on sale. Staying overnight at school beforehand to prepare was also forbidden.

But it was still a significant event that people got genuinely excited for. It wasn't about scale or quality. The school enjoyed the cultural festival more as a symbol, as a break from the mundane.

That's what they do.

The festival fervor permeated my own classroom, too. Already, the barker wars had begun, making it difficult to even squeeze through the halls. Groups handing out flyers and pamphlets paraded along in cosplay that looked like they'd bought it from a discount retailer. Ugh, obnoxious.

Once the opening ceremony cleanup was done, I came back to the classroom to find a flurry of noise and activity. They were in the home stretch before the big performance.

"Makeup! What are you doing?! That greasepaint is too thin!" Ebina roared out.

Meanwhile, Miura was going around talking to each and every person present.

"What're you all nervous for? You're killing me here. I'm, like, seriously laughing my ass off. I mean, everyone's all here to see Hayato anyway. There's not even any point in getting so worked up, right?" It was a mean thing to say, but it did seem like it would make them less nervous.

Looking around at my classmates, I saw they were all working hard to make sure to complete their work. I figured this past month and a half had strengthened all their relationships. They might laugh, they might cry, they might even yell or nearly come to blows, but even so, they'd come to realize one another's true feelings and finally become one...I guess. I wasn't a part of that, so I have no idea.

I had no tasks at the moment, so I loitered around the entrance to the classroom, muttering "I see, hmm…" as if I were working.

"You've been pretending to be busy for a while now. Nothing to do?" At a question befitting a real supervisor, I turned around to see a supervisor indeed, or rather, our cultural festival boss, Ebina. "If you're free, then can I ask you to do reception? Or are you going to get on out there?"

Nope, nope. I replied with a shake of the head.

"All right, reception, then. Tell guests about the performance time. All you've got to do is tell them that, if anyone asks."

"Uh, but I don't even know when it is, though."

"It'll be fine. It's posted by the entrance. Really, you just need to be there 'cause it's lame if no one's outside. You just have to sit there. We're counting on you."

For real? I just have to sit there? What kind of dream job is this? I'd like to take advantage of this experience to find employment of this sort in the future.

I accepted her offer and left the classroom to see that there was indeed a long, folded-up table and two or three folding chairs sitting there near the door. *Hmm. Guess I'll set this up, at least.*

The long table rattled as I extended the legs, the chairs snapped into place, and setup was done. Despairingly cool! Maybe this is part of being a boy, but I love transforming things like these. I like disassembling them and stuff, too. During class, I'll unconsciously take apart my ballpoint pen and then put it back together again.

On the wall was the poster with the performance schedule written in large font. If I sat right next to it, I doubted anyone would go to the trouble of asking me about it.

It was about five minutes until the doors would open. As I stared off into space, the commotion in classroom 2-F got even louder. I peeked in just a bit, figuring something must have happened.

"All right! Time for a huddle!" said Tobe.

Everyone was like, "Huh?" and "Seriously?" but they started forming a circle anyway. If this were recess, they'd be about to start a game.

"We're never gonna get things started unless Ebina takes the lead!" he insisted. "Come on, over here, over here! Come to the middle!"

You're all in a circle, so there isn't really a more prominent position. Or so I thought, but Tobe was pointing to the spot beside himself. He'd found a legitimate way to position himself so that he and Ebina would have their arms around each other's shoulders. *Not bad, Tobe. Quite the strategist.*

As if in support of his plotting, Miura pulled Ebina in by the arm. "C'mon, Ebina. Go into the middle." And then she shoved Ebina into the actual middle. The center of the circle. With everyone else around her. Tobe was about to cry.

Ebina spun to look at everyone, and then her gaze stopped on one person. Standing alone in a corner of the classroom was Kawasaki. Ebina gave her a broad smile and called her over. "Come on. You too, Kawasaki."

"M-me? I-I'm fine…"

"There you go again. You made the costumes, so you've got to take responsibility for that."

"Responsibility…? You said *you'd* take responsibility." But even as Kawasaki grumbled, her feet were carrying her into the huddle.

Once everyone but me had assembled, Yuigahama turned to glance at me. I smiled back at her and shook my head. She frowned, a little unhappy.

It was fine, really. When you haven't actually done anything, it's way more uncomfortable and awkward to join in. If I couldn't stand there with confidence, it was best if I didn't participate. I mean, Sagami was looking pretty ashamed herself after all.

Indeed, her expression as she stood in the huddle was not very cheerful. Her recent failure would probably stick with her for a while, but even more than that, I think she was bothered by her own low participation.

People with a habit of assigning ranks end up doing it to everyone. That was why Sagami was considering her own rank right then. She was a ways away from Miura and Hayama's group, but she wasn't directly in front of them, either, probably staying out of their line of sight. She was rather off to the side, which I think was an expression of how she felt her rank was right then. The psychological distance was embodied in physical distance.

By that measure, Ebina occupied the center of the group and the center of the cultural festival. When Ebina called out, everyone responded.

Watching the complete huddle from the outside was surprisingly not so bad.

×　×　×

The classroom was surrounded by blackout curtains and jam-packed like a can of sardines.

Ebina judged that they probably wouldn't be able to fit in any more guests, so she fired off instructions to hang the FULL HOUSE sign on the door. Once I'd done so, I moved the reception table in front of the door to cut off anyone else who wanted to get in.

The door was left open just a crack for ventilation, and I peeked in.

Finally, the curtain rose on stage. The performance began with a monologue from the Narrator, played by Hayama. As the spotlight shone down on him, the audience bubbled up momentarily. It sounded like many of Hayama's friends and fans had descended upon us.

The set consisted of an airplane with a desert in the background. The pictures drawn by the Narrator were played by boys in full-body costumes, like mascots. Two of them represented the illustration of a boa constrictor wrapping around its prey by tangling together with each other. The audience roared with laughter at the silly interpretation.

Then...

"If you please—draw me a sheep." Totsuka's line sounded from offstage.

"Huh? What?" Hayama hadn't managed to pick up the quiet, whispery request.

So once more, the Prince repeated, "Draw me a sheep." Then the spotlight struck Totsuka, standing near the edge of the stage. His adorable clothing and lovable visage sent the audience into another tizzy.

And so the two met, and the story proceeded smoothly from there.

When the Prince recounted the tale of the Rose on his planet, a boy appeared in a green full-body tights suit with a red shampoo hat on his head, talking with an effeminate lisp. Everything after that was over-the-top, too. All the flashbacks to the various planets the Prince had visited were basically visual comedy gags.

The blustering King, so desperate to maintain his authority, was wrapped in layer upon layer of fancy carpets a bunch of the students had brought from their homes. Yamato was sweating buckets.

The Vain Man, who demanded reverence and recognition, was covered head to toe in aluminum foil. Tobe was so sparkly he was hard to look at.

The Drunkard, who drank to forget the shame of his addiction, was surrounded with sake bottles and boxes for high-alcohol-content liquor, as if to say, *Take that!* Oda or Tahara or whoever it was must have been nervous, because he was as bright red as a real drunk.

The Businessman recited numbers and yelled out, "Listen, I'm a very important person!" The class rep actually cut a fine figure in a suit. Perhaps this was the fruit of Ebina's direction.

The Lamplighter, bound by the rules to light the lamps and extinguish them again, was wearing dirty overalls made to look sooty. His role of spinning round and round the lamp was perhaps somewhat fitting for a complaisant weather vane like Ooka.

Maps and globes surrounded the ignorant Geographer, who recorded what explorers taught him without ever taking a step outside his own study. Oda or Tahara or whoever it was reading them looked fairly scholarly.

Everyone had contributed their opinions for the creation of these costumes (probably), Kawasaki had worked hard on them (surely), and the audience seemed to find them hilarious (yay).

And then the play got to the part when the Prince leaves the earth.

He'd arrived in the desert, met a snake, seen many roses, and realized that what he'd had was truly common and nothing special at all.

I could hear sniffling in the audience at Totsuka's mournful delivery. Totsuka was so precious...er, rather, the prince was so piteous, I wanted to give him a hug right that instant.

That was when a man in a fur coat and a fox mask appeared.

—*Oh, this is my favorite scene.*

The prince offered the Fox an invitation. "Come play with me. I am so unhappy," Totsuka said sadly, his face downcast. So good, gets me right here. By the way, the first draft of the line in Ebina's script was *Why don't we just do it?* Seriously, what was that woman thinking?

The Fox replied to the Prince, "I cannot play with you... I am not tamed."

I love that line: *I am not tamed.* It's such a simple and realistic description of the act of becoming friends.

Making friends is, in fact, a lot like being tamed by a variety of things: the person themselves or the social atmosphere that tells you to get along with everyone and not rock the boat. Then your life and even your heart are tamed. Your fangs are removed, your claws broken, your thorns pulled out. You treat everyone carefully, like something swollen, so as not to wound or be wounded. I like the expression because it's kind of taking a dig at such "friendships."

As I was mulling over these thoughts, the scene continued.

"First, you will sit down a little distance from me—like that—in the grass. I shall look at you out of the corner of my eye, and you will say nothing. Words are the source of misunderstandings. But you will sit a little closer to me, every day..." The Prince and the Fox conversed more and more. And so they both tamed each other.

But even so, it came time to part. At the end, the Fox told the Prince a secret. This is probably the most well-known part of *The Little Prince*.

—*What is essential is invisible to the eye.*

After parting with the Fox, the Prince once again went to visit various places, and the scene changed back to the desert. The Narrator and the Prince were again searching for a well.

"What makes the desert beautiful is that somewhere it hides a well," said Totsuka, and the audience gave a sigh of lament. This was also a classic line from the book. Many of the people present must have been familiar with it.

In the end, after their hearts touched through many conversations that they themselves touched on at many points in time, it came time for the Narrator and the Prince to part. By the way, in Ebina's original script, they touched lips and bodies, too. That girl, seriously...

"Ah, little prince, dear little prince... I love to hear that laughter..." Hayama's line got all the women excited. If I recorded that on mp3 and distributed it, I could make a killing.

"We'll be together forever..." Hayama's next line turned the audience into a sea of satisfied sighs. *That's it—I'll make a Hayama pillow talk CD. And it'll come with a body pillow. I've got a hunch this'll be big business.*

Then finally, the farewell scene came.

Bitten by the Snake, the Prince fell without a sound. Totsuka's fragile performance, like he was about to vanish, made the audience hold their collective breaths.

The screen turned black.

A single spotlight hit Hayama, and the Narrator's monologue brought the final scene to a close.

Then the audience exploded in thunderous applause. The curtain closed on the memorable first production of *The Little Prince: The Musical*, a massively successful, sold-out show.

But that wasn't a musical, was it? It was just a play... There wasn't any singing or dancing.

× × ×

When the performance was on break, I closed the classroom doors.

It seemed my role also meant staying behind to watch things, so while my classmates were taking their breaks or going out to see the other classes' plays, I was sitting on the folding chair by the entrance.

I'd have to be walking all over the place the whole next day as a part of my recording and miscellaneous tasks for the cultural committee, and the first day was the only time I'd have to participate in the class stuff. I hadn't been able to join in the preparations for this, and I couldn't help run the event on the second day, either, so I was stuck there with no way out for the whole day. In fact, if I could call this my participation in the class play, I'd even have liked to thank my classmates for coming up with and approving this role for me.

Well, not many people out there would go to such lengths for me, so I had a good idea of who had come up with this.

"Hey." A plastic bag thunked down on the table, and I looked up to see Yuigahama. I unfolded a chair that was still leaning against the wall, and she took a seat on it with a little *oof.*

Are you an old lady or what?

"How was it?" she asked.

"I'd say it was pretty good. The audience enjoyed it."

Leaving aside its quality as a contribution to the dramatic arts, the audience actually had seemed pretty into it. I don't know if it met super-producer Ebina's expectations, but I think it had worked fine as entertainment focusing more on humor, as Tobe had proposed.

And as a cultural festival play put on by high school students, there was really nothing to complain about. And also, though I wouldn't call it favoritism, exactly, I think they were able to take full advantage of the fun that comes from knowing the performers by casting people with a broad circle of acquaintances, like Hayama, Tobe, and Ooka.

There's an appeal to seeing someone you're normally friendly with play a completely different character, as well as catching glimpses of their real personality, and these elements bring about a completely different sort of enjoyment compared with your standard entertainment. I could indeed say that musical was good, in those respects. Also, above all, Totsuka was cute.

"Yeah, 'cause everyone put a lot of work into it," Yuigahama said while arching her back in a stretch with a "Hnn!" I could tell just how much effort all this had taken from the emotion behind her words.

Thanks for all your hard work, seriously. But...more importantly, when you arch your back in that T-shirt, it draws my attention to your chest and belly button, so I'd kinda like you to not. "Well, I guess. Maybe you were all working a lot. But I wasn't there, so I don't really know."

"You were busy with the committee. You couldn't join in with the class stuff, so there's no helping that. U-um...are you bothered about being left out of the huddle?" Yuigahama touched her index fingers together, looking at me with upturned eyes. It was a habit of hers, something she did when she was hesitant about asking something. Yet again, she was worrying herself about things that didn't matter.

"Aw, no way. And, like, I didn't even do anything, so it would've been wrong for me to join in." Regardless, I'd made her concerned for me, so I answered her with uncharacteristic honesty.

Then she breathed a short sigh that sounded like an exasperated chuckle. "I knew you'd say that."

"How?" *It's kinda embarrassing when you read my mind like that. Stop it.*

Yuigahama flopped back into the chair, and it made a bashful *kyeep!* "Y'know, Hikki, you're serious about the weirdest stuff. I can tell by looking at you."

"You're looking...?"

Her chair gave a shocked *ack!* I looked over to see that Yuigahama was half standing, waving her hands violently in front of her chest. "Ah, no, actually, forget that. I'm not. I'm averting my eyes pretty hard."

"Um, well, you can if you want to, though..." Reflexively, I ended up scratching roughly at my head. Both of us suddenly fell silent.

Our silence made the noise of the classes to either side of us sound especially loud. Both Classes E and F seemed to be quite popular. Class E in particular. It had a roller coaster or something, and their line was very long. A few people were whining about having to wait their turn, and I could tell the students from Class E were struggling.

It's funny. Lines beget lines. And this principle isn't just limited to lines. Whenever something's selling, its popularity becomes another form of advertising, and it sells even more. Class E was no exception to this rule, and even more people were joining the rear of the crowd.

"Whoa, that looks like a handful," Yuigahama murmured.

"I dunno if they're gonna be able to manage all that, at this rate," I agreed. From what I could see, Class E was understaffed, as they clearly couldn't control all their guests. It was only a matter of time before the hallway would be blocked.

And then it happened—the shrill *tweet* of a whistle. When I looked toward the sound, I found Meguri. "Handle this, guys," she said. And from thin air, student council members shuffled into existence, and in the blink of an eye, they began to organize the line, while some of the people at the back were shunted off somewhere.

Are you guys Comiket staff or what?

Yukinoshita was among the newcomers. "Is the representative for Class E here?" She immediately called for their rep, asked about the situation, and discussed how to manage it.

"Yukinon is so cool…"

"Well, the kids in Class E are clearly scared of her, though." From where we sat, she was just the same old Yukinoshita, but for someone who didn't interact with her much, her cold, intimidating aura had to be fear itself.

"She's cheered up a bit, though, huh?" Yuigahama remarked.

"…Yeah."

Once Yukinoshita was done dealing with the matter, she breathed a small sigh. Then she lifted her head and glanced at us for an instant. But then she immediately averted her eyes again and strode briskly away. She must have had something else to handle next.

As we watched her go, I said to Yuigahama beside me, "Hey, can I ask you something?"

"Hmm? What?" she replied, without turning to look at me. She was resting her chin in her hands, elbows on the table.

"When we went to Yukinoshita's place, did you talk about anything?" I asked.

Yuigahama *hmm*'d and considered a little, then opened her mouth. "Nooothing at all."

"What?" My reaction demanded an explanation.

So Yuigahama started telling me the rest of what had happened that day. "After you left, Hikki, we were hungry, so we ate together and watched some DVDs, and then I went home... So she didn't say anything you'd want to know, Hikki." The last sentence seemed rather cold.

"Oh...it's not like there's anything I'd want to know anyway."

"Really? I wanted to know."

"So then why—?" I was about to ask why she hadn't asked, then, but looking at her profile, my voice withered. She was so focused on the far end of the hallway where Yukinoshita had left, I hesitated to say any more out loud.

"You know, I've decided to wait for her. 'Cause Yukinon will probably try to talk and get closer...so I'll wait."

That was a very Yuigahama-like response.

This was Yuigahama. She always met people halfway. So I was sure she'd wait. And Yukinoshita knew that, too, so she'd try to take that step in and not leave her hanging.

"But if waiting is never going to work with someone, then I'm not going to wait," she said.

"Hmm? Well, yeah, there's no point in waiting for someone hopeless."

That was when Yuigahama smiled just a little. She twisted her head a bit, still leaning on her hands, and gave me a long look.

There was nothing happening in this classroom, so the river of people flowed by at high speed. Students were coming and going, hurrying through the hallway to their new destinations or attempting to bring in more guests. There was no need to differentiate all the individuals from the restless mass, and the commotion was heedless of us, too. In other words, it was background, environmental noise.

That was why I could hear her voice so clearly. She spoke slowly, sounding more mature than usual.

"That's not what I mean. I won't wait… I'll be the one to make the first move."

My heart skipped a beat. It hurt so bad, I thought it would tear me open from the inside.

Looking into Yuigahama's dewy eyes, I was on the verge of parsing what those words meant. But if I were to think about that, I'd probably find myself in deep trouble. And that would most likely lead to mistakes. I've made many of those in my life, but I didn't want to mess this one up, I don't think.

That was why at this point, I still didn't have the words to respond. "Oh…" I gave her a vague, meaningless nonanswer.

She replied with a shy smile. "Uh-huh, yep." I took that shy smile to mean that this conversation was now over. The both of us sighed a little bit and looked away from each other.

That was when the plastic bag on the long table caught my eye. "So anyway, what's with the bag?"

"Oh, I forgot. You haven't had lunch yet, right?" She rustled around in the bag, and then another package arrived, a paper box. Opening it, she pulled out something else from inside. *Huh, that's a rather odd* matryoshka *doll.* Or so I thought, but apparently, that was not the case.

It was some kind of bread. A round, chubby loaf of bread.

There was whipped cream layered on top, chocolate sauce drizzle, and colorful chocolate sprinkles. But it was basically bread—round and chubby. Actually, it was just sandwich bread. It wasn't a pastry or anything special, just something you'd describe as plain bread.

But Yuigahama held up the bread à la whipped cream and said proudly: "Look! Honey toast!"

Ohhh…so this was that super-popular honey toast from everyone's favorite, the Karaoke Pasela. What, is this some limited-edition special item? It's not? It's not a special? They're not making deluxe drinks with deluxe coasters to go with it? I'm happy with Karaoke no Tetsujin, too!

I shot Yuigahama a casual look that said I appreciated the gesture, and maybe that was why she sounded a little exasperated when she said, "It's nothing that unusual. There's a Pasela in Chiba, too."

"Oh, I don't go to karaoke much in the first place, so."

Guess this is the quality you get when an amateur makes honey toast. The real thing is definitely better than this. Actually, this is just bread. Seriously. Not gonna put in a bit more effort to erase the breadiness of it? It's bread all over. Totally bread.

"Here we go!" With far too much gusto for serving food, she served me up some on a paper plate. With her bare hands… Not like I minded. I decided to accept the piece of torn-off honey toast.

"So good!" Yuigahama stuffed her cheeks, with a little whipped cream on her face. That blissful expression could only come from someone with a sweet tooth. Watching her, I got the feeling that I could come to like honey toast, too.

A little excited, I put it in my mouth.

It's…so hard… The honey hasn't soaked all the way to the middle… There wasn't enough whipped cream, and at a certain point, the density was a form of punishment… And worst of all was Yuigahama's taste for picking this out for lunch.

However, Yuigahama herself seemed to be enraptured. Did anything about this taste good?

"I love the whipped cream!"

Hey… Hey… Was there a need for this to be honey toast, then? And besides, you stole that whipped cream from my part, didn't you? I had mountains of complaints, but in front of Yuigahama's zeal, I couldn't bring myself to say any of them. At the end, she washed her meal down with some tea.

…Okay, well, I guess it's…kinda okay?

Yuigahama seemed to be done eating, and she gently wiped the whipped cream from her mouth with a tissue. Her lips were glossy, shimmering in the light of the sun. I looked away.

Even with both of us going at it, there was a lot of honey toast. I mean, it was a whole loaf of bread...

And as a whole loaf, it must have cost a commensurate price. You might as well call it money toast. "So how much was it?" I asked, pulling out my wallet.

But Yuigahama stopped me with a hand. "Don't worry about it! It's no biggie."

"Come on, I can't accept that."

"Don't worry about it!" she refused stubbornly.

At this rate, I couldn't see this dispute ending soon. "...I do plan to have someone support me financially...but I'm not going to accept charity!"

"Huh? Your sense of pride makes no sense!" Yuigahama groaned, then she paused a moment in thought. Finally, she grumbled quietly, "Agh, Hikki, you're such a pain... All right. Then later, you treat me to some honey toast...at the Pasela in Chiba."

"You're picking out a place?" My reply was sharp, but I caught her drift. Yet again, I had failed to distance myself from Yuigahama.

I do think we were closer than before. I'm not immature enough to insist on denying it. It was a major factor in the whole episode with the class application documents, too. I could have asked anyone to fill it in for me, but I'd deliberately sought out Yuigahama and chosen her to help.

I, myself, had allowed that. It was easy to rely on Yuigahama.

But.

That was exactly why I had to restrain myself. Uncontrolled, unguided trust is dependence.

I couldn't cling to Yuigahama's kindness. I couldn't take advantage of her gentle heart. Her compassion was like a knife cutting you open, making you worry and suffer, bleeding you dry. I knew that. That was why I couldn't so easily yield to it.

And if her behavior wasn't out of kindness or thoughtfulness but some other feeling, then that goes double. Because then I'd be taking advantage of another person's weakness.

Manage your emotions.

Keep a suitable distance.

So…maybe it's fine to just take one step closer.

A cultural festival is a celebration, and a celebration is a break from the mundane. And because of that change, your value judgments might be a little different from normal. Hey, on a day like today, even I might make a call that's a little suspect.

"Are you…fine with something else?" I asked.

"Yeah, that's fine." She grinned. "So…when'll this be?" There was a strange intensity in her smile.

"U-um, I'm sorry, please let me think about this a little—a lot…" I suddenly found myself acting oddly polite.

Yuigahama huffed out a breath in reply, apparently reluctant to accept my response.

It was still the first day of the festival. But the end was sure to come.

The clock counted out the seconds, telling us that the time we spent then would also eventually end.

In the Hikigaya household, the evening after the first day of the cultural festival

Oh, you're looking something up again. What's it this time?

Well, you know, stuff. Hey…if you wanted to hang out somewhere, where would you go?

I think Destiny Land is a safe choice. Or LaLaport.

The standard course for the Chibanese… Anything else?

What about Mother Farm?

Huh? Is Mother Farm an option? Then is Narita Dream Farm an option, too?

Yeah, yeah! Or the Tokyo German Village!

And, like, the Funabashi Andersen Park?

And Ostrich Kingdom!

Ohhh, then I'll give my vote to the Ichihara Elephant Kingdom.

Nice, Bro; you're pretty good at this. Then Komachi's going with Kamogawa Sea World!

If we're talking aquariums, then Kasai Seaside Park isn't too far away...though it is in Tokyo.

Yeah, aquariums are pretty nice. Zoos, too

There's the Chiba Zoo.

Yep, and they have an amusement park with a scream machine.

They do?

Yeah, on the way there.

That's the Chiba monorail. I mean, riding it *is* a bit of a thrill. And the modern cars are very snazzy.

The Chiba monorail is the best in the woooorld!

It's the longest hanging monorail in the world, too.

There's lots of places for family trips and dates. Yes! Explore Chiba! ...What were we talking about again?

Huh? This was a Chiba ad, wasn't it?

Beyond, **Yukino Yukinoshita** has her eye on someone.

We'd reached the second day of the cultural festival.

That day was open to the general public, so neighbors, friends from other schools, and entrance exam hopefuls were pouring in. It being a Saturday, the place was bustling with people on their day off.

Things were different from the first day, which had felt more like a private party and rehearsal, and where many more issues came up. But since all the members of the cultural committee were handling it, there was nothing to worry about even on this heavy-flow second day. We even had side-groove channels and wings.

And thus, I would be doing committee work for the whole day.

Our clientele was quite diverse: We had many middle school kids from the neighborhood, but there were also families with children and fancy madams, local seniors, and kids who were like, *I don't really get what this is, but I just kinda showed up!*

We were supposed to register all the guests, more or less, but from what I could see, that was largely not happening. Frankly speaking, considering how invisible I was in my class, I suspected I could've gotten in without any check at all. The kids on duty for Health and Sanitation and the male gym teacher had gotten together to set up reception tables in front of both school gates. So I doubted any real weirdos would come in.

As the school started getting congested, my work was to take pictures. My main task for that day was to record each class's presentations and the guests, as well as the general excitement of the cultural festival that year.

So, photography. I'd thought I could just snap some photos of whatever and scratch it off the list, but I was encountering a few roadblocks. As for why, when I began actually taking pictures, people kept on saying, "Um…could you please not take pictures of us?" *Ouch…* Every time that happened, I'd show them my CULTURAL COMMITTEE: RECORDS armband, and for some reason, I always ended up having to apologize for it.

I'd managed to take a bunch of photos at last when something swooped down on me to slam into my back. "Bro!"

"Oh, Komachi." I turned my head around to see my sister attached to me. When she acts all clingy like that, well, her big brother doesn't feel so bad. *Whoo-hoo, my little sister is so cute!*

"A hug after so much time apart! I think this could be worth a lot of Komachi points."

"What? Is this Heathrow Airport or something?" All those foreigners hug too much in the airport, in my opinion.

Komachi was being kinda manipulative, so I peeled her off. The ensuing whimpers were even more manipulative.

Though Komachi didn't have school that day, for some reason, she was in her uniform. Speaking of which, why do high school girls always wear their uniforms? Even though it was a weekend for other schools, everyone around was in uniform. Well, not having to pick an outfit is easier, I guess.

Komachi's outfit must have gotten mussed when she'd glomped me, as she was adjusting the collar of her sailor dress. Something about it struck me as weird.

Oh. The other guests had come in groups, but she'd come by herself. *So that was it, huh?* "Did you come alone?"

"Yeah, I mean, I just came to see you, Bro. That just now was worth a lot of Komachi points, too." Komachi seemed to notice the chilly look

I gave her, as she cleared her throat with a deliberate little *hem-hem*. "Well, to be honest, I just felt shy about inviting friends when everyone's so tense. It's right before entrance exams."

Oh yeah. She was such an idiot I tended to forget, but Komachi was, in fact, coming up to her entrance exams. And Soubu High School was her first choice, too.

Well, it was true that coming to the cultural festival of the school she was applying to might help get her motivated. That must have been part of her reasoning in coming all this way.

She must also have been curious about things in general, because she was glancing all around. "Where are Yui and Yukino?" she asked.

"I think Yuigahama's in our classroom. I dunno about Yukinoshita."

"Why aren't you in the classroom? Do you not belong there?" She didn't even seem to care that it was cruel.

How rude. I do have a place I belong. My desk and chair is my native territory. But I belong nowhere else, so while the cultural festival is going on and the desks are removed from their places, I'm a total nomad. A wanderer. "...An aloof, wandering soul needs no place to call his home."

"Whoa, sounds cool," Komachi replied in the flattest monotone ever. "So what're you doing?"

"Work...," I replied.

Komachi blinked her eyes, two, three times. "So what're you doing?"

"I said, I'm doing work." Why was she asking me exactly the same question again? I'm gonna write a note that says *Komachi needs to listen to what other people say* and give it to Mom.

"So what're you doing?"

"Are you a CD? Do you have a scratch? I'll polish you with abrasives. I'm working, seriously."

"My brother is...doing work...," Komachi muttered, deeply impressed. After three repetitions, it finally seemed to sink in. "My brother, who never worked part-time jobs for long and generally flaked out and gave ridiculous excuses and told them *Well, my parents are all* *like, y'know, about exams…*is doing work…" Then I saw something sparkling bright in her eyes. "Komachi is so happy… But wait, this is weird. It's like you've gone far away. I'm having mixed feelings."

Hey, I don't know what's up with that parental look, but stop it. It's super-embarrassing, and it's making your big brother feel like he might be able to reform his entire attitude toward his lifestyle and correct his ways to lead a decent life for his family's sake.

In an attempt to shake off Komachi's warm gaze, I steered us back on course. "Well, I mean, yeah, it's work, but it's like a low-ranking gofer position. I'm totally replaceable."

"Oh, that makes sense." *She's nodding pretty damn hard there.*

In spite of myself, I smiled wryly. "Right? Makes sense to me, too."

First Hayama, and then my own little sister said it… I must really look like a lackey. Well…I guess I do. I think I have the eyes of a flunky to a real pirate, or a bandit, or highwayman, if I do say so myself.

Komachi and I strolled together down the hall. She walked a few steps ahead of me through the fairly large crowds, checking out the decorations in the classrooms, the students' outfits, and other things, and she seemed surprised by all the energy. She gave an impressed sigh. "…High school really is kinda different."

"Well, middle school doesn't even have cultural festivals."

"Yeah, yeah, just choir recitals."

That term brought unpleasant memories to mind. How could they be so quick to decide someone wasn't singing? I *was* singing! Or did they just not know what my voice sounded like 'cause normally I wouldn't ever talk to them? Was that it? If I made a recording of my own voice, would they think it was a ghost?

Suddenly, Komachi's feet stopped. Then she stretched her back in an exaggerated fashion and shaded her eyes with her hand as she peered into the distance. A second later, she folded her arms and fell into thought, *hmm*ing. "Komachi's gonna go look at a bunch of stuff now. See ya, Bro," she said, immediately scampering away down the hallway and up a staircase.

I was suddenly abandoned. "Wh-whoa…," I replied like an idiot, though I doubted she could hear me anymore. A girl from another school who was walking by twitched and jumped about fifty centimeters away from me.

She may be my own sister, but she could be mysterious. Komachi knows just how to get along with people, but she actually likes doing stuff on her own more than you'd think. She's a next-generation hybrid loner model. She has the gift unique to younger siblings of learning from her older sibling's failures. Having grown up with a specialist in solitude like me, she has a good understanding of the positives and negatives of lonerdom.

Well, there's a wide variety of sibling relationships out there. Being a younger sister with an older brother like me who will inevitably fall short of most standards might actually lift some of your burden. Comparisons won't hurt you.

But if I were an exceptionally accomplished person, I wonder what Komachi would have thought of me.

Perhaps the reason I'd ended up with that question on my mind was that I found *her* there ahead of me. Even among the surging crowds, I could pick her out. Yukinoshita was taking her time, slowly examining each and every one of the classrooms. Her eyes were a little warmer than usual.

No matter why or how things got this way, it was thanks to her that this cultural festival was proceeding without a hitch. Yukinoshita had to know that, and I was sure she was proud. I guess that would put a kinder look in your eyes. She'd gotten real results for her diligence.

Yukinoshita's gaze continued on to the next classroom. Then it seemed that I appeared in her field of vision. She seemed a little surprised, and then her gaze quickly flashed cold. Why? Suspicious, she strode straight over toward me. "You're alone today, I see."

"Well, I'm basically always alone, though. Oh, but I was with Komachi until just now."

"Oh, so she's here, too? You're not exploring the festival together?"

"She just kinda ran off. I figure she was being considerate, since I'm on the job now."

"…On the job?" Yukinoshita tilted her head dubiously.

"It's not obvious?"

"That's why I asked," she said nonchalantly.

So it wasn't obvious… *Hachiman's a little shocked. Well, now that she mentions it, I'm not working at this very moment…* "So anyway, what about you? Work?" I asked.

"Yes, I'm doing inspections."

"Weren't you doing that yesterday, too? Not worried about your class?"

"…I'd rather work than be forced to participate in that," Yukinoshita replied with an extremely dour look.

I'd heard Class J was doing a fashion show or something. Class J, the international curriculum, was over 90 percent girls. If they wanted to have an easy time bringing in guests, they just had to put their good looks front and center. So it was inevitable they'd want to rope in Yukinoshita. Whoa, yeah, she'd hate that. Actually, I'd kinda like to see Yukinoshita forced into fancy clothing, even if she did hate it.

Since Yukinoshita was doing inspections, she constantly had her eye on any number of things, and she came to a halt at one classroom. "…Their presentation. It's not what they wrote on their application." The walls of class 3-B were decorated to look like a cave, and the sign hanging there had an Indiana Jones–ish typeface that read Trolley Olley.

"What's their presentation?" I asked.

"You should at least get an understanding of what every class is doing."

That's kind of an extreme demand, Yukinoshita.

She pulled a neatly folded cultural festival pamphlet out of her chest pocket and then offered it to me. I took it without a word and opened it. *Okay, the warmth of this pamphlet is getting me a little excited. Please don't let your guard down like this.*

To distract myself from my passions of the flesh, I quickly searched to see what Class 3-B was supposed to have on display. *Um, 3-B, 3-B…*

And there it was. Apparently, the concept was to "show off the decorations and dioramas of the room in a slowly moving trolley."

But from inside we could hear screams ("Eek!") and a furious
rattling.

It was clearly a roller coaster… They must have noticed the popularity of Class 2-E's roller coaster the previous day and suddenly changed
their concept. These guys were quick to seize an opportunity.

But there was no way the vice-chair would allow that. Immediately, she called for their representative. "Is your class rep here? It looks
like your presentation isn't the one described on your application," said
Yukinoshita, and immediately, the 3-B girls all blanched.

"Crap!" "They found out it's high-speed!" "J-just make them get on!
Just move it along to avoid an inquisition!" As if we'd poked a beehive,
the class flew into chaos, and some third-years grabbed both Yukinoshita's arms firmly and tried to drag her into the trolley.

"H-hey!" Resisting, Yukinoshita shot a glance at me, like she
wanted me to save her. But here, that had the opposite effect.

Up until then, I'd been pretty much invisible, but now the gazes of
all of Class 3-B locked onto me. "…That one's on the committee, too?"
"He's got an armband!" "Toss him in!"

Some rough older boy immediately captured me. *Hey! How come
I'm not being grabbed by a third-year girl?! This isn't fair, is it?!*

They dragged me into the classroom. *Hey! Who touched my butt just
now?!* The inside of the classroom was decorated like a cave, too. It was
pretty elaborate, with ore shining via LED lights, crystal skulls, boul-
ders made of Styrofoam, and spiders dangling from string.

I only had a moment to be impressed, though, and then we were
shoved into the trolley—a modified cage dolly with decorations on it.
Hey! Seriously, who is it?! Who's been patting my butt this whole time?!

Finally, they gave us a vigorous shove as if to make doubly sure
the trolley would go, and the impact sent both me and Yukinoshita
tumbling to the floor. I'd resisted at the last second, so I was able to
avoid colliding with Yukinoshita, but the resulting position was still
uncomfortable.

... *Too close!* Yukinoshita and I both shifted to the opposite corners of the small trolley.

"Um, thank you very much for riding the Trolley Olley today. Please enjoy the mysterious underground world" came the announcement, and immediately, the trolley started moving. A group of four athletic-looking boys dressed in black like stagehands were pulling it forward. Looking closely, I noticed two more backing them up.

The course was made of desks and tables, wooden boards, and a collection of sheet metal and iron plates, rattling under us as we proceeded at a decent clip. They'd created ups and downs, too, and I could really feel it when we dipped.

This is scary... And scariest of all was the fact that this was all done by hand...

Suddenly, I felt something catch on my clothing. I looked over to see Yukinoshita gripping my sleeve.

As we were shaken and jolted, violently flung this way and that and sometimes even lifted up, I kinda came to understand how clothes feel in the washing machine. Finally, the trolley stopped as we reached the end.

Still leaning back against the wall of the vehicle, Yukinoshita was stunned.

"How was your underground journey? Come visit us again!" The third-year from 3-B officially ended the experience, and finally, me and Yukinoshita both rebooted. We looked at each other. Yukinoshita immediately released my sleeve.

Then they practically chased us out of the classroom. After the darkness, the light of day was blinding.

"How was the ride?!" someone materialized to ask us proudly, someone who I assume was the representative for 3-B.

Yukinoshita, a little unsteady on her feet, shot them an icy look. But her wobbling dulled the impact. "Never mind how it was. It was different from what was on your application."

"Just a little! We were flexible! We just made some on-the-spot judgments!"

That's called "getting carried away." You can waste your time scolding people like this, but they're not going to listen. The representative wasn't at fault, not necessarily. It's just the way groups are. They pick a direction, and once they're in motion, you have a hard time getting them to listen to anyone else. So it would be best to keep adjustments minor. Course corrections. "Well, it looks like lots of people are enjoying it, so I say it's fine. As long as there's no safety issues," I said.

Yukinoshita considered that a bit. "Yes...well, please present additional application documents, then. And explain things fully to your guests. Post a notice by the entrance and provide a verbal explanation before they use the attraction."

"Um...well, if that's all, then okay," said the representative.

"Thank you." Yukinoshita bowed, then left. As she began walking, she glanced back at me. She seemed irked, and I could see the hint of a glare. Maybe the redness of her cheeks was the fault of the sunlight streaming in. "...Records, do your work. Or...will you slack off if you aren't monitored?"

"No..." *Don't you underestimate me. When I slack off, I do it right, even under surveillance. That's who I am.*

× × ×

In the end, I had no choice about the matter, and I took a few photos under Yukinoshita's direction.

We made the rounds inspecting each classroom and recording the event at the same time.

When we got to classroom 3-E, which was pretty close to the gym, Yukinoshita stopped.

PET PLACE: MEOWY WOOFY

Apparently, the students had all brought in their pets from home.

They had photos posted up on the wall for clients to choose from, just like a host club. Of course, there were the basics like dogs, cats, rabbits, and hamsters, but there was also a ferret, a short-tailed weasel, a weasel snake, and a turtle... That's a lot of long torsos there.

Yukinoshita's eyes locked onto one particular photo among the collection.

Oh-ho, the Ragdoll, huh? A Ragdoll is a specific breed of cat, largish with thick, soft fur, hence the name "Ragdoll," in English. The word means "stuffed toy," although admittedly it sounds close to something more risqué. There are also small breeds like the Singapura and the Munchkin. Some people call them "singers" and "munchers," but I promise it's not obscene.

Yukinoshita peeked into the classroom, then looked at the photos again. Rinse and repeat.

…*Oh, this is no good. This is not a good sign. I can see where this is going.* "Why don't you just go in?" I said, even though I knew what was about to happen.

But surprisingly, Yukinoshita shook her head disappointedly. "…There's dogs."

Oh, that's right—you've got a fear of doggos. Then that makes this a no-go, huh?

"Besides…people…would see…," Yukinoshita said with incredible embarrassment. She was blushing bright red, her head lowered.

Well, yeah, the way you coo over cats is a little off-putting, too. She isn't just like, *Aw, how cute!* She gets really into it. She's uncompromising about it. She makes it an art form, really. If people saw her doing that, her dignity as the vice-chair of the cultural committee would instantly evaporate.

This wasn't a legit pet shop, so of course, it wouldn't be the same. People were watching, too. "Well, just head out to Carrefour later, eh? If you go to the pet shop there, you could get a lot out of it."

"I know. I'm a regular."

Oh… She has all she needs…

"Then we're done here, right?" I asked.

But Yukinoshita gave no indication she was about to leave. In fact, she pointed at the door. "Records. Work."

Are you Mr. Popo? Don't talk in one-word sentences.

Anyway, Yukinoshita was very tenacious when there was a cat

involved, and it didn't look like she would budge. Obediently, I gave in and devoted myself to a little photo session. *Nice, nice, why don't you try lifting your leg there?* After a few minutes, I was freed from my duties as her errand boy.

"Come on, is there even a point in taking multiple photos of a cat?" *Well, whatever, I guess...*

Yukinoshita took the digital camera from me and began checking through it. She chuckled in satisfaction at the number of photos I'd taken under her finicky instruction from afar. Watching her, I thought it was kinda dangerous to be walking and messing with a digital camera, but she never came close to bumping into anyone because, strangely, everyone was moving in the same direction.

Ahead of us was the gym. The doors were wide-open, and beyond them I could see a fairly large crowd had gathered already. When Yukinoshita heard the cheers ahead, she returned the camera to me. "...It's just about time."

"For what?" I asked, but she didn't reply.

She marched straight on toward the gym, as if she was searching for the answer to something. Without looking back, she called my name. "Let's go, Hikigaya."

"Hm, uh-huh." Well, no matter where I went, I had my job as Records and Miscellaneous, so I had no objections. And since I was taking photos under the direction of the vice-chair herself, nobody could whine, *Hey, we can't use these!* afterward. It was easy enough, for what it was. I followed Yukinoshita through the gym doors.

The rows of folding chairs were all filled. There were lines of people standing in the back to watch, too. It was quite an audience; the event must have been announced a while ago.

"Oh, Yukinoshita. Perfect timing." One of the volunteer managers stationed in the gym came up to her. "We don't have enough chairs, and people are standing to watch. Do you think we should do some line organization?"

"I think it'll be fine."

"But won't things get noisy?"

"…It'll quiet down soon." And sure enough, just as Yukinoshita said, the chatter gradually faded away. Perhaps the audience sensed that the show was about to start, or perhaps they were awed by the high and dignified presence of the classical instruments on stage.

Before the show began, we moved to the very back with the standing audience. As we shuffled over to the far corner, there was a momentary outbreak of murmurs.

On the stage, I saw women in fancy dresses holding various musical instruments coming onto the stage one after another. Applause welled up from the audience.

The last one onstage, walking with an easy stride, was Haruno Yukinoshita.

Her long, slim dress emphasized the contours of her body, and the dark fabric fluttered with each step she took under the brilliant spotlights. Everyone who saw her was mesmerized. She wore two black rose corsages, one on her chest and one as a hair clip, beautiful even from a distance, and the glitter of pearls and sequins brought out her own radiance as a woman.

Haruno plucked up the corner of her skirt and did a graceful curtsy. Then her high-heeled feet stepped up onto the conductor's podium, where she took a baton in hand. Gently, she raised it up, then paused. All who watched her fell still at the graceful gesture.

Then she brought the baton down sharply, like a rapier. Instantly, the music was on.

The glittering brass instruments under the brilliant spotlights sent out their bursts of air, and the vibrating strings and bows created tones as sharp as arrows. No sooner had the thought occurred to me than the notes of the woodwinds stirred like the evening wind.

Haruno swiped across the air in front of her, and the violinists stood up, bowing with passion. Next, the flutists, piccoloists, oboists, and other performers behind them stood and stepped to the music without a break in the light melody. The clarinetists and bassoonists also raised their instruments high and stood up in alternation. The trumpeters and trombonists pointed upward to indicate a climactic moment, twinkling with an especially brilliant luster. The contrabassists spun their instruments around, while the timpanist twirled dramatically in time with them.

It was a spirited musical introduction, and one that seemed to contradict their classical attire. Their aggressive and dramatic choreography was unconventional, too.

The audience was shocked, like they'd suddenly been punched in the face.

But the rhythm was familiar, the melody stoked a fire inside you, and the choreography created a sense of affinity with the performers. All of it helped you get lost in the music. Before long, the whole audience was keeping rhythm on their knees.

What was this tune? I'd heard it before. It was one that concert bands tend to do a lot…

Right as the answer reached the tip of my tongue, suddenly Haruno raised her hands high and waved them in large motions from side to side. That gesture didn't match the harmony of the orchestra, and attention gathered on her hands. Her thin, long fingers were counting down.

Then a familiar phrase reached our ears. Everyone in the venue had to have recognized the song. Haruno faced sideways once more and arched her back. Baton toward the performers, her free hand toward the audience, she waved energetically.

At that signal, everyone onstage and in the audience leaped up, yelling, "Mambo!"

Still burning with enthusiasm, the performance plunged forward. One more time, the call came in like a raging wave: "Mambo!"

It didn't seem like it had been years since they'd last performed. Not at all. I'd thought the alumni had retired from playing with orchestras, like Haruno had, but under her conducting, they were creating an incredibly vivid performance. They had the audience worked up like what you'd see in a club or a live music bar. It was like they were pulling the audience into their inner circle, almost winning them over against their will. And what let the audience get sucked in was the practiced talent of the orchestra and of the conductor, Haruno Yukinoshita.

We were at the very corner of the standing audience, and that was why I could observe it all calmly. If I'd been in the middle, it probably would've been horrible. I probably would have obliviously stayed in my chair, and then people would have glared at me about it afterward.

The orchestra was still sprinting toward the finale.

"…ess." I heard a murmur beside me, so quiet it was nearly erased by the impressive performance.

"Huh?" I hadn't been able to hear most of what she'd said, so I tilted my head a bit, pointing my ear toward her.

Yukinoshita inched her body just a bit closer and moved her lips in toward me. "I said, I'd expect no less." The whisper amid the sea of sound told me we were close in the darkness. Her clean scent wafted toward me, and I reflexively withdrew.

Then I reconsidered and moved just half a step closer. *It's okay. As long as her face isn't too close, I won't get too nervous.* "I'm surprised to hear you complimenting her."

"…Oh? I may not seem like it, but I do think highly of my sister." Now that we were closer, it was easier for us to hear each other. But her next remark was so quiet, I nearly missed it. "Because I once felt I wanted to be like her." Her eyes were fixed on the stage. Up there was Haruno, wielding her baton as freely and magnificently as a sword dancer.

The conductor's podium was a step above the stage. That place, underneath the spotlight, was right where Haruno belonged.

"…You don't have to. Just stay like you are," I quietly replied.

Maybe my words were drowned out by the applause and cheers from the audience, because Yukinoshita didn't reply.

**And so the curtain rises
on each stage.**

I changed the batteries in the camera installed on the gym catwalk and checked the space left on the memory card. Recording the volunteer groups' performances was another part of Records and Miscellaneous's duties. We'd even have to edit the video files later in Final Cut Pro or whatever that program was on the student council's Mac. They'd taught me the basics, but it was a perpetual pain in the ass, and a Windows guy like me was never gonna get a Mac to work right anyway. The most I could do was stick in some captions.

We sure had a lot of equipment, though, including the Mac and Final Cut Pro. They must have bought it with the school's money, since the camera was apparently a pretty good one, and the mike was properly sensitive. I touched the display to check that everything was good and ready to record.

Once I was done, next I had to prep for the ending ceremony. Unlike the previous day, all I had to do this time were odd jobs, which was a load off my mind.

I came down from the catwalk into the stage wings. The volunteer group that came right before the ending ceremony, the last performance, was Hayama's band. Preparations had begun backstage for the ceremony, which meant the stage wings were packed with people.

"Urk... Aw, oh man, I'm getting nervous." Miura was hanging her head, looking haggard. She was apparently in this volunteer band, too. Looking around at the others, I saw Hayama strumming his guitar with the cable unplugged, warming up. Tobe was smacking invisible drums with a pair of drumsticks. The other one, Yamato, was frozen with a bass in his hands. Ooka was staring at the keyboard onstage with intense concentration.

The only one who seemed calm was Hayama, and the others were all pretty close to the breaking point. Tobe was swinging his head around more than the drumsticks.

Some people were loitering with the band members, too.

"Ummm, stage drinks… Oh! I guess they'd be easier to drink with straws."

"Yui, with these things, if you stick this right into the cap and wiggle it around, it makes the perfect hole. Then you stick the straw in here."

"Huh? Wow, Hina!"

Are you guys their assistants now?

Once enough headsets had been charged up for everyone, Yukinoshita started scuttling here and there. It was getting extremely annoying.

"Do you need something?" I asked her.

Startled, Yukinoshita answered with a question of her own. "Hey… where's Sagami?"

I looked around. I actually didn't recall seeing her.

"I wanted to have one final meeting with her before the ending ceremony…"

"I'll try calling her." Meguri dialed her cell, but after a few moments, her expression turned grave. "…It says she's either out of range, or her phone is turned off." She repeated the automated message word for word. "I'll go ask some of the others." Meguri made a string of phone calls, but she just couldn't pin down Sagami. She sighed, then spoke into thin air. "Are you there, guys?"

"Right here." All of a sudden, student council members appeared from behind the drop curtain.

Are you guys ninjas? Or assassins?

"Could you look for Sagami for me?" Meguri asked. "I'd appreciate it if you could keep regular contact with me as you do, too."

"Aye, madam."

Seriously, are you ninjas?

The search began with the full might of the student council. But even the ninja masters could only track up to where she'd been around noon. After that, they couldn't find a trace. The trail just suddenly ended.

Once Hayama's group's upcoming performance was done, we'd immediately be starting the ending ceremony. If you took into account the checks and prep beforehand, we didn't have much time.

Yukinoshita folded her arms and squeezed her eyes shut. When Yuigahama noticed, she trotted over to her. "What's up, Yukinon?"

"Do you know where Sagami is?" Yukinoshita asked.

Yuigahama tilted her head. "I dunno. I haven't seen her... Do you need her here?" Yukinoshita nodded, and Yuigahama pulled out her phone. "Hmm, I'll try asking around." Yuigahama stepped away to go make a phone call.

I kept Yuigahama in my field of vision as I made another suggestion to Yukinoshita. "Why not just make an announcement on the intercom?"

"Yes, of course." Yukinoshita contacted the broadcast room and had them do a school-wide announcement, but there was no response at all.

"Yukinoshita." Miss Hiratsuka must have heard the announcement, as she'd quietly come around from the back entrance. "Has Sagami shown up?"

Yukinoshita shook her head.

"...I see. Because of the announcement, the teachers have a general grasp of the situation as well, so if they find her, I think they'll contact you, but..." The teacher's expression was grim. In a roundabout way, she was saying, *Don't expect much.*

The audience was burning with enthusiasm, but the temperature backstage had dropped all at once. The more time passed, the more serious an issue the Cultural Festival Committee chair's absence was becoming.

"This isn't good," said Yukinoshita. "At this rate, we won't be able to hold the ending ceremony."

"You're right…" Meguri nodded, somewhat at a loss.

Concerned about their grim expressions, Yuigahama asked, "Does Sagamin have to be here?"

"Yes," said Yukinoshita. "Greetings, general comments, and the presentation of awards are all a part of her role." Those had always been the job of the committee chair, year after year. No matter what was going on with Sagami, the role assigned to her was not going to change.

"Worst case…we could replace her…" Meguri offered an alternative plan. In that case, it would be either Meguri herself or Yukinoshita taking her place. Considering their positions, either one could be justified in taking up the role. But, well, it would still be awkward.

But Yukinoshita nipped that proposition in the bud. "I think that would be a bad idea. Sagami is the only one who knows the results of the merit award and the regional award vote." Everyone in the conference room had worked on the tally in turns, whenever needed. So though everyone had a fragmentary understanding of the numbers, only Sagami, who had consolidated the final results, knew what those results were.

"Then we could put off the presentation of award results until tomorrow?" I said.

Yukinoshita nodded, but her expression remained severe. "In the worst-case scenario. But if we don't announce the regional award now, I don't think there would be much point." The cultural festival was emphasizing regional ties. It wouldn't be appropriate for the award to be presented a day late on the very year that award had been established.

Whatever the case, we still had to find Sagami. But we still couldn't get ahold of her, and we hadn't tracked down her whereabouts, either.

Yukinoshita bit her lip hard.

"Is something wrong?" Hayama asked, looking calm even though he was about to go onstage. He must have sensed the unrest.

"Yes. We can't find Sagami..." Meguri explained the situation to Hayama.

Hayama immediately moved into action. "Vice-chair, I'd like to request a change in the program. Could you let us add one more song to our act? ...We don't have much time, so verbal agreement is enough, right?"

"Can you do that?" asked Yukinoshita.

"Yeah... Yumiko, can you play and sing for one more song?"

"Huh? Another song? Seriously? No, no, no way, no way! I just can't! I'm totally freaking out right now!" Miura was so tense that the question truly startled her.

"Please." But then Hayama smiled at her, and she moaned hopelessly. Dropping her head into her hands, she groaned again. It was kinda cute.

Yukinoshita took one step toward the agonizing Miura. "...I'm swallowing my pride to ask this of you. I'd be grateful."

"Agh...this is unbelievable, seriously..." Miura sighed in resignation and lifted her head to glower at Yukinoshita. "It's not like I'm doing this for you." That wasn't an attempt to cover up some embarrassment; the hostility was genuine. She spun on her heel and marched off in the other direction. "Come on. Tobe, Ooka, Yamato. Stand by." She whapped each one of them on their heads and swished out onto the stage.

Behind her, the three stooges were going, "For real?" and "Oh man," and "You're kidding me!" but still obediently followed her.

The four of them went on standby for the performance, and the Volunteer Management section leaped into action. They double-checked where each person would be at each point in time and prepared for the extra song in a flurry of activity.

Meanwhile, Hayama had pulled out his phone and was swiftly

contacting various people. I doubted he was just sending simple texts. He had to be working a mailing list or SNS or Facebook or LINE or whatever. After a bunch of typing, he made a few phone calls, too. Once he was finished, he sighed.

"...Thank you," said Yukinoshita.

"Don't worry about it. I want us to look good today, too. Anyway... we can buy you ten minutes with the extra performance. You have to find her before then."

"All right."

"..."

He could buy us ten minutes, huh? If Sagami wasn't answering her phone or responding to the announcement, then she'd been intending to bail all along. It would be impossible to find someone who wanted to hide in such a short period of time.

"I'll go look for her."

Yuigahama tried to leave, but I stopped her.

"If you just search for her at random, you're not gonna find her."

Meguri had already deployed the student council for the hunt. We'd made use of a bunch of connections already. But we still couldn't locate her. I doubted Yuigahama would come across Sagami if she were to go out right then to look.

So it would be more constructive to consider her gone and use the time Hayama had bought us to make our next move. "It'd probably be fastest to have someone else go up and just make up the prize results. The poll numbers aren't publicized anyway," I said.

Everyone seemed shocked.

"Hikigaya..."

"Really..."

"That's a little much..."

"I'm not sure if that's a good idea..."

Miss Hiratsuka, Meguri, Yuigahama, and Hayama of the "good sense" faction expressed their dissent.

...No go, huh? I thought I'd suggested a pretty realistic plan there, though.

Yukinoshita, the one you'd think would be the first one to reject my ideas at a time like this, remained silent. Curious, I looked over and saw her hand was over her mouth. Apparently, she'd been mulling over something this whole time. "…Hikigaya."

"What?" She'd been deliberating long enough that I was now anxious about what horrible insults she would throw at me.

But she looked me straight in the eye. "If we buy another ten more minutes, can you find her?"

"I dunno…" I explored the possibility a little. Miura's group was right about to go onstage. They could only do one extra song. Best-case scenario, they could do a little MCing before and after their songs. Then there was the time it took them to leave the stage, and the time the audience would be able to wait in silence for the ending ceremony. Also, something unforeseen could happen that would shave off some time.

Taking all these things into consideration, Miura's band could entertain the crowd for seven or eight minutes from now. Adding another ten minutes onto that would mean in actuality that they could hold on for a little over fifteen minutes. On foot from the gym, I could go search one place at most. If Sagami had left the school grounds, then we were out. I had no choice but to make my guess and bet on that one chance.

"…All I can say is, I don't know."

"I see. You're not saying it's impossible, then. That's enough." Despite my vague answer, Yukinoshita's reply was clear. She got out her cell phone and took a deep breath. Steeling herself, she made a call. Eyes closed, she waited for the person to pick up. After a few seconds, her eyes flew open. "Haruno? Come to the stage wings now."

How would she buy ten more minutes? Yukinoshita had found the answer.

× × ×

Not long after Yukinoshita's call, the recipient showed up. "Heya, Yukino-chan. What is it? I do want to see Hayato's band, and they're about to go onstage." Haruno Yukinoshita's smile was overflowing with so much self-assurance, it was scary. Apparently, she'd been watching the volunteer bands this whole time. There had been no need to go to the trouble of phoning her, as she'd been surprisingly close by.

Yukinoshita ignored Haruno's complaint and got straight to business. "You need to help, Haruno." Her statement was so direct, Haruno's eyes changed color. Without a word, she regarded Yukinoshita coldly. But Yukinoshita did not avert her eyes; she glared back at Haruno with strengthening determination.

The place where their gazes met was quiet and horribly chilly. It was freezing the air itself around them, like liquid nitrogen had spilled.

Haruno's icy smile split into a giggle. "Oh? All right. Since this is the first time you've actually requested something from me, I'll *graciously* hear your request," she said haughtily. Even if she was acting merciful, nothing about her reply was kind. It was even sharper than a flat refusal.

But Yukinoshita tilted her head at that. Then suddenly, she smiled a little. "Request? Don't misunderstand me. This is an *order*, as a committee member. Didn't you see the organization chart? You should know that according to the chain of command, I have the authority here. You're obligated to cooperate as the representative of a volunteer group—even if you're not part of this school," Yukinoshita retorted with absolute confidence. Arrogant to the last. Even though she was the one who needed something from Haruno, she wouldn't back down from her position of superiority.

It suddenly reminded me of who she'd been six months earlier. Never pandering to anyone, cutting down opposition with the blade of her sense of justice: That was Yukino Yukinoshita.

For her part, Haruno Yukinoshita chuckled and smiled with sincere glee. "So is there any penalty if I reject this duty? You have no power to compel me to do this, do you? It's too late to disqualify me from performing. So what'll you do? Tell on me to the teacher?" She just giggled. She was ridiculing Yukinoshita's righteousness, calling it a childish morality that never works in the real world.

Haruno was being completely realistic, which was exactly why you couldn't argue with her. Yukinoshita was talking about how things *should* be, based on principles. A best-case scenario. It was fair to describe her argument as idealistic. When it came right down to it, that wouldn't mesh with Haruno's realistic approach.

Oh, this isn't good. Yukinoshita was at a bit of a disadvantage. If you want to oppose a realist, that's a job for a nihilist like me. I was about to step in when Yukinoshita sensed this and quietly restrained me with a hand. Then she turned her head slightly and smiled gently.

With that one expression, she told me it was okay—she could be strong.

She turned back to Haruno and spoke again, with more force. "There would be no penalty...but you would benefit from cooperating."

"How, exactly?" Haruno chuckled as if she found this all quite amusing.

Yukinoshita brushed aside the pressure from Haruno's beautifully twisted grin and put her hand to her own chest. "You'll earn a favor from me. It's up to you how you take that," she declared.

Haruno froze in place. "Hmm..." She wasn't smirking anymore. She was just staring at Yukinoshita with a cold look. "You've grown, Yukino-chan."

"No." Yukinoshita smiled back at her. "I've always been like this. Haven't you noticed after seventeen years together?"

"Oh..." After a brief reply, Haruno quickly narrowed her eyes. The expression prevented me from easily reading the intent behind it.

"...Ha." In spite of myself, I laughed.

"...What?" Yukinoshita demanded.

"Nothing..."

Yukinoshita glared at me, and I laughed again.

Yeah, this is exactly it. This is who Yukino Yukinoshita is.

Haruno folded her arms to collect herself. The gesture made her look a lot like her little sister. "So what do you plan to do?"

"We're going to buy some more time," Yukinoshita replied briefly, but that wasn't an answer.

Frowning slightly, Haruno asked another question. "But how?"

"With me, you…and two others, we'll manage. If possible, one more." Yukinoshita glanced over to the greenroom by the stage wings. It gave me a general idea of what she planned to do.

"Hey, Yukinoshita, are you serious?" I blurted in surprise.

Like me, Haruno must have seen through her in a glance, because she smirked. "Oh, that's a fun idea. So what song?"

"We won't be able to practice, so we have no choice but to do something we already know. Can you still play that song you did before at your cultural festival?" Yukinoshita asked.

Haruno showed us she could still sing whatever that song was. I guess I should say I was impressed, but not surprised. She was just humming, but I ended up lost in the music.

Yuigahama went, "Ohhh, that song," too, impressed and entranced. If even I knew that song, of course Yuigahama would have known it.

After Haruno finished her casual rendition, she grinned boldly. "Just who do you think you're talking to? What about you, Yukino-chan? Can you do it?"

"I can do just about anything you've ever done."

…*She must have been practicing in secret.*

When Haruno heard that, she nodded. "I see. Then we just need one more person, and we'll be good to go," she said.

We all looked at one another. *Hey, hey, just a moment ago, you said you needed two more, right? This is an issue even more basic than failing simple addition…* Or so I thought, when I heard a very large sigh close by.

Then Haruno called the source of that sigh by name. "Shizuka-chan."

"…Guess I've got no choice," said Miss Hiratsuka. "I'll play the bass. I think I could still play that song I did with you before."

Oh yeah. When I saw Miss Hiratsuka during summer vacation, she mentioned how Haruno made her play in a band for the cultural festival or something like that…

Then Haruno spun around and said, "Meguri, you can do a backup keyboard, right?"

"Yes! Leave it to me!" Meguri replied with energy, both her hands balled into determined fists. Not only had she seen Haruno perform live before, she was older than us and accustomed to standing up in front of a crowd. There was no hesitation in her reply.

"So now I guess we just need vocals, huh?" said Haruno.

Expression brooding, Yukinoshita said quietly, "…Yuigahama."

"Wha—?!" Yuigahama must not have been expecting to hear her own name as a part of this. A genuine and rather amusing yelp of surprise left her mouth.

Yukinoshita took one step in to stand close to her. "Could I rely on you for this?"

"Uh, um… Er, I don't feel very confident about it… I don't think I could probably do it very well, and I might actually just make the whole thing worse, to be honest…" Yuigahama touched her index fingers together, looking away and mumbling in embarrassment.

But…

After she trailed off, she squeezed Yukinoshita's hand tight. "I've… been waiting for you to say that to me."

Yukinoshita squeezed back delicately. "…Thank you."

"It's okay. B-but…I don't completely remember the lyrics, you know?! For all intensive purposes."

"It's *all intents and purposes*. The fact that you can't even say that right makes me somewhat uneasy."

"That was a little mean, Yukinon!" Yuigahama protested, giving Yukinoshita's hand a little shake.

Yukinoshita broke into a smile. "I'm joking. If you feel you're in trouble, I'll sing, too. So, um, I don't mind…if you rely…on me…" Yukinoshita was blushing hard enough even I could see it in the darkness of the stage wings.

Yuigahama replied with a bright smile. "…Yeah!"

I watched them, then quietly headed from the backstage area to the door connecting to the gym exit. Silently, surreptitiously, I set into action.

"Hikigaya." An unexpected voice came from behind me. "Best of luck."

"You can do it, Hikki!"

I didn't reply to either of them with words.

My only response was a carelessly raised hand as I continued on out the door.

All right, this is my time now. The next ten minutes are up to me.

Onstage, under a spotlight, was not where I belonged.

My stage was an empty path out a dark exit.

A stage for one—Hachiman Hikigaya.

×   ×   ×

The gymnasium exit connected directly to the school building.

School tradition said that every year, the volunteer band expected to draw the biggest audience would be slotted for the last performance. This slightly atypical program would allow them to transition straight into the ending ceremony. It was the most efficient way to move students into the gym.

In other words, right now, there were only a handful of people scattered around the school building.

Either way, it was about time for the ending ceremony, which meant a lot of people would be going to the volunteer concerts to have one last big whoop with everyone else.

The lack of people was convenient. It meant that anyone else out here would catch my attention, even from a distance. You could say the conditions were favorable for tracking down Sagami.

But I still wouldn't be able to visit more than one place. My time was limited. I didn't even have the time to check the clock.

You can't slow down time. You can't move any faster than your own physical limits, either. So the only thing you *can* accelerate is your thoughts.

Think.

Any loner should take pride in their capacity for deep thinking. We use resources that would typically be diverted to interpersonal relations on ourselves, and all that introspecting, reflecting, regretting,

fantasizing, and imagining and daydreaming ultimately leads us to ideology and philosophy.

I would expend all those useless powers of thought to explore every possibility, to disprove and reject any conclusions I could. And then, among the ideas I couldn't reject entirely, I would do my utmost to substantiate them, just like how I do when I'm speaking in defense of myself.

Criticizing others and defending himself are Hachiman Hikigaya's greatest talents.

I just had to do that over and over, and the answer would emerge on its own.

It was simple. Sagami had to be alone right at that moment. So then all I had to do was trace the loner thought processes.

When it comes to lonerdom, I'm not just one cut above her; I'm about a thousand cuts above. I didn't start this gig yesterday. I'm a veteran. Don't you underestimate me.

Sagami is self-conscious; I'm sure of it. When she was in her first year, she was in the A-group, and she got used to being at the top of the heap. But ever since the second year, the presence of Miura and her clique had pushed her down the totem pole. That couldn't have been pleasant for her to swallow. But despite this, Sagami couldn't do anything herself to change the sense of her social class.

So that was exactly why she would seek out people lower on the social ladder than she was. She would try to stand at the top of the B-group, at least. And she had managed that. But once you've experienced the upper-class lifestyle, it's hard to take when it goes down. So she had to satisfy herself with something else.

And then came this cultural festival.

Would the position of chair of the cultural committee have been enough to fulfill her desires? Yes. She'd joined the committee under Hayama's recommendation, and once Sagami was committee chair, even the legendary Haruno Yukinoshita had praised her. Sagami had also gained talented help for the job itself in Yukino Yukinoshita.

But then what would happen when that didn't go well, either? What if Sagami was unable to get what she wanted, and even her alternative fell through unexpectedly? As a member of the committee, she hadn't been able to help with the class project like she'd wanted to. Her discontent had led her to go help anyway, while someone else worked with the committee instead of Sagami—or rather, someone else had fulfilled that role even better than she had. And to make it worse, even Hayama and Haruno, who had given Sagami her confidence boost in the first place, ended up preferring the substitute.

So what about Sagami's pride, her self-conceit, her self-consciousness?

Her woes were quite clear to me. I'd been down that road, too. *You're naive, Sagami. That's a path I know.*

I remember skipping school, wandering around by myself, then getting found and reported to the school and everyone finding out. Back then, my unmanageable, hopeless self-consciousness had exploded, and all I'd wanted was for someone to look at me.

That's why I get it. I know what you want to do. And I know what you want everyone else to do for you. And what you don't want us to do.

You're five years late. I already went through all that back in elementary school.

I can predict where you'll go.

What does someone who has lost a place to belong want? For someone to find that place for them. If you can't seek it out with your own eyes, you have to get help. I just had to apply the principle to my own mental map.

Sagami wanted people to look for her, and she wanted to be found, so she'd be on school grounds. And it'd be somewhere noticeable, too. She wouldn't have shut herself up in an empty classroom, and neither would she lock herself in anywhere.

And one more thing: She'd be somewhere she could be alone. If she became lost in the crowd, then she really would be unfindable. If she had come to feel her own worthlessness, she would already be well aware of how it felt to vanish into a group.

She wouldn't go anywhere she couldn't physically enter, either. From a psychological perspective, she couldn't be too far away.

So what else was left? There were still too many options. I needed a little more to substantiate something, or maybe just rule out some options.

If her self-consciousness had run amok, then I had one more case to examine, aside from my past self.

To follow that lead, I pulled out my cell phone. I guess it was kinda sad… I just called the most recent number in my call history.

"'Tis I."

He freaking picked up before it even rang. *I'd expect nothing less of you, Zaimokuza.* All that goofing around on his phone when he has nothing to do has borne fruit. I'd have liked to commend him for it, but unfortunately, I had no time. Quickly, I asked my question: "Zaimokuza, where are you usually at school when you're alone?"

"Oh, 'tis such an unheralded call! Ba-herm, I am ever in suspend mode—"

"Just answer me. I'm in a hurry."

"…You're serious?"

"Tch. I'm hanging up."

"Wait, wait, wait, waaait please! The veranda by the nurse's office! I'm also in the library a lot! Or on top of the special building." There were people in the nurse's office, and the classes were all using the veranda. The library was locked, too, so you couldn't get in.

On top of the special building… The roof?

"If you're looking for empty spots," he added, "there's the space between the new building and the club tower, I guess. It's shady and cool. And quiet. Just right for meditation… Are you looking for someone?"

"Yeah, the cultural committee chair."

"Oh, the one who made those opening remarks. It seems you are in need of my aid…"

"You'll help out?"

"I have no choice. Where should I look?"

"Around the new building. Thanks! Love ya, Zaimokuza!"

"Aye. As do I!"

"Shut up, creep!" I smacked the call closed.

If she was on the roof, I had an idea about that.

I booked it toward my own classroom. The empty hallway served as a comfortable racetrack. But the lack of people increased the chances that the one I was looking for would also not be there.

Please be there… I dashed up the stairs, practically praying, but fortunately, I caught sight of my target sitting on a folding chair right in front of our classroom. Her bluish-black ponytail drooping moodily and her long legs crossed, she was languidly gazing out the hallway window.

I desperately tried to hide my panting as I called out to her. "Kawasaki…"

"What are you breathing so hard for? I thought you were with the cultural committee?"

I wasn't going to respond to Kawasaki's teasing or her question. "You've been on the roof before, right?"

"Huh? What're you talking about? This is random."

"Just tell me." We didn't have much time, and my impatient reply came out harsher than I had intended.

"Y-you don't have to get so m-mad…" Tears welled in her eyes, and she started fidgeting a little.

I let out a slow breath in order to calm myself somewhat. "I'm not mad. I'm just kind of in a hurry with some committee stuff."

"A-all right, then…" She breathed a sigh of relief.

She's surprisingly sensitive. Oh, no, no, think about the roof right now. "So you were up on the roof before, right? How did you get up there?"

"I'm surprised you remember that…," Kawasaki muttered softly as if it were a fond memory. She caught me in her gaze shyly.

…I told you, I'm in a hurry.

The thought must have shown on my face. Flustered, she got back on topic. "U-um, the lock on the door from the central staircase is broken. A lot of the girls know about it."

Really. So Sagami should know about it, too. That was consistent with the other condition for a location she'd go to: that other people would be familiar with it.

Whatever the case, I had no more time. As this point, it was the most likely suspect.

"So what about it?" Kawasaki asked. She seemed puzzled at my silence. But my feet were moving before I could reply.

But I still had to thank her, at least, even if I was in a hurry. "Thanks! Love ya, Kawasaki!" I yelled over my shoulder as I sprinted off as fast as I could.

As I turned the corner in the hallway, I heard an earth-shattering shriek behind me.

×   ×   ×

The stairs leading to the roof had been used as storage space for the cultural festival, so it was hard to run up them. But there was enough space for a person to squeeze through. Sagami had probably made her way along this same trail through those little gaps. With each step I took in pursuit, the more sure I felt that I was getting closer.

I was positive that Sagami wanted to become like Yukinoshita or Yuigahama: someone who would be recognized, wanted, and trusted. That was why she'd gone for an instant title. She had wanted to affix the label of *chair* to her chest for the sake of the prestige. Then she could label others from her lofty high horse, too, and affirm her own superiority.

That was the truth of the "growth" Sagami had talked about.

But that's not what growth is. You can't cheat and call facile change some sort of maturity.

I hate it when people call something "growth" when it's just a minor shift or a compromise to end the discussion. I hate it when at the end of the road, people give up and then pass that off as "becoming an adult." No one's going to change dramatically overnight or in just a few months. People aren't Transformers.

If you could just become the kind of person you wanted to be, I wouldn't be like this.

Changing yourself and changing others, having changed and having *to* change.

It's all lies.

How could you so easily accept that the way you are now is wrong? Why would you reject the person you used to be? How come you can't just accept who you are now? How can you believe in someone you haven't even become yet?

If I can't be okay with the disgusting person I used to be and the person I am now at rock bottom, then when the hell can I accept anyone? Can you even accept the person you're going to be when you've rejected both who you are now and who you've been all your life?

Don't expect to mature just by throwing your past away and overwriting everything about yourself.

Don't you dare call it growth when you're making it all about the title, crowing over a little recognition, getting drunk on your status, crying out about how important you are from within the shackles of rules you created yourself, all the while oblivious to the world until someone teaches you about it.

Why can't you just say you don't have to change? That you're fine as you are?

The farther I climbed up the stairs to the roof, the fewer obstacles I saw. Eventually, I reached an open landing, the end point. Beyond this door was the end of the line.

Hide-and-seek was over.

× × ×

Just as Kawasaki had said, the padlock on the doors was broken and hanging from the door handles. I messed with it a bit. When it was closed, the doors appeared locked, but a good yank would bust it open. This would make trespassing on the roof easy…

A little rust flaked off, and the door opened, hanging a little askew. It creaked loudly.

Wind whooshed in as blue skies opened before me. Since I was higher up, you'd think I was closer to the sky, but the lack of any reference point just made it feel farther away than usual.

Sagami was leaning against the fence, looking in my direction. Her expression turned to surprise, then disappointment.

No shocker there. She couldn't have been waiting for me to come searching. In fact, she must have wanted someone like me to *not* look for her. On that point, while I was sorry for failing to meet her expectations, I hadn't exactly wanted to come pick her up, either. I hoped she could let it slide, and we'd call it even.

Anyhow, in our current circumstances, we were approaching this from similar angles. So we could start this conversation on equal terms.

"The ending ceremony is about to start, so go head back." I told her briefly only what I'd come for.

She drew her brows together, unhappy. "It's not like I really have to be the one to do that, right?" she said, turning her back to me to indicate she didn't really want to talk.

"Unfortunately, you actually do, for a couple of reasons. There's not much time. It'd help if you'd hurry it up." I think I'm pretty shit at convincing people, if I do say so myself. But though it might not have seemed like it, I was actually meticulously avoiding the words Sagami wanted to hear.

"Not much time— Wait, hasn't the ending ceremony already started?"

So she knew. It annoyed me a little. "Yeah, normally, it would have. But we're managing to buy some time. So."

"Hmm. Who's doing that?"

"Um…oh yeah. Miura. Yukinoshita and some others," I replied. But Miura's band would probably already have been done performing by this point. It was about time for Yukinoshita's band to go on standby.

Sagami clutched the fence tight. "Oh…"

"Now you know, so you should go back."

"Then Yukinoshita should just handle it. She can do anything anyway."

"What? That's not the issue here. You've got the vote results. You have to announce those, and a bunch of other stuff, too." As I'd predicted would happen, Sagami and all her obnoxious replies were getting on my nerves. But I didn't have the time to be spending on this conversation.

"They can just recount the tally results. It's not that much if you all worked on it together…"

"We can't. None of us have that kind of time right now."

"Then just take the vote results and go!" The chain link fence shook as Sagami hurled the paper with the tally at me.

For an instant, I actually thought about just taking the paper.

But I couldn't do that.

The request that Yukinoshita and the Service Club had accepted was to support Sagami in her job as committee chair. In other words, it was to ensure that Minami Sagami fulfilled her obligations. If not for that request, I wouldn't be there right now, and Yukinoshita wouldn't have become the vice-chair, either. To abandon the request would be to deny all that Yukino Yukinoshita had done.

That was why my job was to make Minami Sagami attend the ending ceremony and stand up on that stage as committee chair, to give her the honor of being the chair, and also to make sure she would experience the associated frustration and regret.

So what would I have to do to accomplish that?

If I could get Sagami to hear what she wanted to hear, from the person she wanted to hear it from, that would be enough. But unfortunately, I couldn't do that.

I could keep on talking with her, but she was stubborn. I doubted she would budge.

Should I let someone else know she was here and have them come? But who? My contacts included Yuigahama and Miss Hiratsuka, who would be onstage by then, and I got the feeling that calling Totsuka or

Zaimokuza wouldn't change much. I never would have imagined that my lone-wolf lifestyle would backfire on me at a time like this.

So I got this far, only to reach a stalemate, huh...? I unconsciously balled my hands into fists with aggravation.

That was when it happened.

A loud creak. I turned to look, and Sagami probably did, too.

"Here you are... We've been looking for you." Coming through the door was Hayato Hayama.

Behind him were Sagami's two cultural committee friends. Hayama had probably brought them here.

"Hayama... Guys..." Sagami said Hayama's name, then gently looked away. This was probably what Sagami had actually wanted. What she'd hoped for.

Hayama continued to fulfill those hopes, taking one step forward, then another. "We couldn't get ahold of you, so we were worried. We were asking around everywhere, and then a first-year told us they'd seen you go up the stairs."

So Hayama had done what Hayama did best and made use of his personal connections to trace that thin thread here. All I could say was *Impressive as always.*

Despite all Hayama had done to get to her, Sagami was still digging in her heels. "I'm sorry, but..."

"Let's go back now, okay? Everyone's waiting. 'Kay?"

"That's right!"

"They're all worried," her friends added.

Hayama also knew full well that there was no time, and he earnestly told Sagami what she wanted to hear in an attempt to convince her. As you might expect, all three of them working on her at once would wear her down. She took her friend's hand, and they shared a moment of mutual warmth.

But that still wasn't enough.

"But it's too late to go back now...," she moaned.

"No way, everyone's waiting for you," said one girl.

"Let's go together, okay?" said the other.

Hayama watched their exchange, but just for a second, his gaze flicked to his wristwatch. He was impatient, too. "That's right. Everyone's really trying to make this work for you, Sagami." He knew he didn't have her convinced; this wasn't just extra prodding. He was using everything at his disposal to try to win her over.

"But...I've caused a lot of trouble, so I don't know how I'd even face everyone..." Surrounded by her friends, Sagami's eyes watered, and she sobbed. They all attempted to soothe her, but Sagami's feet didn't move. The only thing moving here was the needle on the clock.

Same results, even with Hayama here, huh...?

The seconds were ticking away.

Our time was almost up. What was the fastest and most efficient way to get her going?

Force her?

No.

That might have been possible if it were just me and Hayama. But the two girls would definitely have stopped me. That would clearly just lose us time.

Besides.

That wasn't the way Yukinoshita would have wanted it done. Ultimately, I had to get Sagami to walk out of there on her own two feet.

Yukinoshita has her own way of doing things, and she's always stuck to it: meeting things head-on, holding on to her pride while demonstrating her abilities to the fullest.

So then, I...

I suppose I have no choice but to stick to mine.

Meeting things spinelessly, crassly, and spitefully. Fair and square.

What would I have to do to get some actual communication going with Sagami?

There are only two ways people at the bottom can communicate with each other: They can lick each other's wounds, or they can drag each other down.

I had one option.

I took a good look at Sagami and Hayama.

Hayama was still encouraging her, kindly, in an attempt to somehow urge her along, baby step by baby step. "It's okay. Let's go back."

"I'm such garbage…," Sagami spit in self-loathing, and her feet stopped again.

That meant this was the moment. *Good grief. I honestly disgust myself—both for always coming up with ideas like this and for not actually hating that I do it. Aghhhh.* I blew out a deep, long sigh of irritation.

"You really are."

No one moved, and no one spoke.

Four pairs of eyes gathered on me. An audience of four.

A great turnout, for me.

"Sagami, you ultimately just want people fawning over you. You're doing all this for attention, aren't you? And what you really want right now is for someone to tell you, *No, that's not true!* It's no wonder no one treats someone like *you* as the committee chair. You really *are* garbage."

"What are you talking—?" Her voice was trembling.

But I cut her off. "I'm sure they've all figured it out. I don't even know you, and I can tell."

"Don't act like I'm anything like you—"

"You're just like me. We live together in the lowest tier."

Sagami's eyes weren't wet anymore. They were bone-dry, burning with hatred.

I chose my words carefully to build a solid argument. Everything so far had just been what I saw from my subjective experience. All that could do was anger her. "Think about it," I continued. "I don't give the slightest damn about you, and yet, I'm the one who managed to find you first." It was stating *objective* facts that would get things going. "Which means…nobody was really looking for you in earnest."

Sagami's face paled. The color from her anger and hate faded, and shock and despair took their place. Her mixed-up feelings forgot how to express themselves, and all she could do to show them was bite her lip in pain.

"You get it, don't you? That's all you—," I began, but I was cut off. The words were replaced by a wheezing noise from my throat.

"Hikigaya, stop talking." Hayama's right hand was clenched around my collar where he had shoved me into the wall. The shock of the impact had knocked the breath out of me.

"...*Ha!*" I pasted on a desperate smile to cover up how he'd winded me. Hayama's fist gripping my collar shook. He sucked in a shallow breath and blew out a deep one in an attempt to calm himself. For a few seconds, we glared at each other.

As the tension shattered, the girls began to move again and rushed in to stop him.

"H-Hayama! That's enough! Just leave him. Let's go, okay? ...Okay?" Sagami put her hand on Hayama's back.

At that, Hayama expelled one last great sigh and turned around, letting go of my collar. He avoided looking at my face. "...Let's get going," he prompted the others, his tone calm.

Her two friends surrounding her like a convoy, Sagami left the roof.

As they went, the girls conversed as if they wanted me to hear. "Are you okay, Sagamin?"

"Let's just go, okay?"

"And wow, who was that? Wasn't that mean?"

"I dunno. What was that?"

The three of them left, and at the end, Hayama began to close the door behind him. "...Why is that the only way you can manage things?" he muttered, as if to himself. His words stung.

Alone on the roof, I leaned my back against the wall and slid down onto my butt.

The sky was clear and far.

It's a good thing you're a really cool, good guy, Hayama. If he hadn't gotten mad, he wouldn't be Hayato Hayama. *It's a good thing you won't let it go when someone's getting hurt in front of you. It's a good thing you won't let someone hurt others.*

Look, it's easy—a world where no one gets hurt is complete.

Hayama was probably right, and this way of doing things was wrong.

But right now, this is all I can do.

But I think that even I will change someday. I'm sure it's inevitable. Something will change me. No matter what I want, the way others see and understand and appraise me is sure to change. If everything is in constant flux and the world is always changing, then the world around me, my environment, the standards of judgment themselves will distort into something with it, changing the way I am along with it.

So that's why.

—That's why I don't change.

"Agh…" I breathed a deep, deep sigh.

…It was about time for the ending ceremony.

I sent a short e-mail that read *Resolved* to Zaimokuza and forced my heavy body up to leave the roof.

×   ×   ×

I hurried automatically toward the gym. It wasn't that I needed to know how things had gone. Frankly speaking, I really didn't care what happened to Sagami.

It was that the attention of the people in the hallways was all directed toward the gym.

The low-frequency bass reached all the way into the hall, encouraging both students and guests to instinctively seek out its source. Their feet were carrying them to the gym nearly against their will.

It actually felt like the sound was filling the whole school building. It was a low, crawling sound, probably the bass and the bass drum. But the vibrations shaking the pit of my stomach came from more than that.

It was the cheers.

The living pulse of clapping hands and stomping feet. Their vibrations, their heartbeats, were creating a rhythm throughout the whole school.

There weren't many people left outside. The students and teachers were all gathered for the ending ceremony.

I put my hand on the gym door.

When I opened it, I was greeted by a rush of sound and light. Searchlights danced around as the disco ball hanging from above scattered the myriad beams.

And within the luminous vortex were the girls.

The bassist beat out notes with a voracious eagerness. The drummer asserted her presence with a whimsical, funky beat. The stock-serious guitarist picked with incredible accuracy as if attempting to restrain the wild and free rhythm section. She regulated the band as a whole. And then there were the carefree vocals. There was the occasional hiccup, but the vocalist sang each and every word and note with earnestness and care.

The guitarist took a step forward to center stage and leaned in close to the vocalist. The both of them must have gotten changed earlier, since they were wearing matching T-shirts as they supported each other to weave the melody together.

Some in the audience were waving their arms back and forth, some were headbanging, some were swaying their cell phones side to side like sea lilies glowing pale, and some were so caught up in the moment they were diving from seat to seat and being lifted into the air. The crowd was as enthusiastic as they would be for professionals… No, they were so passionate precisely because the performers were amateurs.

When the drums sped up provokingly, the guitar raced with them neck and neck, strings thrumming. When it seemed like the music was about to fall apart, the slap bass scolded them. And then, reaching out as if to embrace it all to her chest, the vocalist extended her arms and belted out the song with everything she had.

The song had a vocal call, and the crowd yelled back. Waves surged across the crowd from right to left. The brilliant glow sticks shone like countless stars scattered about the gym.

In that moment, in the darkness, they had all become one.

Nobody noticed when I came in.

Of course, I doubt they could see anything from up onstage.

Amid that obnoxiously powerful enthusiasm, I leaned against the wall. Everyone was fighting to get close to the stage, so there was extra space at the back. No one was around there.

This was the final performance of the long, long cultural festival. Everything was over now.

Oh yeah, I was in Records and Miscellaneous, wasn't I?

So I'd remember this, at least. I doubt I'd forget that sight. I wouldn't be able to.

I'm not on that radiant stage. I can't join in with all the jumping.

I'm alone at the very back, just watching.

But I know I won't forget.

Finally, **he and she** find the right answers.

The ending ceremony proceeded without any issues.

But Sagami's closing remarks were a mess. She got flustered and bungled her lines, of course, skipping over parts, and she even forgot to announce the merit award, too. Each time she made a mistake, Yuki-noshita was there, calmly holding up cue cards. And finally, tears began to spill from Sagami's eyes.

Everyone else must have thought she was crying because it meant so much to her. People called out to her with all kinds of remarks: "You can do it!" and "It was great!" and "Thank you!"

I didn't believe for a second that she'd been crying because she was touched. I think she was crying either over her own worthlessness or in frustration, like, *Why is this happening to me?* But I do think that when she cried afterward, when she was done with her formal remarks and general comments, she was genuinely touched. The kind words people said to her after she'd hit rock bottom would leave the deepest impression. Though I did find this rather regrettable, since I was the one who had made her feel like crap in the first place.

As Sagami walked offstage to the wings, her makeup smudged and streaked, she looked exhausted. Her retinue of friends immediately rushed to her side like she was a marathon runner who'd reached her goal.

"Are you okay?"

"Things would've been fine if he hadn't said anything."

"That really messed you up, huh?" It seemed news of my deeds had traveled, and the entire cultural committee was glaring daggers at me.

The intelligence must have circulated to my classmates, too, as everyone in 2-F was glancing at me as they conversed in hushed tones. It was quite a bed of needles.

There were a number of familiar voices among the murmurs. "Yeah, right? Hikitani's a real jerk! He did the exact thing before, too, during summer vacation."

Damn you, Tobe...

"Well...he does have a sharp tongue. He doesn't come off that way if you really talk to him, though."

"You're so nice, Hayato." That was Miura.

"Hayato is sticking up for Hikitani... Yesterday's enemy is today's homo*bfshhht!*"

"Hey, Ebina, keep it under wraps, seriously. Look, your nose is bleeding. C'mon, blow, blow."

Yuigahama was laughing nervously the whole time, while Totsuka shot me a look of concern. I smiled back to say this was nothing to me and watched my classmates leave the gym.

Even after all the classes were gone, there was still committee work left to do. I busied myself retrieving the sound and video equipment from the stage area and backstage. The full committee participated in the final job of the day. To an outsider, it seemed they'd somehow gained a real sense of unity. Well, it's kinda weird to say I was "an outsider" as a member myself, though.

"Committee, attention!" shouted the gym teacher, Atsugi, once we'd finished most of the work. He was sort of in charge of this cultural festival stuff, so we all shuffled in to gather in front of him. "Okay, it looks like there's still some more cleanup left to do, but first: nice work, kids. This was a pretty good cultural festival, and I've seen quite a few. Don't get carried away at the after-party and get up to trouble. See ya, folks." Considering how authoritarian he'd sounded when he first spoke to the committee, his remarks were pretty kind.

There was a cheer, then some applause. Everyone thanked everyone else for their trouble and praised one another for their efforts, creating a unified storm of emotion. Meguri found Sagami off to one side and gave her a light push on the back. "Go on, Chair."

"Huh? But…"

Apparently, Sagami realized Meguri was asking for a speech, and she hesitated.

At the beginning of it all, she'd been a poor manager; in the middle stages, she'd confused everyone; at the end, she'd even abandoned the whole committee; and once it was over, she'd ended up a mess. It was no surprise she was hesitant now.

"You're the chair," Yukinoshita said coolly, stating the obvious fact. If the failures and the regrets of the chair belonged to Sagami, then the honors and commendations did, too.

"…Yeah." Sagami gave a small, pensive nod. "Um, I'm sorry for causing so much trouble…but I'm glad everything ended well… Thank you so much. Good job, everyone."

"Thank you!" There was one last crisp formality, and then we were dismissed. The girls hugged, while the boys gave each other high fives. Sagami turned to Yukinoshita and dipped her head in a tiny bow.

It was finally over…

Leaving the circle of the cultural committee, I breathed a long sigh.

While everyone was chatting, I went back to the classroom. They were talking about the after-party that night, too. I would likely not be invited. Someone could invite me out of kindness or formality's sake or hating leaving someone out, but even if I did go, there would be nothing for me to do but eat anyway.

Waves of exhaustion slowed my pace. Everyone was passing me by.

That included Sagami and her friends, and for an instant, their conversation stopped. Their eyes were kind of fixed forward as they avoided looking in my direction at all.

You aren't going hard enough here, Sagami. If you're really going to ignore someone, you do it without even being aware of it.

I discovered Meguri in the flow of people, and she noticed me, too. She walked toward me. "…It's over, huh?"

"Yeah."

Her expression dark, she commented, "You really are thoughtless and nasty."

She must have heard about what happened from Sagami, or from her friends. Well, even if she didn't, her impression of me couldn't be good. I couldn't argue with what she'd said. All I could do was apologize. "Sorry…"

"…But I had fun. I'm glad that my last cultural festival was a good one. Thank you," she said, and then with her pleasant smile, she waved good-bye and left.

This had been Meguri's final cultural festival. I think as the student council president, there were some things she couldn't yield on. Maybe that wasn't why, but she must have been glad there were no large external issues, at least. I felt relieved, just a bit.

"Are you fine with this?" The question came from behind me.

I shot back the obvious answer. "Yeah. This is fine."

"I see."

Misunderstandings can never be resolved. But you can ask new questions. If you ask again, the answers you'll get may not be right, but they're the answers I like. So this was fine.

I slowed my pace a bit.

The gym was almost entirely empty when the steady footsteps tapped closer, and Yukino Yukinoshita walked up to my side. "…You really will save anyone, won't you?"

"What?" I asked back. I didn't get what she meant.

"Normally, Sagami wouldn't have gotten away with abandoning her responsibilities and running off like that. But once she came back, *she* was the victim of your cruel remarks. She had testimony not only from her own hangers-on, but from Hayama, too. Indisputable."

"You're reading too much into this. I don't think that far ahead."

"Oh? But that's where things went, ultimately. So I think I can safely say you saved her."

No. What I did shouldn't be acknowledged in that way. My actions shouldn't be approved of or admired. They should be decried and denounced.

By the time we'd reached the gym exit, I finally came up with an appropriate-seeming reply. "Well, even if you're right, none of it would've worked if Hayama hadn't been there. So you can't really say it was because of me."

Yukinoshita fell silent, frowning slightly.

"Ohhh, so modest, as usual!" The voice resembled Yukinoshita's somewhat, but when I turned toward her, she was shaking her head as if to deny she'd said anything. And then suddenly, I noticed.

"...Haruno, you're still here?" said Yukinoshita. "Why don't you just go now?"

Haruno Yukinoshita and Miss Hiratsuka stepped out from beside the door to the gym. Miss Hiratsuka was standing with a cigarette in one hand, while Haruno was changed and ready to leave. It looked like the two of them had been hanging out there, chatting.

Haruno smacked my shoulder a couple of times. "Oh, you really are something, Hikigaya. Everyone's been telling me about it. I love how you play the heel like that. You might be wasted on Yukino-chan."

"What's being wasted is *my time*, in this conversation. Leave, already," Yukinoshita snapped haughtily.

Haruno pretended to be deeply wounded. "How cold, Yukino-chan! Didn't we play in a band together? We're such close sisters!"

That clearly irked Yukinoshita, as her eyebrows twitched upward. "I'm impressed you can say that after you sped up the way you did. You know, I was forced to keep up with your tempo."

"What's the problem? It got us all pumped up! Right, Hikigaya?"

"Yeah, everyone did look pretty into it," I said.

Yukinoshita blinked her eyes two, three times. "...You were watching?" Apparently, she'd assumed I hadn't been there. It was true that I'd come back pretty close to the end, so she must not have known about it. She wouldn't have been able to tell from the stage anyway.

"Just at the end. Well...you know. I guess it was pretty good. I was impressed." I'm sure I should have been complimenting her for a thousand other things, but I couldn't find the words. All that came out was a halting, clumsy review.

As I offered my vague and meaningless remarks, Yukinoshita jerked her face away. "Th-that... It... It was pretty far from perfect, considering I made more than a mistake or two, and the worst part was that we weren't at all together—the audience was excited for it, but it might have been unlistenable under calmer circumstances, and the reason for all this was our lack of practice, which played a major role, but the issue was rooted in the band's general lack of cohesion, and even saying that, I should have been carrying the melody, but I ended up holding back the piece as a whole, and as a result..."

"Ohhh, someone's being shy! You're so cute, Yukino-chan!" Haruno teased her.

Yukinoshita cleared her throat, then glared at her sister. "...Why don't you go now, Haruno?"

"Yeah, yeah, I'm going! See you later, then. That was fun. I'm sure our mother would be surprised to hear about today...don't you think?" Haruno smiled as if testing her younger sister, and Yukinoshita's expression stiffened. Haruno eyed her, then turned away and marched off. I don't know what Yukinoshita thought of Haruno's parting remarks. Their circumstances were still a mystery to me.

Once Haruno was some distance away, Miss Hiratsuka rolled up her sleeve to check her watch. "...It's just about time for the final homeroom class. You head back to the room, too."

"All right. Bye, then." Yukinoshita unfroze, said a casual farewell to Miss Hiratsuka, then started walking away.

I followed after her. "I'll get going then, too."

"Hikigaya..." Miss Hiratsuka called out to stop me. Her voice was heavy.

When I turned around, I saw her giving me a worried smile. "I wonder what I should say. There was your slogan suggestion and then the incident with Sagami... Ultimately, I think you've played a large role in this. It was your actions that got the cultural committee functioning and made you Sagami's scapegoat." She cut off there. She must have been pausing to prepare—not because she wasn't ready to say it, but because I might not be. "But I can't bring myself to honestly commend you for it." Suddenly, her hand reached out for my cheek. She touched me gently, not allowing me to look away.

"Hikigaya, helping someone else is no excuse to hurt yourself." Her soft fingers struck an odd contrast with the faint smell of her cigarettes. Her moist eyes seemed to pierce my soul.

"Eh, it's not like that was enough to hurt me, though…"

"Even if you're used to it…you need to realize now that some of us find it painful to watch you get hurt." She patted my shoulder. "That's it for my lecture. Go."

"Uh-huh…" My reply was a farewell that didn't even count as words. Then I headed for the classroom.

But even after turning in to the hallway, I felt as if her kind eyes were still watching me go.

×　　×　　×

The enthusiasm of the cultural festival had yet to die down in the classroom. It was abuzz with chatter and activity. The end-of-day homeroom was just a formality, so once the class rep was done with his closing remarks, the whole class just talked about the after-party.

That meant it had nothing to do with me. I even felt the wordless implication that I couldn't come, even if I wanted to. If someone were to invite me out of sympathy, refusing would make me feel bad, so I quickly collected my things and left the classroom.

Suddenly, I wondered which after-party Sagami would join, the committee one or the class one. It was a pointless thing to be worried about.

The wreckage of each class's friendships and passions were strewn about the hallway.

The next day was Sunday, a holiday. Monday was a holiday to replace the Saturday we'd spent at school. On Tuesday, all classes would be using the whole first half of the day to clean everything up.

Everything would probably be left here until then, monuments to our memories. Then, once it was all cleaned up, they'd immediately go to work again preparing for some new high school event. I was bound to get roped into helping with the cleanup, too. As of now, my excuse of being on the Cultural Festival Committee was invalid.

…Well, even if it was, I still had some miscellaneous work to deal with.

I adjusted my bag on my shoulder. Inside it were some reports and memos that my section had to sort out. The rest of the Records and Miscellaneous crew had entrusted these papers to me, and aggregating all these notes into a final report was to be my last job. Before I *clickity-click*ed it all into the computer, I had to sift through all the information and scribble together a summary of the contents.

I knew I'd fall asleep if I did this at home, and it was Saturday, so all the family restaurants would be crowded. There might be other kids there killing time until the after-party, too. I wanted to avoid working on this there.

My feet automatically carried me to a quiet place where I'd be able to concentrate. As I walked down the empty hallway of the special building, I noticed a chill in the air. We were getting deeper into fall. It had been six months since I'd begun walking through this hall because of club.

I arrived at the Service Club room and put my hand on the door. Suddenly, I realized I didn't have the key. Usually, I wouldn't be the first to arrive, so I'd never worried about it before. But that day, there was no guarantee that another person would be there.

I figured I'd give up and go home, and I was about to pull my hand away from the door—but the handle felt oddly loose.

Resolutely, I opened the door.

It was quite a normal room, nothing strange about it.

What made it feel so different was the presence of the girl inside. She was quietly running her pen along a page in the slanting rays of the sun. The sight was so picturesque, I even began to fantasize that after the world ended she was bound to remain right there, doing the same thing for eternity.

When I saw her, I stopped, body and soul.

—In spite of myself, I was entranced.

Yukinoshita noticed I was just standing there, and she gently laid her pen on the table. "My. Welcome, Sir School Pariah."

"Are you trying to start a fight?"

"What about the after-party? You're not going?"

"Don't ask me that when you already know the answer," I shot back.

Yukinoshita smiled pleasantly. She was sure to say something infuriating again, with that charming smile on her face. "So? Your thoughts on having everyone genuinely hate you?"

"Heh. It's nice to have people acknowledging your existence," I said.

Yukinoshita put her hand to her temple to relieve an apparent headache and sighed. "I don't know whether to be shocked or exasperated. You really are strange…though I don't really mind how you acknowledge your own weaknesses."

"Yeah, neither do I. In fact, I love that about myself." *Yay, I'm the best. I'm so cool for trying to do my job well, even when people are sniping at me.* If I didn't encourage myself, I think my spirit would break.

I pulled all the memos out of my bag and began sorting them. I'd been about to forget why I'd come. Speaking of which, why was Yukinoshita here? "So what're you doing here?"

"I have to fill out my career path form. I was so busy preparing for the cultural festival, I just wasn't able to find the time. Things have finally calmed down enough for me to fill it out," Yukinoshita replied, and she picked up her pen. But her hand remained still. Her mouth moved instead. "What did you come here for?"

"To put together a report. I wanted a quiet place where I could concentrate," I answered as I scribbled away with my pen.

Yukinoshita stared at my hand. "I see… We were thinking along similar lines."

"Loners choose from a narrow set of options. It's just the result of our convergent evolution. It's not that we're similar at all."

Yukinoshita and I had most likely just come to this room in search of a quiet place. Neither of us had a wide range of behavior in the first place, so this sort of thing only happened because our habitat range overlapped. In actuality, if she lived the next town over, we would hardly ever encounter each other at all. We were only meeting like this because we went to the same school.

I'd put it this way: Even if we were both alone, Yukinoshita and I were completely different creatures.

That's right.

We're not alike at all.

I think that's why these conversations we have always feel so refreshing and comfortable.

I felt the lingering heat of the festival smoldering inside me. I'd asked the question over again and derived a new answer. Now it had become a proper conclusion.

—So then...

—She and I...

"Hey, Yukinoshita. Me and—"

"I'm sorry; it's impossible."

"Agh! I didn't even finish saying it!"

Having rejected me pretty damn firmly, Yukinoshita was giggling in amusement. "Didn't I say it before? You and I are never going to be friends."

"Is that right?"

"It is. I never lie." Though her tongue may slip, and she may speak without thinking.

But I couldn't let her comment slide. I'd made up my mind that I wouldn't force my ideals on people. I figured it was about time for me and Yukinoshita to be released from that spell.

"Well, you can lie if you want. I lie a lot, too." In fact, I lie and lie and lie relentlessly. That's me. "It's no big deal to say you don't know about something when you actually do. What's weird is forcing it out of you."

That alone would probably be enough to make her understand—what, and when, I was talking about.

The morning of the entrance ceremony.

On the first day of high school, I got into a traffic accident. I'd gotten myself so excited for the entrance ceremony and my new life that I'd left home an hour early, and that was where my luck had run out.

It must have been around seven in the morning. Yuigahama had been walking her dog near the school, and she had let go of the leash. Then, right at the worst moment, a limousine had come along with Yukinoshita inside.

That was how the accident had happened. And that accident was how Yukino Yukinoshita had met Hachiman Hikigaya.

But even after that, Yukinoshita had claimed not to know me. She'd never brought up the accident—Yukinoshita, the one known to say more than was strictly necessary in her crisp, brusque way.

A long, long silence went on.

Dusk was closing in on the clubroom, and Yukinoshita's head was still tilted down. She was motionless. Only her voice came toward me. "…I wasn't lying. I didn't know you." It seemed to be like a do-over of some conversation we'd had once before.

But what came next was different.

She lifted her head. She looked me straight in the eye and smiled. "But…now I do."

From that expression, finally, I understood. "Is that right?"

"It is," she said triumphantly.

It's no use. I can't beat her. If she's gonna be so cute when she says that to me, I can't argue with her.

Suddenly, the words of the fox crossed my mind: *Words are the source of misunderstandings.*

That's exactly right.

Misunderstandings can't be undone. There are no take-backs in life, and when you get the answers wrong, you're stuck with the consequences. So that's why you tirelessly ask the questions over again—so you can discover newer, more correct answers.

Yukinoshita and I hadn't known each other.

What does it take to be able to say you "know" someone? I hadn't understood that—even though if I'd just looked at us both, I would have gotten it. What is essential is invisible to the eye—because without even realizing it, your eyes have shifted.

I—

We—

We'd finally come to know each other, over the course of nearly six months. Our character portraits were just names and fragments of impressions, pieced together into a mosaic of false perceptions. I'm sure our impressions didn't reflect the truth. But...

Well, for now, that was fine.

The long vacation and short festival were over, and finally, the trivial and hopeless mundanity had come back.

A light rapping sounded on the door, like the footsteps of our humdrum lives returning. "Yahallo!" Yui Yuigahama opened the door.

But I couldn't think of any reason she would come here. Shouldn't she have been out at some after-party right about then? "Yuigahama? Do you need something?" I asked.

"Nice work on the cultural festival, guys! So let's all go to the *kouyasai*!"

"No. What is a *kouyasai* anyway?"

"You didn't even know, and you still turned it down?! Hey, so, Yukinon, let's go!" Yuigahama plopped down in her usual seat next to Yukinoshita and, like a spoiled child, shook her by the shoulders.

Yukinoshita's expression said she was mildly annoyed, but she didn't push Yuigahama away. "I don't really know anything about it, either. What is it?" she asked.

Yuigahama looked up into the air for a few moments. "U-um... kinda like a really big after-party, sorta...?"

"You're not even sure yourself," I muttered. Her carelessness made me shudder.

Yukinoshita put a hand to her chin with a *hmm*. "Based on the sound of the word, can I take it that it's the opposite of a *zenyasai*?" That is to say, the party on the eve of an event.

"That's it!" Yuigahama commended Yukinoshita for the correct answer with a pointed finger. Was that actually right, though? Yuigahama continued her untrustworthy explanation. "Hayato and the others planned it. They said they reserved the live music house near the station! They were talking about how we're inviting not just people from our own class, but lots of other people, too…"

"I see," said Yukinoshita. "So that's why you came to invite Hikigaya as well."

"Uh, but I'm in her class. I'm invited as a member of the former category. Right? Yuigahama?" Uneasy, I ended up double-checking with her.

"Yeah, only just. Hayato was saying you should be invited, too."

"Oh yeah? Does that 'just' have a double meaning? Is he only trying to be fair? 'Cause I'd be the one to turn that down. I don't want Hayama doing me any favors." There's nothing more painful and sad than being invited out of pity. I think the superficial politeness just makes both parties unhappy. It should hurry up and go out of style.

As if to calm my anger, Yukinoshita admonished me in a slow and quiet tone. "You don't have to refuse him so aggressively. You should be thankful for his offer. Why don't you have them let you into their clique? As their foil."

"Hey, what would I even be foiling? Their attempts to have fun? And why am I getting cast as the foil here? Could you not just slap a role one me without my consent?" Someone like me couldn't even be a foil in the first place. At best, I'm an NPC, and at worst, a lackey. There's the possibility I don't even have a role at all.

"H-hey, come on, now," said Yuigahama. "We've got this chance, so let's go!"

"I'm fine. If I went, I'd just be alone in the corner leaning against the wall anyway. My presence would kill the vibe, and then I'd feel bad," I said, going back to putting together my report.

Work is nice… It's an extremely convenient excuse to refuse things. Once I become a corporate slave, it'll accelerate my lonerdom.

"He has a point," Yukinoshita agreed. "Besides, the *kouyasai* isn't organized by the cultural committee, so I can't see any reason to go."

"Huh? Hikki's doing work, so there's no helping that, but you, Yukinon..." Yuigahama trailed off.

Yukinoshita then started writing something.

"What're you writing, Yukinon?"

"I'm filling out a career path form."

"Hmm... Then I'll wait until you're done!"

"I never said I'd go...," Yukinoshita replied, somewhat bewildered.

But Yuigahama was watching over her, grinning. It looked like she had set herself up to wait.

Oh, Yuigahama's gonna drag her away, all right. If she says she's gonna wait, she really will do it. She's a loyal dog.

The red light of the setting sun was streaming into the clubroom.

The festival was over.

There are no take-backs in life. Even this one hopeless act in the play of life will eventually be gone.

Certain I would regret that loss one day, I concluded my report.

Afterword

Good evening. I'm Wataru Watari.

We're moving further into autumn. Autumn of reading, autumn of the arts, autumn of exercise: There are lots of autumns out there. What sort of little autumns have all of you found?

Autumn's end—
how does my
neighbor live?

Can't you tell? I'm working.

Autumn of labor. Autumn of corporate slavery... I'm sick of this already!

And so I have humbly delivered to you *My Youth Romantic Comedy Is Wrong, As I Expected*, Volume 6. The story is moving into autumn, too, and though the going is slow, things are gradually proceeding.

It's been a year and a half since I began writing this series, and within the story's timeline, it's been six months. But only recently has it come to me that I myself have only finally gotten to know all the characters—though I'm sure that even now, I only feel like I know them.

Well, there's still a long road ahead. I hope from this point onward, we can just slowly get acquainted with them, bit by bit. I hope all you readers will continue on with me for a little while longer, too.

And below, the acknowledgments:

To Holy Ponkan⑧: With every single book, your beautiful illustrations reach a new stage of evolution. Are you Psaro? Do you hold the secret formula to evolution? Thank you very much.

To my editor, Mr. Hoshino: I'm very, very sorry for always forcing such a mess of a schedule on you. No, you've got the wrong idea! This is because of, you know, *cough, cough*. Thank you.

To Mr. Koushi Tachibana: Now that I think of it, you were the one who came up with giving this series the abbreviation of *-gairu*. Thanks to you, things are a confused mess. Is the series nickname *Hamachi*? Is it *Oregairu*? I'll never forgive you for the comments you made on the book band.

To all the writers: I was barely keeping up with things this time around, so you weren't able to invite me to those drinking parties, but Wataru Watari believes that it's not because you hate me, but because you were being considerate. Thank you.

To everyone at Media Mix: Thank you so very much for a whole bunch of things I can't fit in here. I'll be counting on you moving forward, too.

Also, in writing this book, I made reference to *The Little Prince* by Antoine de Saint-Exupéry, translated by Natsuki Ikezawa, published by Shueisha.

And at last, to all my readers: This series has gone by fast, and we're already at Volume 6. Thanks to all your support, I've finally reached a turning point. Thank you so much. It'll keep on going for just a little longer, y'know?

Now then, on that note, I will set my pen down here.

On a certain day in October, in a certain place in Chiba, on a long autumn night, while sipping *hot* MAX Coffee,

Wataru Watari

Class 2-F Cultural Festival Presentation Proposal

P. 3 **"...has a *hard* crash landing *deep* in the desert."** In Japanese, "crash landing" is *fujichaku*, and here, it's written with *fu* from *fujoshi*, meaning "rotten girl" and referring to the Japanese counterpart of the slash fangirl. Replacing *fu* syllables with the "rotten" character is a common sort of wordplay among *fujoshi*.

P. 3 **"...the *shota* 'Prince'..."** *Shota* refers to youthful male characters, often in the context of attraction to them. The male counterpart of a loli.

Chapter 0 ⋯ **Hina Ebina**'s musical is homoerotic, as expected.

P. 5 **"...*Lovely story.*"** *Ii hanashi da naa* (what a nice story) is an Internet meme, a sort of ironic or sarcastic way of showing your appreciation for a story. It's often paired with ASCII art of the protagonist of Ikki Kajiwara's manga *Karate Baka Ichidai* shedding manly tears.

P. 5 **"*Definitely not.*"** *Sonna wake aru ka desu*, literally meaning "there's no way that's true," with an added polite/cute copula *desu* at the end, is a quote from the protagonist of the anime *Humanity Has Declined*. In episode eight, she encounters an assistant who behaves so outrageously, she speculates that he must be from another planet and then follows that thought up with "There's no way that's true."

P. 5   **"With a title like that, I was expecting more over-the-top tennis matches."** The Japanese title for *The Little Prince* is *Hoshi no Ouji-sama*, meaning "prince of the stars." While *myu* is often used as short for "musical" in Japanese, the *hoshimyu* portmanteau is particularly evocative of *Tenimyu*, the *Prince of Tennis* musicals, of which there have been over a dozen. Unlike the *Prince of Tennis* manga, which was ostensibly *shonen*, *Tenimyu* is unabashedly there to bait fangirls.

P. 5   **"...Prince of Curry is a related product..."** This joke also makes more sense when considering the Japanese title of *The Little Prince* translates to *Prince of the Stars*. Prince of Curry is a brand of instant curry marketed at children.

P. 6   **"But the one thing that was different about this script..."** This line is a reference to the opening narration of the Japanese adaptation of the 1960s American TV show *Bewitched* (which was popular in Japan). The original line goes, "But the one thing that was different about their family...was that the wife was a witch."

P. 6   **"...eight hundred different varieties of stars!"** This is in reference to a line from Gin Ishida in *Prince of Tennis*: "My *hadoukyuu* technique has eight hundred different varieties!"

P. 6   **"A certain pilot and a pervert prince..."** This is a combination of the title of two light novel series: *Remembrances for a Certain Pilot* and *Hentai Prince and Stony Cat*.

P. 6   **"...Miss Naughty."** In the Japanese, Hachiman says, "Fraulein (meaning 'perverted young lady')." Like with the "crash landing" earlier in the story, the *fu* in the Japanese pronunciation of *furoirain* is written with the character for "rotten/perverted."

P. 6   **"...Shiki Theater Company..."** Shiki Theater Company is one of Japan's largest and most well-known theater troupes.

Chapter 1 ··· In the storm, **Hachiman Hikigaya** continues to slide.

P. 10   **Bonchuu** is a character in the manga *Seikimatsu Leader Den Takeshi!* (Legend of the End-of-Century Leader Takeshi). His trademark is yelling out some variation on his own name when he punches, like "Bonchuuaaaagh!"

P. 10   **"...balls flying over Marine Field..."** ZOZO Marine Stadium, also known as Chiba Marine Stadium, is a stadium in Chiba city. It's near the sea, so it's quite windy.

P. 10   **"...I'd wondered if there was a Pokémon under there."** This is one of the lines from the Japanese opening of the original Pokémon anime, *Mezase Pokémon Master*: "Capture those Pokémon! / From the fire, from the water, from the grass, from the forest / from the earth, from the clouds, from under her skirt (eek~!)."

P. 10   **"Were they doing maintenance on your grid all summer or something?"** In the Japanese, Yuigahama mistakes *shakou* (light blocking) for *shakou* (social life).

P. 11   **"Light-blocking clay figures"** is the literal translation of *shakouki doguu,* a specific type of humanoid clay figure made during Japan's prehistoric period (the jomon period, 14,000–400 BC).

P. 11   **"Whoa, that was a pretty M-2 way to put that."** M-2 syndrome is *chuunibyou*, or "middle school second-year disease." Afflicted persons become absorbed in their dramatic, anime-inspired fantasies.

P. 12   **"I guess even the great outdoors is tired of this."** In the original Japanese, the onomatopoeia is *byoo*, which is how a Japanese speaker might pronounce the word *view*. Hachiman says, "*Byoo, byoo*—you'd think it was a spy for JR." View Plaza is the name of Japan Rail's travel center.

P. 12   **"Are you Lemon-chan or something?"** Lemon-chan is a mascot for Melon Books, a bookstore that sells manga, *doujinshi*, and related goods. It might also refer to an anthropomorphization of the lemon drink C.C. Lemon.

P. 12   **"How very like you, Hikikomori-kun."** A *hikikomori* is a shut-in, someone who never leaves the house. Generally, they're younger, and their parents support them. They're sometimes called *hikki* for short.

P. 13   **"...Amaterasu Oomikami went full shut-in."** In Shinto myth, Amaterasu, the sun goddess, locks herself in the Ama-no-Iwato (heavenly rock cave) in a fit of fury and grief due to her brother Susano-o's misdeeds.

P. 13   **"...I will become the god of the new world."** This is an infamous quote from Light Yagami, the protagonist of the manga *Death Note*.

P. 16   **"...like a blazing fire!"** Here, Hachiman says *rekka no honoo*, which literally means "a blazing fire," but it's also the name of the manga by Nobuyuki Anzai, localized under the title *Flame of Recca*.

P. 16   **Osamu Dazai** was a renowned author of twentieth-century Japan and author of *No Longer Human*, a novel with autobiographic elements. It's generally about depression and misery.

P. 18   *"The wind drags me away, ah, like a yacht."* This is a reference to the poem "Earth" by Tatsuji Miyoshi, a twentieth-century poet: "An ant goes / dragging a butterfly wing / ah / like a yacht."

Chapter 2 ··· **Minami Sagami** aggressively makes a request.

P. 19   **"But it was not to be…"** In the Japanese, this says, "On the contrary, *dosukoi!*" a reference to a LINE sticker of a sumo wrestler giving the viewer a sidelong glance. *Dosukoi* is a meaningless phrase used by sumo wrestlers to intimidate their opponents.

P. 19   **"…the sun was shining bright and perfect in the sky, and I was doing so, so great."** This is a line from "We Gotta Power," the second opening theme song of the *Dragon Ball Z* anime.

P. 19   *Kiteretsu Daihyakka* (*Kiteretsu Encyclopedia*) was a long-running children's manga by Fujiko F. Fujio. The fifth opening theme song for the anime is titled "Lack of Sleep."

P. 20   **"…of the year?"** Sayaka Suzuki from *Pani Poni* has the particular habit of adding "of the year" to her various descriptions of people.

P. 20   **"If Totsuka had been holding bread in his mouth…"** A *shoujo* manga cliché.

P. 22   **"…leering at me."** This is in reference to the "Leer" skill from the Pokémon games, which reduces enemy defense.

P. 22   *"Even dull-skied London turns to Paris…"* This line is from the ending song, "Que Sera, Sera," of *Ashita no Nadja* (Tomorrow's Nadja).

P. 23   *"Gyawaa! This is conspiracy!"* This line is from Father, the mysterious alien protagonist in Ken Nagai's manga *Shinsei Motemote Oukoku* (Holy Kingdom of Sexy).

P. 23   **"That's war…! It doesn't count…! It doesn't count!"** In the second season of the gambling anime *Kaiji*, one character in the show is busted for cheating and yells, "It doesn't count! It doesn't count!"

P. 24   **"…pressing the wrinkles of each hand together is happiness."** This is from an ad for Hasegawa, a company that makes home Buddhist altars (used for praying for deceased family members).

P. 24   **"*Naamuu.*"** Short for *Namu Amida Butsu*, or Amitabha. Mindful repetition of this buddha's name is a central part of Pure Land Buddhism, one of the most widely practiced forms of Buddhism in Asia. In Japan, *naamuu* is often just colloquial shorthand for any form of Buddhist prayer.

P. 24   **"Iron out your wrinkles before you work on mine."** In the Japanese, this line says, "The wrinkles came together," which is an idiom that means "I saw the negative consequences."

P. 25   **"…were you born in a temple?"** This is a reference to an Internet copypasta called "T-san, who was born in a temple." T-san is completely amazing and resolves bizarre phenomena one after another.

P. 25   ***"Now, now. Go ahead, Glasses."*** *Maa, maa, megane douzo* is a line from Haruna Kamijou, a character in the social game *The Idolmaster: Cinderella Girls*. In the context of the game, it means, "Now, now, go ahead [and take these] glasses," and it's become something of a meme that she forces glasses on people. The meaning in this context is different, and he's using *glasses* as a form of address.

P. 27   **"The only kind of ship I've got is me/Totsuka, apparently."** In Japanese, Hachiman makes a pun with the Japanese pronunciation of "leadership" (*liidaashippu*) and "cold compress" (*reikanshippu*).

P. 28 **"Is this Jigoku no Misawa now?"** Jigoku no Misawa is a comic artist whose shtick is drawing obnoxious people who say obnoxious things, especially a lot of humblebragging.

P. 33 **"...end that sentence with a *See ya, folks!*"** In the Japanese, this was *jaano*, meaning "see you" in the Hiroshima dialect. *Jaano* became popularized when the Hiroshima-born former pro boxer and world champion Shinji Takehara would always end his blog posts with the word, so it's gained a more vigorous and macho image than the original meaning.

P. 35 *"Committee chair: Sumo."* Meguri made a mistake with the kanji in Sagami's name. It should be 相模 (pronounced "Sagami"), but instead, she wrote 相撲 (sumo), which looks very similar. E. Honda is a character from the Street Fighter video game series and a sumo wrestler.

P. 36 **"...carry the beat with some castanets, though. *Untan ♪, untan. ♪*"** This refers to a scene in the band anime *Kei-On!* In the Japanese, this line is a pun between "transport" (*unpan*) and *untan*.

P. 37 **"... or *wanyaka pappa yun-pappa*."** These are lyrics from the *Galaxy Angel* song "Egaite A-so-bo!" The Japanese words for "gentle" and "fluffy," *honwaka* and *funwari*, sound a lot more like these nonsense syllables than the English does.

P. 38 **"...Fight! Fight! Chiba!..."** This is a song by Jaguar, a musician who is mainly active in Chiba prefecture only, with a sort of 1980s visual-*kei* aesthetic and a calm, whispery singing voice.

P. 38 **"...I don't mean the one from *Pyu to Fuku*..."** *Pyu to Fuku! Jaguar* is a gag manga about recorders, aspiring musicians, and their daily lives.

P. 38 "**...sparkling, glittering...rock-paper-scissors...**" *Sparkling, glittering, rock-paper-scissors* is the catchphrase of Cure Peace from the anime *Smile Pretty Cure!*

P. 39 "**...so sporadic I started wondering if I was in a field of mushrooms.**" In the original Japanese text, the pun here was between "sporadic" (*sanpatsu*) and "haircut" (*sanpatsu*). Hachiman says, "The conversation was so sporadic, even a hairdresser wouldn't do that much haircutting."

Chapter 3 ⋯ **Hina Ebina**'s musical is homoerotic, as expected. (Part 2)

P. 44 "**...stud-studded...**" The Japanese here is a reference to *Doki! Marugoto Mizugi! Onna Darake no Suiei Taikai* (Heart-pounding! All swimsuits! The all-girls swimming show!), a spin-off of the *Swimming Show* pop-star variety show that began in 1970, with swimming as a theme.

P. 44 "**...perversely—er, assertively—**" This is another example of the *fu* wordplay, in which the *fu* in the word "bold" (*futeki*) is replaced with the character that means "rotten/perverted."

P. 46 "**...identifiable by their footsteps are Tarao...**" Tarao, often referred to as Tara-chan, is Sazae-san's son in the long-running manga and anime series *Sazae-san*. The sound effect for footsteps is a sort of cartoonish rattling, squeaking noise.

P. 47 "**...picking away like *pokasuka-jyan*.**" Pokasuka-Jyan is a trio of comedians who use musical instruments to primarily make musically oriented jokes. *Pokasuka-jyan* is also a sort of onomatopoeia for strumming wildly.

P. 47 "**...*bom-boko-bom-boko*—what, is this a tanuki battle?**" The Japanese title of the Studio Ghibli movie *Pom Poko* is *Heisei Era Tanuki Battle: Pom Poko*. The change to *bom* from *pom* implies a lower, heavier sound.

P. 49 *"Unlimited Double Works…"* This is referencing Unlimited Blade Works, a special ability of the protagonist of the *Fate/stay night* visual novel and the name of the first Fate movie.

P. 49 **"What Marble Phantasm."** In the Type-Moon universe (which includes the Fate series), "Marble Phantasm" is the special ability to materialize a phantasm, to configure the world according to your vision of it.

P. 49 **"But a sigh escaped me. *I just don't want to get a job.*"** This is a reference to some lyrics from the opening song of the anime *Attack No. 1*, a late-1960s *shoujo* anime about volleyball, and the first girls' sports anime ever to be televised. The line is "But the tears escaped me. I mean, I'm a girl."

P. 59 **"What was the source of this difference…? Pride, and a different environment…"** This is an Internet meme that originated from a newspaper article about baseball players. There was a thread on 2ch that also used this name, leading to this line often being used online when making comparisons.

P. 59 **"YuruYuri *is one thing, but if it's full-blown* yuri, *I can't entirely back you up there.*"** *YuruYuri* is a manga and anime series about a group of girls in their middle school's Amusement Club.

P. 61 **"Listen with amazement! Prostrate yourself with rapt attention!"** This is playing with the catchphrase of the Oni Child Trio from the children's anime *Ojarumaru*. When they stand in a tower, they call out, "Listen and be amazed!" "Look and laugh!" and "We're the minions of the Great King Enma!"

P. 62 **"…they made the one in black the main character…"** Nagisa Misumi, also known as Cure Black, is one of the protagonists in *Futari wa Pretty Cure,* the magical girl anime.

Chapter 4 ··· Suddenly, **Haruno Yukinoshita** attacks.

P. 71   *"You kinda look like a housewife…"* Traditionally speaking, in Japan, the housewife takes care of all family finances, taking her husband's paycheck in full, managing all expenses, and doling out an allowance to him. It's considered household affairs and, therefore, women's work.

P. 73   "We're counting on you…" In the Japanese, she says *yoroyoro* instead of *yoroshiku* (counting on you), which is a verbal quirk from the character Ami Futami in *The Idolmaster*.

P. 76   **"But incidents don't happen in conference rooms. They happen at the scene."** This is a line from *Odoru Daisousasen* (*Bayside Shakedown*), a police drama. When there's a chance to arrest the culprit, the higher-ups order the protagonist to wait until the investigators from the head office show up so that they can take credit for the effort. The protagonist, Aoshima, responds with this line.

P. 77   "…I thought she was talking about super robots…" Hachiman is referring to *Super Robot Wars: Original Generation*, a GBA-era RPG in the Super Robot Wars franchise.

P. 77   "…revealing her history with gangs…" In Japanese, he says "Australian meat," since in Japanese, *Aussie* is pronounced like "OG."

P. 78   *"Is it the end of the century?"* The manga *Fist of the North Star* is set in an apocalyptic landscape at the end of the century, and the phrase *end of century* is thrown around constantly in the story. *Fist of the North Star* is also infamous for having a lot of strange, invented yelled sound effects, including *hya-hah*, a cry of joy you hear from various minor characters.

P. 86   "…Decree of Return to Farming." This was an order by the shogun in the 1700s that farmers who had left their farms to go to the city for economic reasons be forced to go back to their farms and do agricultural work.

P. 88   *"Taka, taka, taka. TAAAN!"* This is in reference to a particular manga by the comedy artist Jigoku no Misawa, in one of his series of one-panel gags that feature people doing mildly obnoxious things. In this comic, a man taps away and then slams the enter key hard with the distinct sound effect *taan*.

P. 88   **"…doesn't it?! Nooo!"** The wording of this phrase, which is rather more obvious in Japanese, is a reference to an Internet meme that goes, "Rainy season ended yesterday?! It won't rain anymore? Yaaay!" with the following line being, "Rainy season isn't over, is it?! Nooo!" The meme is often accompanied by ASCII art. It originated from a brief NHK interview with a beachgoer.

P. 89   **"…seniority by length of service."** Traditionally speaking, in Japanese companies, promotion is largely based on age (which is equivalent to length at the company, since it's traditional to only accept fresh university grads as new employees), not competence, and you're obligated to follow the orders of anyone who has been with the company for longer than you. This tradition has also been slowly dying.

P. 89   **"I Can Be a Corporate Slave!"** This is a reference to the light novel *Nareru! SE* (I can become a systems engineer!) by Natsumi Kouji.

Chapter 5 ⋯ **Meguri Shiromeguri** is pleasantly trifled with.

P. 94   **"…Characteristic Genre Name…"** Hachiman is parodying the Tales series of RPGs and their tradition of giving every single one a "Characteristic Genre Name" (a term coined by the producers) along the lines of "RPG to enforce justice" (*Vesperia*), "RPG to know the meaning of one's birth" (*Abyss*), "RPG called destiny," (*Destiny*), etc.

P. 104 **"…It was meee!"** This line is from Youji Haneda of the visual novel *We without Wings*. This line is from when he gets a friend to call up someone and string them along, only to reveal it was just a prank call from Youji.

P. 106 **"Since the majority of the nicknames were written in phonetic katakana or hiragana letters, the formal kanji characters stuck out like a sore thumb."** All Japanese surnames, and most Japanese given names, are written in kanji (Chinese characters). Writing a name in hiragana or katakana, the phonetic syllabaries of Japanese, makes it look softer and more like a nickname.

P. 106 **"What's more, they even added a friendly little *kun* honorific in katakana…"** *Kun* is a standard honorific for boys of equal or lower status, and it's considered polite to add it at the end of the names of all your male peers. It's typically written in kanji, so writing it in katakana is just a blatant attempt to make it look more like a familiar nickname when it's really just what you'd use for everyone. In this series, most of the people in Hikigaya's class refer to him using this honorific, as "Hikitani-kun." Honorifics have generally been removed from these novels in the name of readability.

P. 108 **Mother Farm** is a farm-themed theme park in Chiba prefecture, while **Orandaya** is a Chiba-based business that makes both European-style sweet pastries and Japanese-style sweets (*wagashi*).

P. 111 **"…must have eaten a translation jelly…"** Translation jelly, called *honyaku konnyaku* in Japanese (translation konjac), is an item in the children's anime *Doraemon* that the titular character pulls out of his stomach pocket. When eaten, you can understand any language.

P. 111 *"I can't understand what's going on here. I don't understand, Masked Niyander."* The original joke here was a segue into the title of the children's anime *Nyani ga Nyandaa Nyandaa Kamen*, which loosely translates into "I don't get this, Masked Niyander" with meow sounds inserted into all the words. Since the title is so untranslatable, it's generally localized as *Mighty Cat Masked Niyander*.

P. 112 *"...After two turns, I'll give it back to you double."* This is referring to the skill "Bide" in the Pokémon games, which does exactly what Hachiman describes.

P. 114 **"Don't underestimate the power of the Jagan eye..."** This is a line from Hiei in the manga *Yu Yu Hakusho*. His third eye (often just left as *jagan* in translations, which literally means "evil eye") gives him a number of supernatural abilities.

P. 114 *"There's no seat for your ass anyway!"* This is a line from Midori Iwamoto in the J-drama *Life*. She says it to her former "bad friend," Manami Anzai, when she dumps her graffiti-tagged desk and chair out the classroom window.

P. 115 **"It was so brazen I started wondering if she'd been taking metalworking classes."** The original wordplay here is based on the Japanese word *rokotsu*, meaning "blunt" or "blatant." The characters in the word literally mean "exposed bones." Hachiman says, "The bones are so exposed, it's like, *Where'd this skull come from?*"

Chapter 6 ⋯ Unusually, **Yui Yuigahama** is indignant.

P. 119 **"...even the famously overworked poet Takuboku Ishikawa would have to admit it."** Takuboku Ishikawa was an early twentieth-century poet who died young of tuberculosis. Overwork was a contributor to his death. One of his poems goes, "I work / and work and yet my life / remains / impoverished as ever / I gaze at my hands."

P. 131 *"Fun! So fun!"* The original slogan is *Delicious! So delicious! Juumangoku Manjuu. Manjuu* is a type of sweet bun. The company is, as Hachiman says, based in Saitama prefecture.

P. 132 *"Friendship / Effort / Victory"* These are commonly known as the "*Shonen Jump* values," the sort of values sought for in manga that run in the wildly popular magazine *Weekly Shonen Jump* (titles like *One Piece*, *Slam Dunk*, and *Hunter X Hunter*).

P. 132 *"...Hakkou Ichiu."* *Hakkou Ichiu* is an Imperial Japanese slogan. The literal meaning in its original context, the *Nihon Shoki*, is roughly "I shall cover the eight directions and make them my abode" (referring to the emperor). This was later used as justification for imperialist expansion, essentially the Japanese version of "manifest destiny."

P. 133 **"Is she making caramel sweets in there?"** Hanabatake Bokujou (meaning "field of flowers farm") is a brand name for caramel sweets. The inside of someone's head being a field of flowers is a Japanese idiom describing someone who's thoughtlessly optimistic.

P. 135 **"...the character for 'person' is two people leaning on each other..."** Hachiman is referring to the kanji for "people," which looks somewhat like a wishbone, or an inverse *V*. This is a famous quote from the teacher Mr. Kenpachi in the J-drama *3-nen B-gumi Kinpachi-sensei*, a classic teacher drama about middle school with a lot of Very Special Episodes, rather like the Japanese *Degrassi*. Linguistically speaking, this is not actually the origin of the character but rather a modern pop interpretation.

P. 139 *"Chiba's famous for dancing and festivals!"* This is a line from "Chiba Ondo," a traditional-style song and dance that is the official dance of Chiba prefecture. It's typical for every region in Japan to have a dance like this, which volunteers perform during local festivals.

P. 140 **"My time is now!"** This is a famous quote from Sakuragi, the protagonist of the basketball manga *Slam Dunk*. The full line is "When were your glory days, old man? Back during the nationals? My time... My time is now!"

P. 142 **"I hate perceptive kids, you know?"** This line is a *Fullmetal Alchemist* reference, a quote from Shou Tucker, a man who engaged in some heinous alchemical practices, speaking to Edward, the protagonist, who has figured out just what he's done.

P. 142 **"Was she about to say 'thenceforth' instead?"** The Japanese gag here was based on the word *jaa*, which means "then." He says, "If she wasn't saying it like she just had an idea, then all she could be talking about is Zojirushi." Zojirushi is a popular brand of rice cookers, which are *suihan-jaa* in Japanese.

P. 143 **"They're called corporate slaves because they don't disobey..."** This is a play on a quote from Shiori Misaka in the visual novel series *Kanon*. The original line is "They're called miracles because they don't happen." The parallels are more obvious in the Japanese, as he's mimicking her speech style.

P. 144 **"Get on out there, you!"** A quote from Johnny Kitagawa, president of Johnny & Associates, that is famous partially because the "you" is said in English. Johnny & Associates is a very prominent talent agency that produces boy bands and male idols, and they're behind some of the biggest pop stars in Japan.

Chapter 7 ··· This is the moment **Soubu High School** is festivaling hardest.

P. 150 **"Was it Mil Máscaras who had a thousand faces?"** Mil Máscaras is a famous *luchador*, and his ring name is Spanish for "thousand masks." On the other hand, Nyarlathotep, the deity from the Cthulhu mythos, is known as the God of a Thousand Forms or the Faceless God.

P. 155   **"Despairingly cool!"** This is the line that comes during the next-episode previews of *Chousoku Henkei Gyrozetter* (*Super high-speed transforming Gyrozetter*). It's about transforming robots.

P. 163   **Comiket** is a massive biannual *doujinshi* (fan work) convention in Japan, with an attendance of over half a million. It's no exaggeration to say the entire convention is just a series of lineups, and a large portion of staff is present purely to manage lines.

P. 165, 166   **Karaoke Pasela** and **Karaoke no Tetsujin** are both just karaoke parlor chains.

P. 167   **"You might as well call it money toast."** The original line here in Japanese is "It's not a burrito." In Japanese, the words sound similar: *honitou* and *buritou*.

Chapter 8 ⋯ Beyond, **Yukino Yukinoshita** has her eye on someone.

P. 178   **"…TROLLEY OLLEY."** This is a reference to a *Yu-Gi-Oh!* card, Express Train Trolley Olley.

P. 183   **"…sounds close to something more risqué."** Hachiman is referring to "love dolls," human-sized mannequins used for sexual purposes. In Japanese, the terms sound a lot more alike: *ragudooru* and *rabudooru*.

P. 183   **"…'singers' and 'munchers'…"** The Japanese nicknames for the Singapura and Munchkin are *pura-pura* and *chikan*, which mean "jiggly" and "groper," respectively.

P. 183 *"Are you Mr. Popo?"* In Japanese, Mr. Popo in *Dragon Ball Z* speaks in a truncated, Tarzan-like manner.

Chapter 9 ⋯ And so the curtain rises on **each stage**.

P. 200 *"…this is my time now."* This is a play on the iconic quote from Kouta Kazuraba, the main character of *Kamen Rider*. He says, "This is my stage now."

Chapter 10 ⋯ Finally, **he and she** find the right answers.

P. 227 **"…I lie and lie and lie relentlessly. That's me."** This is a play on a line from the opening song of the *Tottemo! Luckyman* anime. "I'm lucky and lucky and lucky relentlessly. That's me." The gag here rests on a pun between *uso wo tsuku*, "to lie," and *tsuku*, "to be lucky."

P. 231 **"Does that 'just' have a double meaning?"** The Japanese pun here is on *giri* (barely) and *giri* (obligation).

P. 231 **"…what would I even be foiling?"** In Japanese, Yukinoshita calls him "Hikitateyaku" (meaning "foil") and he responds with "Hey, don't just smoothly get my name wrong." The word sounds a lot more like his name than *foil* does.

Afterword

P. 233 **"Autumn's end—"** This is a haiku by Matsuo Basho in 1694, written a few weeks before his death.

P. 234 **"Are you Psaro?"** Psaro is the final boss of *Dragon Quest IV*.

P. 234 "Is the series nickname *Hamachi?* Is it *Oregairu?*" This series has two different popular abbreviations in Japanese.

P. 234 "It'll keep on going for just a little longer, y'know?" This is a quote from Master Roshi in the *Dragon Ball* manga, after Piccolo's defeat. Some at the time felt the manga might end there, but it ended up going on for quite a long time after that.